I0822257

K.C. MCMILLIAN

Kiana (K.C.) McMillian

SPECIAL EDITION HARDCOVER SEVENTEEN & EARTH MAGIC IS REAL SERIES

Cover designed by Getpremades.com

Editor for Seventeen: Caron Pescatore

Mashal High/ Mashalville Logo:

SR Illustrations
3/11/22

Editing/Beta Reader: Shalinie Rohit

Editing/Proofreader for Earth: Alicia Marcia

Claudette, Kevin, and Eli Artwork by @irdeinfierno

Dagger Pictures/Character art Fire & Ice Sisters: Aethrastic Designs

Special Edition Hardcover ISBN: 979-8-9878723-4-5

Dedication

Every little girl who has always wanted to follow their dreams but was too afraid to do so!
This is for you!

NOTE:

This book contains references to depression, suicide, sex, and murder that some readers may find disturbing.
Readers' discretion is advised.

If you or someone you know is experiencing suicidal thoughts and is at immediate risk of hurting themselves, please call 1-800-273-8255 or 988. You are not alone, and help is available.
Please do not lose hope. Your life matters!

All spells in this book are a figment of the Author's imagination and are purely fictional.

NOTICE:

Table of Contents

Claudette

Chapter 1

Claudette

My father recently married one of the world's worst women, and lucky me, she has twin daughters who are eviler than she is. You know how you eat a peanut butter and jelly sandwich and peel off the ends of the bread because that's something you don't want to eat or be bothered with? Well, yeah, that's what they are, something that should be peeled off and thrown away. Far, far away. Honestly, they are a pain in my neck! It's as if their entire mission in life is to ruin mine, and ever since my father married that dreadful woman, all I have wished for is emancipation. Emancipation is when you divorce your parents, and I have wanted to do it since my father returned from the Islands with her and those twins. But before we get to that, let me introduce myself.

My name is Claudette Richardson. I am sixteen years old, and I will turn the unimportant age of seventeen in two months. I have dark skin, light-brown eyes, a curvy frame, and dark-brown sister locks cascading past my shoulders. Oh, and I am five-three, which many consider short these days. I have two best friends, Spencer, a drama king and always like fifty percent hype, and Nicolette, my calm, laid-back friend. Neither of them treats me differently because I don't have a mother. Spencer is five-ten, handsome, with pale skin and red freckles, while Nicolette has flawless dark skin and a round face. She is slim, is the same height as me, and wears her hair in box braids.

When I was five, my mother died from a heart attack, and my father worked two jobs to keep our house. We lived in a small suburban town with white picket fences, *like in the movies*, and extremely nosey neighbors. Of course, we had an extraordinary golden retriever dog named Buddy, whom I loved so much. I remember how he would greet me and lick my nose when I came home from school, his tongue wet and slimy. I loved it.

Autumn was approaching, the leaves were changing color, and the holiday season was just around the corner. My mom's friend Mirna picked me up from school along with her daughter Sky, which was odd because it was a Thursday, and typically on Thursdays, my mom would pick us up. Mirna seemed nervous or stressed when she arrived, as if she had a lot on her mind. I mean, how do you tell a five-year-old that their mom is dead? I cannot begin to fathom how she must have been feeling.

A dozen police cars surrounded my house, and my father looked devastated as we pulled up. I had no idea what was going on. I ran out of the car down the brick walkway to our home, and I saw the medical examiners walking out with a body covered up that I later found out was my mom. At the time, I didn't exactly know what death meant, but I was sure about to find out.

As my dad sobbed in the bathroom on the day of my mother's funeral, I stood outside the door, covering my ears. I knew that "*death*" was terrible, but come on, I had no idea that when they said my mom was dead, I would never see her again. I remember seeing her beautiful golden-brown face sleeping peacefully, and I thought maybe she was resting. I didn't know I would never see my mommy again.

When my dad finally opened the door, his eyes were puffy and red. My father was tall, about six–one, and had a short fade cut. I remember he looked like he was in his twenties, even though he was in his late thirties then. His skin tone was caramel, and he had a muscular build because of his frequent visits to the gym. According to all my current classmates, my father is an "*old hottie*," which disgusts me.

After my mom's funeral, my dad took us to Evi's, our favorite ice cream shop. I did not know it then, but that would become one of our rituals on Sundays, Wednesdays, and Fridays.

As the years went on, I realized and better understood what death meant. Whenever I asked my father what had happened to mom, he would disappear into his office for days. Eventually, I gave up asking since it upset him so much. Later, Mirna told me my mom had a heart attack.

We didn't have any other family; my mom was an only child, and her parents died a few years before she met my father and had me. My father was an only child too, who had lost his parents when he was younger. *Note to self: when I find the love of my life, be sure to have at least three kids.*

Back to my point: it's January, and tomorrow we're moving to Mashalville, Long Island. From what I know, it is an imaginary place since I've never heard of it before. However, my stepmom Gabriella wants to move there and begin a new life. Luckily, my father has found a job as an accountant, and his salary can afford to pay for our home. *No more two jobs*!

Gabriella is a clothing designer; she custom-fits middle-class women. She is your go-to if you're attending a dinner party and want to be the best-dressed person. As much as I hate her, I can't deny that she is a talented seamstress. Gabriella has light-brown skin with hazel eyes and curly red hair. She is also curvy; now that I think about it, so was my mom. I guess my dad has a type.

My birthday is two months away, and instead of celebrating my seventeenth birthday with my best friends that I have known all my life, I have to celebrate in a new town, at a new school, around evil step vermin. *Just great*. It's my last day of school, and this woman, *Gabriella*, insisted that the twins and I should go. I would much have preferred to skip the last day and hang out with Nicolette, Spencer, and Mitch.

I check myself out in the mirror. I'm wearing a long black sleeve shirt, with black tights under ripped denim jeans. I have on black suede boots and black leg warmers over my jeans. Black is my favorite color.

"Let's go, girls!" Gabriella screams from the bottom of the stairs. The twins come rushing out of their room, and Marissa bumps into me.

"Get out of my way, freak!" she hisses. Crissy, standing beside her, eyes me warily.

I can't stand Marissa and would turn her into an ant and squash her if I had powers. She is five-nine with light-brown skin, green eyes, and short, purple, and black curly hair. Crissy, her identical twin, has long, black, and green curly hair. They are both attractive and popular at school, and they know it. Sadly, colorism plagues them. They think being light-skinned makes them more attractive than dark-skinned women, and the fact that most of the guys in school chase after them only makes their heads even bigger. *I hope it's not like this at our new school.*

You would think that colorism had died down during this generation, but unfortunately, it hasn't. I can't tell you how often I've been told I was beautiful for a dark-skinned girl. Whatever that means. I roll my eyes and follow the twins downstairs.

Gabriella drives us to school every day. She said we… I mean, *her daughters* are too good to ride the public school bus. Whenever my father is around, Gabriella declares we are queens and should be treated as such. She only includes me in this scenario to present this loving me as one of her own to my dad and everyone else. In truth, Gabriella hates me, and I know she wants to get rid of me by how she treats me.

I'm allergic to peanuts, and she put them in her sweet potato pie last Thanksgiving. I mean, who puts peanuts in sweet potato pie? Is that like a new ingredient? She vowed she didn't know I was allergic, but I'm sure I'd mentioned it before—over ten times! She gave my dad a little twirl, licked her lips, and he was hypnotized. We also had to get rid of Buddy because *she* was allergic.

I sit in the backseat on the right side of the car and rest my head on the window, wishing I were anywhere other than here with people I despise. I plug in my Air Pods, so I can't hear what the idiots are saying and think about when my dad first met Gabriella.

About two years ago, my dad and I were on vacation. We went surfing on the beach, and I was learning new maneuvers I wanted to show him when this woman approached. Seeing her eyeing my dad from a mile away, I watched as she put the moves on him. Mostly, my dad ignored the women who would throw themselves at him, but when I saw his lips curve into a smirk, I knew that was it. The next thing I knew, he was leaving me with my friend Nicolette and her family while he visited Gabriella on the Islands every chance he got. He did it so often that it became infuriating. Once he made it known that he and Gabriella were dating, all the other women in the PTA were disappointed, and the free meals they usually plied him with abruptly stopped. The first time I met the twins, Marissa spat her gum in my hair, and my dad had to cut my hair shorter because it wouldn't come out.

Gabriella said Marissa suffered from anxiety, so she acted "*nervously*" when we met. *What did that have to do with her spitting gum into my hair*? I wondered. Eventually, I decided just to let my hair lock up.

Crissy is creepy; she doesn't speak and follows Marissa everywhere like a shadow. They have this weird twin bond thing. Honestly, I don't understand it, but I am an only child. Either way, I don't like them. They are bullies and pick on me, my friends, and other kids. This one time, they bullied this girl so badly that she stopped coming to school. The next thing I knew, she was dead, and her mom and dad moved away. I am pretty sure she committed suicide because I overheard a few parents whispering about a note she had left. *Either that or the twins murdered her.* I was sure the twins had something to do with her disappearance.

When we arrive at the school, Gabriella kisses Crissy and Marissa on the cheek and tells them she loves them. Times like this make me wish my mother were alive. I walk away swiftly to find my friends.

Walking down the hallway, I take in the scent. It smells like a sweaty wrestler. I glance around at my classmates; some I will miss, and some I absolutely will not. I will miss the nice kids, the small conversations I usually have with some of my peers before classes begin, and the terrible sloppy joe sandwiches the lunch ladies make. And I will definitely miss Mr. Edwards! I hate math, but wow, he makes suffering through that class worth it. When he turns to face the board, we can see his firm butt. Oh my! I love watching him solve for X because he goes slow, and all the girls, including myself, watch how he moves his arms on that whiteboard, flexing his muscles. I was in lust. Man, I wish I were that board whenever he used scented markers and would lean in to smell them. But thinking about it now, that is a pretty weird thing to do because who leans into a whiteboard and smells the marker scent? Getting flustered from thinking about Mr. Edwards, I lean against the locker, close my eyes, and take in the aroma—a little tear forms at the corner of my eye. I have been living here all my life and will genuinely miss it.

Chapter 2

Last Day

Tears fall down my face, and I am full-on crying. I don't want to leave my home and start over again, especially in the middle of the school year. What would make my father accept a new job offer now?

"Move it, Blacky! You're in my way," Marissa screeches, shoving me aside.

Okay, granted, I was standing in front of her locker, but was there a need to shove me? Let alone call me Blacky? Technically, I am dark brown; I am not black. Black is a color, but again, *whatever*. I do not say a word; I just let her shove me. I know if I retaliate, her shadow will get involved, and although we were leaving this school, I am sure she would send her minions after me.

I motion toward her locker as if she is a Queen, and I am clearing the way. She gives me a sadistic smirk, and I walk to Spencer's locker to wait for him to arrive at school. Classes start at nine, but we have homeroom for fifteen minutes, and I usually walk with him and his boyfriend, Mitch.

Mitch and Spencer have been together for two years and are each other's first. When they came out, it was the talk of the school, and kids bullied them for it, but Nicolette and I stood our ground and continued being his friend. Which ultimately resulted in our demise. We were once popular, but when we did not participate in bullying Spencer, that was it for us. I was not into that; I love everyone who loves me back. I do not believe in bullying someone just because they are different. We will be friends if you are an incredible person and we vibe. I do not care about race, religion, or sexual preferences. But the people I go to school with are dissatisfied with themselves, and they take it out on others.

"Hey, Claudette, what's up?" Spencer grins as he approaches.

I groan. "Do you really need to ask?"

"What did the demon twins do to you now?" He shakes his head, sighing.

"The usual." My voice is flat.

"They're unhappy with themselves and insecure about their looks and skin color. That is the only reason they make fun of you."

I am confused by his statement. "Everyone thinks they are the most beautiful girls in school. Why would they be insecure?"

"Everyone is insecure about something, Claudette." He wraps his arm around me as we head toward homeroom.

"Hey, Spence?" I look up at him.

"Yeah?"

"Where's Mitch?" Those two are never apart.

Spencer frowns. "He sends his apologies. He's out sick, so he will miss your last day."

"Oh, aw, that sucks! I was looking forward to seeing him today." I pout. "But I hope he gets better soon." Mitch is hilarious; he is the one I go to when I feel down. He is an excellent match for Spencer.

We walk into the classroom; Mr. George is writing his plan for the history class on the chalkboard. We listen to the school announcements, say the pledge of allegiance, and then it is time to start the day.

By the fourth period, I am exhausted from smiling and engaging with everyone. My teachers decided that today would be the day they focused on the fact that I was leaving. Any other day they did not care that the girl with no mom existed, but oh, because today is my last day, let us make a spectacle out of it.

Fourth period I have math, and I can't wait! I saw Mr. Edwards during the second period, and he wore those slim-fit dress pants that curved his butt in the right way. He has what I describe as "a firm, perky bootie" that sits up effortlessly. I am obsessed with my high school math teacher, which is terrible, but it's an innocent crush. I know nothing would ever come from it, but I hope to find an eye candy nearly as hot as him when I get to my new school.

"Hello, class." Mr. Edwards claps his hands to get our attention. "Please take your seats."

I always sit right in front to have the perfect view of him.

"Claudette, today is your last day with us. How are you feeling?" he asks in his husky tone. *Oh no! Not again*. I want to become invisible. I am so tired of answering that question. I would have skipped classes today if I had known this would be such a huge deal.

"I am feeling okay; thank you for asking, Mr. Edwards," I reply.

"Glad to hear it." He claps his hands again, then turns to write on the chalkboard. "Okay, students." Mr. Edwards pivots his attention back to the class. "Today, we will go more in-depth with the quadratic formula; please pay attention!"

The rest of that math lesson is a blur to me. Mr. Edwards sounds like he is saying, "blah, blah, blah." I am too distracted gazing at him instead of listening to what he is saying. So embarrassing! I am unsure how far along my new math class is, so perhaps I should have paid more attention to what he was teaching us rather than staring at him.

After the bell rings, I run out of the classroom so quickly you would have thought smoke was trailing me. I head down the hallway to my locker to put my books away. It is my lunch period; thankfully, I have lunch with Nicolette and Spencer. Spencer has lunch during the sixth period, but because this is his free period, he eats with us and goes to the library during his actual lunch period.

In our school, everyone is part of a clique. You have the cool kids, who are the ones who have wealthy or very successful parents and don't want to attend private school. You have the intelligent kids; all classes they take are

AP. You have the jocks comprising basketball, soccer, football, and tennis players. Parents and the school district fought over separate teams because male and female basketball, soccer, and tennis players could not play together. Parents wanted a female football team, and the school board compromised and settled for girls' flag football instead. They take up two long tables in the middle of the lunchroom because there are so many of them. Of course, you have the cheerleaders who sit with the jocks. You have the nerds, which you would think would be the smart kids, but in my school, the nerds are the goofy individuals who are only good at math and science. There are the awkward kids who drink, smoke cigarettes and weed, and wear black clothes. And then there are us, *"the outcasts."* Which means we used to be a part of a clique but got kicked out. It is ridiculous.

Nicolette and I head to the lunch line to grab our food. Today is sloppy joe Thursday, and for dessert, they are giving away mini cheesecakes thanks to Trina, the lunch lady. One day each week, she makes a special dessert and brings it for us to try. She plans to start a "Trina's Sweet Treats Dessert Truck" and uses us as her tasters, I had no complaints because everything she makes is delicious.

Our table is the rocky one no one wants, which is by the water fountains. Five people can fit at this table instead of ten to fifteen.

"Hey guys," Spencer says as he sits beside Nicolette.

"Hey, Spence." Nicolette nudges him with her shoulder. "Where is your other half?" She takes a bite of her cheesecake.

"He is not feeling well today."

"Oh, no!" Nicolette's eyes widen.

While Nicolette and Spencer chat, I devour my food as quickly as possible. I have to meet with my guidance counselor, Ms. Cameau, to discuss my progress and all the information they need to transfer to my new school.

Besides my friends, Ms. Cameau is the *only* other person in the school that I feel comfortable speaking with. She has light-brown skin, bright red hair, brown eyes, and is short, like me. She is also awkward but in a great funny way.

"Hey, guys, I'm going to head to Ms. Cameau's office now. I'll catch up with you two after school."

My friends nod in acknowledgment, still deep in conversation, and I get up and head toward the door to exit the lunchroom.

In the office, I spot Ms. Cameau struggling with her office door. When our gazes meet, she drops the papers she is carrying.

"Would you like me to help you with those?" I say.

"No honey, I got it. Thank you, though. Come on in." She ushers me into her office, quickly picking up the papers from the floor.

I walk in and sit down. Ms. Cameau's favorite color is purple, so everything in her office, besides the desk and chairs, is some shade of that color.

"Have a seat." Ms. Cameau moves to sit behind her desk.

I sit in the brown chair, glancing around her office and smiling. I am going to miss coming here and having our chats. I came here because I needed help to grieve my mother's death and deal with my day-to-day high school life, but I have come to think of Ms. Cameau as a friend.

"How are you feeling today?" She tilts her head and stares at me with genuine interest.

"I am not okay."

She nods and scribbles on her lavender notepad. "Would you like to tell me about it?" Ms. Cameau weighs her luck in getting me to talk more about it.

"Not really," I say deadpan.

"Okay, so what would you like to talk about?"

"I don't know. Do you have anything to talk about?" I look everywhere in the room but at her.

"Well, I have recommended to your father a therapist for you. I believe you would benefit from it."

"What? Where is this therapist located?"

"She is in your new town, which is not far from here. I found three potential therapists, and this one insisted on meeting you. Of course, you can always reach out to me," she says.

I laugh. Here I have been acting like I was moving out of the state and only moving a few towns over. "Yes! That would be great!" I am sure whoever the woman Ms. Cameau recommended has to be just as great as her. Unfortunately, my new school doesn't have guidance counselors; I am unsure why.

"So, how are you feeling about moving away?" Ms. Cameau asks.

"I am not okay with it." I huff. "For one thing, I don't particularly care for my stepmother or her children. For another, we are moving to a new town they chose, which seems like a setup."

She scribbles in her notepad and nods. "I see. What would you say is the issue with your stepmother? From an outsider's perspective, she appears to care about you."

That's what she wants all of you fools to believe! I fidget in my seat. I don't like it when people, especially Ms. Cameau, state the obvious. It seems like Gabriella cares about me, but I know she does not. It was just a matter of proving it to others. But she is so on point with her acting skills I can never catch her slipping. Only my friends believe me.

"Well?" she says, waiting for my response.

Pressing my lips together, I fold my arms. "I don't trust her!"

"I see. And why don't you trust her?"

At that moment, I am so ready for this session to be over. I glance at the clock and see we still have fifteen minutes to go. I decide to change the subject. "How many days will I have to meet with this therapist?" I ask instead of answering her irrelevant question.

Ms. Cameau makes another note in her notepad, giving me a warm smile. "How about we end now since you arrived earlier? I will call your father on Monday to discuss this with him."

"Excellent." I grab my belongings, and we embrace before I hasten out of her office.

The rest of the day goes by in the blink of an eye, and the next thing I know, I am in the car with the demon twins and their evil mother. Spencer and Nicolette arrive to see me off as soon as we get home. Everything is packed, and mommy dearest will cook dinner for us once we arrive at the new house.

"I'm going to miss you so much, Claudette!" Nicolette gives me a bear hug.

"Me too, and I know Mitch will as well!" Spencer cries, joining in on the group hug.

"We will be there for your birthday!" Nicolette blinks back tears.

"I will miss you guys too, and you better be there!" I say, teary-eyed.

"Of course, I already spoke to my mom, and she talked to Spencer's mom. They plan to bring us out there, although we have been trying to find your new town on Google maps, and we can't." Nicolette says.

"That's very odd; perhaps I'll come to you guys instead," I suggest.

"What's your address again?" Spencer asks.

"1103 TK Avenue."

Spencer types the address into his phone, and nothing comes up.

I spot my dad walking toward the car with the rest of our things and decide to ask him about it. "Hey, dad, what is the address of our new home? We can't seem to find it on Google."

"The address is 1103 TK Avenue," he says, showing me the location on his phone. It is peculiar; I can see it on his phone but not on mine or anyone else's.

"Okay, Claudette, say goodbye to your friends. We must head out now because you and the twins are starting your new school tomorrow," Gabriella's voice annoyingly echoes.

Tomorrow is Friday. Who starts a new school on a Friday?

"Who starts a new school on a Friday? That doesn't make any sense," Nicolette whispers, imitating my exact thoughts.

The fact that we think alike is one reason I love her. I smile and hug her one last time. Mommy dearest gives my friends a fake smile while the twins scowl at us as they walk toward the car. Spencer hugs me, and my eyes fill with tears.

I sit inside the car, buckle my seatbelt, and turn around to see my best friends waving at me through the back window. My dad starts the car and drives forward, and I stare out the window at my friends until they are no longer visible. I am going to miss them terribly.

WELCOME TO

Kevin

Chapter 3

New Girl

I am getting ready to head to my new school, Mashal High, and dreading the first day. To make matters worse, we must wear uniforms. *Who wears uniforms in a public school*? Burgundy, gold, and black are the school colors. Females must wear burgundy, black, and gold plaid skirts with thick black stockings and burgundy button-up long-sleeve shirts with this strange Sun, Moon, and Earth logo. It is odd because when we first entered the town, there was a sign that said, "Welcome to Mashalville," with the same Sun, Moon, and Earth symbol. *What is with this town and that symbol*?

I finish getting dressed, place my locks into a bun, and head down the spiral stairs to await the demon twins and mommy dearest. My dad had already gone to work and told me he would be late for dinner. I felt utterly alone. My dad and I used to do everything together, but since he married Gabriella, we have no alone time. I cannot remember the last time we went to Evi's for ice cream.

"Are you girls ready for your first day?" Gabriella asks as she walks to the closet and grabs her car keys and purse.

"Yes, Mom!" Marissa drags her feet as she walks from the kitchen with a raisin muffin, Crissy hovering behind her.

When we arrive at the school, I am stunned; it looks like a miniature castle from a movie. The architecture combines ancient and modern, and a gold sign with the Sun, Moon, and Earth symbol hangs over the school's entrance.

"Have a great day, girls," Gabriella squeals before she speeds away.

I glance at Marissa and Crissy, noticing they seem nervous. In our previous school, they always exhibited confidence, so how should I feel if they are worried now? As we walk through the doors, a weird gray smoke circles us, and I cannot breathe for a few seconds. *What is happening*? I cough uncontrollably. The twins look worried about me for a change, yet they are not coughing like I am.

"Hey there, are you okay?" a strange girl standing behind me asks.

"Yeah, I think so. What was that?" I respond in a strained voice.

"Oh, I am not sure how to answer that," she says.

Um, what? What does she mean she's not sure how to answer that?

"What?" I frown. "What was the smoke for?"

"Calm down; the smoke is our way of checking for weapons," a tall, pale-faced man explains. "Hello, I am principal Deanwall. Nice to meet you."

"Nice to meet you, too." Marissa shakes his hand.

"You have a firm handshake, young lady! Follow me. I will show you to your escorts." Principal Deanwall turns and starts walking away.

Escorts? What type of school is this?

All eyes are on us as we walk by. I feel like a fish in a bowl, or worse, like a fish out of water, grappling for air.

The girls look amazing in their uniforms, while the boys have me tripping over my feet. Almost every guy is attractive, wearing fitted khaki pants and burgundy button-up shirts. Suddenly, I notice a tall, green-eyed, muscular god staring at me. He must be at least six foot one. When our gazes meet, he smirks, and my jaw drops. *Is it hot in here?* In response to his gaze, Marissa rolls her eyes at me. I can feel her jealousy radiating at me.

"Please take a seat; your escorts will be with you shortly," Principal Deanwall says once we arrive at his office.

"Are we each getting our own escort?" Marissa asks.

"Yes, you are all three separate individuals who require three escorts," he answers matter-of-factly.

"My sister and I do everything together, so we only need one escort. Thank you." Marissa's tone is firm.

"I'm sorry. Did I give you the impression that you had a choice? You will each have your own. Whatever crap you pulled at your old school will not work here," Principal Deanwall says, dismissing her request as he hurries away.

Marissa stands there with an annoyed expression, shocked that, for once, she has not gotten her way. The little princess is not used to that, and I try my hardest not to laugh. After a moment, three individuals enter the office. The twins and I are speechless when we notice the sexy god from the hallway. He walks in with one female and another less attractive male. *Please let that sexy one be my escort!*

"Hi, my name is Kevin Evans. Nice to meet you all," the sexy god says in a deep, husky voice, making me want to melt. I peek at the twins, probably convulsing in their pants, just like me.

"Which one of you is Claudette?" He flashes a sexy smile, glancing at his clipboard. This is the one time I have ever been super excited that my name is Claudette. I raise my hand, moving closer to him. I can see the twins' death glares out of the corner of my eye.

"Follow me." He flashes me another spine-tingling smile.

"With pleasure," I whisper, licking my lips and winking at Marissa.

"What was that?" Kevin asks.

"I said sure." I bite my lip, hoping he hadn't seen the wink.

Kevin and I leave the office and walk down an old hallway that needs renovation. I do not see any other students, so I assume they are already in class. Kevin stops in front of a locker and puts in his combination; I stand, shuffling my feet, waiting for him to say something. I swear I am lusting over him because he is so fine. He is a mouth-watering sight to see. I am completely enamored with him. *Pull yourself together, girl!* My inner voice, which I like to call Detta, is clamoring.

He rests his tall, slender body against his locker. "So let me explain this school to you." I do not know if he has a six-pack or eight under that button-up shirt, but I know I would not mind exploring more. He reaches into his pocket and grabs a pen, flexing his muscles. *He is doing this on purpose!*

"Our school is divided into two wings—East and West. This wing we are in now is the East; after your seventeenth birthday, you will understand the significance of this wing compared to the West."

I have no idea what this beautiful man is talking about, but I listen intently. After the silence between us stretches for a few seconds, it clicks.

"Wait! I'm sorry, what does my seventeenth birthday have to do with anything?" I furrow my brow.

"My apologies, Claudette, but I can't reveal that to you until then," Kevin says.

"I don't understand."

"I will explain that to you after your birthday."

"How old are you?" I ask him.

"I'm seventeen." His full lips curve into yet another sexy smile.

"I thought you were supposed to be my escort. Doesn't that mean you should explain everything to me?" I challenge him, but internally, I am swooning over his smile.

"The only thing I can tell you, for now, is that all your classes are in the East Wing. After your seventeenth birthday, you will have a decision to make. That is when you will stay in the East Wing or move to the West. I'm sorry, but I can't say anymore. But I can show you where all your classes are. Students from the East and West wings only interact during lunch and gym periods."

"You are being very vague, sir, but okay." I shrug.

He licks his lips sensually, making me bite back a groan, and I nearly faint when he grasps my hand. I am confused. He is incredibly charming, but I do not understand why he is holding my hand. He must have noticed my facial expression because he lets go immediately. I glance down at his hand and mine, then look into his beautiful green eyes.

"I'm sorry. I should have asked if I could touch you," he says.

You can do whatever you want to me. I blush. "It's no worries. Lead the way."

"The hallway is very slippery sometimes, so watch your step," he advises.

I follow him down the dark hallway and listen while he tells me about the teachers, the classes they teach, which ones he thinks are cool, and the ones he does not like. What I really want to know is if he is single. At my other school, all the guys were duds, and I could not connect with any of them. I want someone I can spend most of my time with; I am still a virgin, but despite my non-existent sex life, my sex drive is extremely high. That makes little sense, but Nicolette would always say that whenever I was attracted to some guy. Spencer and Nicolette are not virgins, but they always tell me I should wait until I find someone with whom I have a genuine connection. I know absolutely nothing about Kevin, but one thing I know for sure is that I want him.

I trail Kevin to my first class, which he also has. English is my favorite subject, so it is my only advanced class. I look at him as he opens the door and ushers me inside. All eyes are on me as I enter the room, and I feel very exposed. I don't like it. At that moment, I wished I was stranded somewhere in a desert, swallowed whole by quicksand.

"Miss Richardson, nice to meet you," a loud, deep voice says from behind me. I look at the sizable frumpy man and smile.

"Please take a seat," he says.

I sit next to Kevin. Apparently, when you are assigned an escort and have the same class as them, the other kids automatically have to leave two spots open. *Go figure.*

"My name is Mr. Rogers. Please review our syllabus and let me know if there are any books you haven't read."

I skim over the syllabus, and from what I can tell, I have read all the books listed. I smile and inform Mr. Rogers that I have read them. In return, he announces that we have a pop quiz, and by the looks on everyone's faces, it seems as if it is my fault. *Oops!*

Each class is supposed to last about thirty-five minutes, but it seems to take the bell forever to ring, and when it does, it is different. It is a *ding, ding, boom,* which sounds like an off-key tune I can't quite catch. Kevin takes my books and insists on showing me to my next class.

"Are you going to show me to all my classes?" I peer at his handsome face from beneath my lashes.

"Yes. I am your escort, so I have to *escort* you to all your classes for the day." Kevin winks.

"And how long are you supposed to do this for?" I cock my head and look at him, trying not to stare at those full lips.

"We're only obligated to do it for a week, and then you're on your own."

"What made you sign up to be my escort?" I ask, unsure I want to know the answer. Suppose he is just being nice to me, and we have no connection!

"I didn't sign up to be *your* escort. I signed up as *an* escort, and the principal assigned you to me."

My face flushes a bright red, and I gaze at my feet. *Duh, Claudette. Obviously, he did not sign up to be* your *escort. Where is that quicksand when you need it?*

"Here is your history class. We only have English, gym, and lunch together. I will see you after history to take you to your next class." Kevin hands me my books and walks away. I take a deep breath and enter the classroom. It is a small class; there must be about ten students here, and they are all chit-chatting. My entering does not stop the conversation. I spot a desk in the back corner and sit there. I take out my phone and send Nicolette and Spencer a text message, telling them I miss them, and quickly snap a sad-faced picture of myself as proof. The weird off-key bell rings, and the teacher walks in. She begins to write on the chalkboard without looking in my direction, not even bothering to introduce herself to me.

When that class ends, I am ready to see Kevin again; he is so hot. The next class is science, which is pretty quick as today they are taking a test on the homework given to them yesterday. Since today is my first day, I just read the previous chapter. Lunch is next, and Kevin meets me at my science class. While walking to the cafeteria, we pass through the West Wing, and I cannot help noticing the twins and their escorts. The twins are already seventeen, so I assume that is why they are in the West Wing. But then again, Kevin is also seventeen. *This school is strange.*

"Hey, so everyone has a specific place where they sit," Kevin says, breaking into my reverie.

If it is anything like my previous school, I already know that the popular kids sit on one side, and then you have all the other groups. Although, by the looks of this cafeteria, it seems much worse.

All West Wing students sit on the left, and the East Wing sits on the right.

"Never cross paths with the students on the left. They will destroy you!" Kevin looks at me, his eyes fierce.

Huh? I am unsure how I am supposed to take that; this school is full of teenagers; how much destruction can they do? Without saying a word, I nod.

"I don't always eat lunch here; I am going to my car today. Would you like to join me?" Kevin offers.

Woah! My knees feel weak, like Jell-O. Of course, I want to join him, but we just met, so it is not a smart idea. He looks me in the eye when the silence lingers between us for more than a few uncomfortable seconds. "It's okay, Claudette, you can say no."

"Maybe, another time," I murmur. Kevin nods, grabs his food, and heads out of the cafeteria. I look around, trying to determine where I should or could sit. I get my food, which I have to say is a better selection than at my old school.

There are sandwiches like actual cold cuts that look scrumptious, potato salad, all selections of salads, and peanut butter and jelly. *Wow!* What lunchroom serves potato salad? I take one and head to the outside court. Few students are out here, and I have no idea which side is West versus East, so I sit in the middle, looking around to ensure I am not breaking some obscene rule.

Feeling lonely, I take out my phone and text Nicolette and Spencer in our group chat.

Nicolette:

I cannot stand my friends; they always have to be extra. When I am about to respond, I notice a young olive-toned girl with curly hair standing in the window a few stories above me. She looks like she is under the influence. *Oh my God! She is about to jump!*

I run inside screaming, "She is going to jump! She is going to jump!" No one so much as budges. I do not know where the girl is or on what floor. I focus on how many windows up I saw her. It's the fifth window. That means it has to be on the fifth floor. I run down the hallway, searching and praying that I am not too late. I finally reach the bathroom where she is. She is standing on the ledge outside the window; her face is wet from tears, and streaks of black eye makeup run down her cheeks. *What could have happened to her to make her want to jump?*

"Hello… Why are you standing outside the window?" I try to make small talk with her.

"Don't come any closer!" she bellows.

"Okay, I am not." I raise my hands at my side, palms facing forward as though in surrender. "I am going to stand right here. My name is Claudette. I am new here; what's your name?"

She glances at me but does not say a word. When her focus is no longer on me, I move closer. I carefully place one foot in front of the other, trying to be as quiet as possible.

"Trust me. You don't want to be in this school! It's full of evil witches!" she hisses.

"I am sure all schools have evil witches; it doesn't mean you have to jump to be rid of them." I do not know what she means by witches. She can't be serious.

"No! You don't understand." She frowns at me.

"Well, how about you come back inside and explain it to me? I am having a hard time fitting in," I say, trying to reason with her.

"How can I trust you're not like everyone else here?" she asks. I can see the pain in her eyes as she questions my intentions.

"It's hard trusting someone. I don't believe I am like everyone else, but that's something for you to determine. You will only know if you come back inside. This is not the way. Trust me, *I know*. I have been where you are," I confide. "I wanted to end my life; I wanted the pain to be over. But believe me when I say someone needs you."

She turns to face me, steps back inside the window, and falls into my arms, sobbing. I know how she feels. A little after my father married that woman, I felt overwhelmed and alone. I wanted to die, so I took pills and hoped for the best. Fortunately, I didn't take enough; they only made me extremely sick. That was why I started seeing Ms. Cameau five days a week instead of the original two days. They even discussed whether I should see a therapist outside school, but I told my dad it was unnecessary. He agreed and repeatedly told me how much he loved me and did not want to lose me. I felt terrible, but sadly, that was not the only time I attempted suicide.

"What's your name?" I ask warily, wondering if she will tell me.

She lets me go and wipes her eyes. "Isabel Garcia." Her voice is low and husky.

"Nice to meet you, Isabel."

She gives me a soft smile and regards me with beautiful green-blue eyes. She has honey-blonde curls, thin eyebrows, a round face, and a curvy body. I do not know what would make her want to end her life, but I know it has something to do with this weird school.

"Today is my seventeenth birthday." Her Spanish accent shines through.

"Oh, happy birthday, Isabel." I smile.

"It's not a happy day because I have an important decision to make," she says, and my smile falters.

"I am sure whatever decision you have to make shouldn't make you want to end your life."

"How old are you, Claudette?" Isabel eyes me curiously.

"I am sixteen." *What is this town's obsession with my age?*

She backs away from me slowly, frowning.

Her response and the change in her energy bewilder me. *What did I do? What did I say?* "What is it?"

"Oh, mama! You're sixteen; when do you turn seventeen?"

"My birthday is March twentieth. I don't understand. Why do you look so worried?" I push for answers.

"I'm sorry, Claudette, but I can't tell you. You will know once you turn seventeen. I have already said too much." Isabel gives me the same vague response Kevin had.

When I am about to say something else, a girl bursts into the bathroom with other students. They ignore me and escort Isabel out, asking her if she has revealed anything to me. She tells them she did not.

What am I missing? I am so confused, but before I can dwell on it anymore, the bell rings, and it is time for my next class.

Chapter 4

Fitting in With the Cool Kids

The rest of the day is a blur. I can't wait to be home in bed and away from this eerie school. The weekend has arrived, and I want to read over some class assignments to prepare for Monday. My thoughts turn to Kevin, how sexy he is, and how he invited me to have lunch in his car. *Has he asked other girls, or is it just me?* But then again, there is no reason for me to feel special. Suddenly my phone beeps, notifying me of a text message from an unknown number.

Unknown:

Hi, this is Kevin. I got your number from the system.

Woah! Stalker much? But I couldn't lie; it was as if I manifested it to happen. I was smiling from ear to ear. After smiling for way too long, I reply.

Me:

Number saved.

I didn't know how to respond. I want to seem cool and not extremely thirsty because, trust me, my mouth is watering.

Kevin:

For you, handsome, I am never busy.

Me:

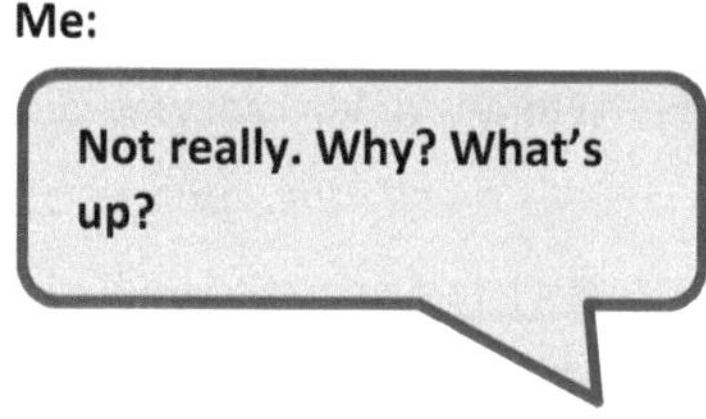

Smooth.

Kevin:

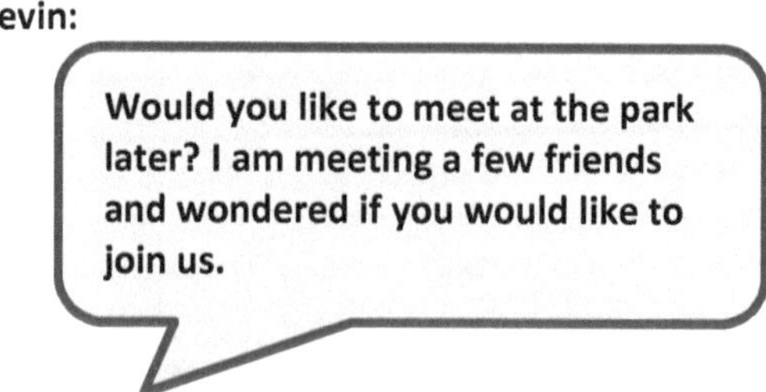

As much as I want to join, I know it isn't a good idea, and I also know that my dad will not allow me to go, even if other people are around. My father doesn't have a problem with me dating. He just wants to have dinner with the guy beforehand, get to know him, and embarrass me a little. I just met Kevin and am unsure if he is attracted to me or only wants to be friends. I must get to know him better and see if the feeling is mutual before putting myself through the embarrassment with my dad.

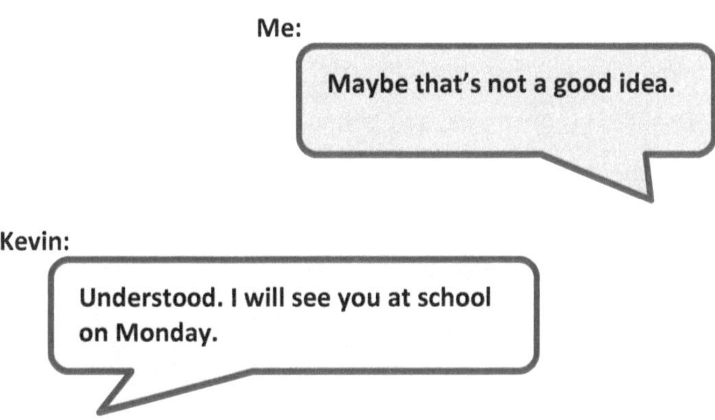

I throw my phone aside, turn onto my belly, and plunge my face into my pillow, belting out a small scream. I seriously have a crush on a guy I just met, and I have no idea if he feels the same. A knock at the door distracts me from my lusting for Kevin.

"You can come in," I shout.

My father walks in with a stern expression.

I roll over and sit up, biting my lip. "What is it, dad?"

"Ms. Cameau called me yesterday and suggested you see a therapist. Is everything okay with you? Please let me know if you feel overwhelmed, like when we were back home. I love you and need you in this world. Please don't do anything to hurt yourself again. I know the move—"

"Dad, I'm fine. I don't intend to hurt myself; I understand that suicide is not the way. But I should speak to a therapist. I feel a little overwhelmed with this new school and have a lot to sort out." I give him a reassuring smile.

"Honey, I am sorry we had to move, but there is something that you will find out once you turn seventeen. Just know that I am always here for you."

"Okay! What is it, dad? Seventeen is not an important age, yet you and everyone in this weird town have been making such a huge deal! What am I missing about the significance of turning seventeen?" I cross my arms, pressing my lips together.

"I am sorry, honey, but I can't tell you that." He looks away briefly, and then our gazes meet. "Trust me when I say it will all make sense on your birthday. This town is my home, and although I left, I decided it was best to move back so that you could make a vital decision on your own."

"Dad, what are you talking about?" I scrunch up my face. "What decision do I have to make?" I question for what seems like the millionth time since moving here.

"When the time comes, you will know." His response is vague, like everyone else's.

"Dad, you are being so vague and creepy, but okay." My shoulders sag. I already feel exhausted from this topic.

"I love you, Cheetah!" My father kisses me on the cheek. He calls me a cheetah because it's my favorite animal.

"I love you too, Dad," I reply.

"Okay, get out and meet some new people. Don't stay cooped up in this room all weekend. But you know the deal with boys. They must have dinner with the family before you spend time with them alone!" he instructs in a fatherly tone.

I roll my eyes. "Perhaps I will work on that next weekend. Since you and Gabriella had the genius idea of moving in the middle of the school year."

"Okay, I will let you have that one," he says, snickering as he closes the door behind him.

I find it weird that he would tell me I have some decision to make when I turn seventeen. *What decision?*

I spend the rest of the weekend alone in my room, wanting to stay away from Gabriella and the twins. Scrolling through Instagram, I search for Kevin, Isabel, and a few other names of people at my new school. I find them but don't want to follow them immediately. Luckily, their pages are public, so I can stalk them for a while first.

I look over Isabel's feed. She seemed pretty happy until her parents were murdered recently, right before her seventeenth birthday. So far, they have not caught the killers. *No wonder she wants to commit suicide.* Her recent posts are about how much she misses them and wants to join them. Isabel turned her comments off, except for one post of her and her mother. People have been giving their condolences. And her last post is of a prayer in Spanish with a lengthy caption, displaying her hurt about no longer having a family. I like all three posts and follow her, hoping she will follow me back if or when she signs back into Instagram.

I check out Kevin's page next, and from what I can tell from his posts, he isn't close with his parents; he has two friends—Tanya and Tristan—and there is no sign of a girlfriend. I smile.

After stalking Kevin's and Isabel's pages, I head to bed. It is Sunday, and tomorrow is school. I look forward to seeing Kevin and hopefully building a friendship with Isabel.

I wake up early Monday morning, shower, style my locks into a bun, and dress in my Mashal High uniform. It is pretty warm today, so I don't have to wear thick black stockings with my skirt. Not saying a word to the twins or Gabriella, I hop into the car and wait for them to come so we can head to school. But when they get in, they don't say anything to me, which is odd. Usually, Marissa has some sly comment, and Gabriella says something irrelevant. But today, they say nothing.

Once we arrive at school, I decide to try to fit in with the students on the east side. I head to my locker to get my books for my first-period class when I see Kevin approaching.

"Hey Claudette, how was your weekend?" He grins.

"It was pretty good, and yours?" I smile back, feeling butterflies from seeing him.

"It was smooth. Want to hang out after school?" He waggles his eyebrows.

"Um..." I stand frozen, not believing all I have to say is, *um.* Of course, I want to hang out with him, but all I can think of is my father's reaction.

"What is it?" he asks, his eyes concerned.

"So, my father disapproves of me spending time with, you know, boys unless he meets them first, even if it's just as friends," I explain, as I feel my cheeks growing hot.

I added the friend part because, to be honest, I still do not know if Kevin is attracted to me.

He leans closer, and I can feel his warm, minty breath on my face. In a husky tone, he says, "I would not let my daughter leave my sight if she were as beautiful as you."

Um... I'm sorry. What? Did he just say I was beautiful? I swear I am melting, and my underwear feels damp.

"I wouldn't mind meeting your dad. Just let me know when and where." A panty-melting smile traces his very edible lips.

I gulp. "Actually, what I need to know is—"

"I am interested in being more than just friends," he says, cutting me off.

I blink. "I'm sorry. What?" *Did he say what I think he said?*

"I am interested in you, Claudette. It is purely physical because I don't know much about you, but I am interested in getting to know you. And if one requirement of making that happen is meeting your father, then so be it."

I gape at him, not knowing what to say.

This beautiful guy is interested in me, *little old me*. He pulls out his phone, asks for my socials, and follows me. The sound of the bell forces us to break apart, and we head to our classes.

Soon it is lunchtime, and I look forward to seeing Kevin again. This time, I want to eat lunch with him in his car. Although I tell myself I am okay with not fitting in, a voice inside me calls me a liar.

I go to the lunchroom, intent on finding Kevin, but when I don't see him immediately, I sigh and grab a salad. I survey the cafeteria again for him but still don't see him. As I am about to leave, someone seizes my hand. It is Kevin!

"Would you like to sit outside?" he asks.

I nod, and we head outside to sit on the East Side of the courtyard.

"So, this is the side we're supposed to sit on?" I ask.

"Yes, it is. You will understand–"

"More when I turn seventeen. Yeah, yeah, yeah," I say, cutting him off.

"Don't be rude." He takes a bite of his chicken sandwich. Even the way he chews his food is sexy. *Like, does this guy know what he is doing to me?*

"Kevin, I don't understand. What is so special about turning seventeen?"

"I wish I could explain it. I can only imagine how you must feel. But unfortunately, I can't. It's against the rules." He sighs.

"The rules?" I raise an eyebrow.

"Yes, the rules of this town. Turning seventeen is significant here in Mashalville, and you will better understand once you have reached the age," Kevin explains without telling me anything.

I don't know what to say to that. I am so frustrated about this age thing that I don't say another word. I take a bite of my salad and look around, spotting Kevin's two friends from his Instagram posts walking toward us. I sit up straight, trying to exude confidence I don't have.

"Hey, I am Tanya." The girl beams.

"And I am Tristan; nice to meet you," adds the boy, his ocean-blue eyes sparkling. I notice his tragus piercing and wince.

Tristan is very handsome and appears sure of himself, while Tanya seems like a "princess," judging by how prim and proper she is. Her eyes are light brown with a grayish tinge, and she wears a nose ring. She is beautiful.

"These are my only friends in this school; they are on the West Side, though. But I don't hold that against them." Kevin smirks.

They all laugh. Honestly, I don't see the joke, but it probably isn't meant for me to get.

"I thought the West and East Side don't interact with one another." I cross my arms and tilt my head as I look at them.

"Mostly, we don't. But we three hit it off so well in gym class we became friends," Tristan explained.

"Yeah, we have been cool ever since our first encounter." Kevin fist-pumps Tristan.

"So, how do you two know each other?" I look from Tristan to Tanya.

"We met on our seventeenth birthday." She stares intently at Tristan, and they share a long, sloppy kiss.

Well, I didn't see that coming.

"Great, those annoying twins have found me." Tanya scowls when she and Tristan break away from their kiss.

I am about to ask which twins she is talking about when I notice Marissa and Crissy walking toward us.

"I thought norms are not supposed to sit with us?" Marissa grits her teeth.

"I'm sorry, and who are you? You're new here and should tread lightly with what you say!" Tanya retorts, causing a sadistic smirk to appear on Kevin's handsome face.

I feel like I belong for the first time in a long time. Finally, Marissa and her sister are on the other side, but I have to interject because of who I am.

"How about we all sit here and enjoy lunch together?" I suggest.

Marissa and Crissy scowl at me, and the next thing I know, I feel a smack across my face. *I'm sorry. Did she just slap me? I think she did!*

I stand up, clenching my fists. *Crissy smacked me across the face.* Everyone is now standing, and Kevin looks angry.

"I'm reporting you to the principal!" Tanya storms away, with Tristan following her.

What is happening? People are actually sticking up for me.

"Let's go!" Kevin grabs my hand to walk away, and I can't fathom what's happening. Besides my two best friends, no one has ever stuck up to a bully for me before. And even though I want to punch Crissy right in her big mouth,

I let it go.

Once school is over, Kevin offers to drive me home, and he is adamant about telling my dad what happened at lunch today, which is amazing of him because until now, it has been as if the twins are angels when they are really Satan's spawns. Every time I tell my dad some evil thing they've done, Gabriella convinces him it was all a misunderstanding. So, I finally gave up trying.

I arrive home right before the demon twins and inform my dad about what happened with them in school and how Crissy smacked me in the face when I didn't even do anything. He is livid but thanks Kevin for stepping in and invites him to stay for dinner. Instead of the usual "family dinner" with the twins and Gabriella, there is a division for that night. Gabriella, Marissa, and Crissy go out while my dad, Kevin, and I stay in. If I am candid, this is for the best because my father, Kevin, and I get to spend quality time together. We have a great evening, and I look forward to more days like this.

Eli

Chapter 5

New Guy in School

It has been several weeks since Crissy smacked me in the face, and my father and Gabriella have not spoken during all this time. As a result, she sleeps in the guest room, and he sleeps in their bedroom. *If only they would get divorced!* I am grateful to Kevin, Tanya, and Tristan for sticking up for me because Gabriella cannot sweet-talk my dad into accepting her daughter's actions toward me this time. But, of course, it does not last long because soon she is prancing around the house in skimpy clothing and back in the room with my father. *It was good while it lasted.*

Usually, when the twins pick on me—mostly Marissa—Gabriella gives some ridiculous excuse for why they did it. But because Tanya defended me and reported them to the principal, her ploy didn't work this time, and my dad was over it. Still, I do not know what he sees in her.

Kevin is picking me up to go to school, which my father is a little skeptical about at first, but after a few dinner nights, he has become very fond of Kevin. Not to mention so am I, but I do not know what we are. We are more than friends, but neither of us has said if we are boyfriend and girlfriend, although it feels like we are. We text each other every night, or he calls me. So, I feel like I am his girlfriend, but until he says so, I won't think more of it.

Kevin calls to let me know he is outside, and I see the twins give me a death glare as I walk out the door. Since the altercation, Tanya, *the most popular girl in school*, has given the twins a hard time. I can't believe she stuck up for me and has become such a lovely friend. But I do not believe in bullying, and when I voiced my concerns to Tanya, she understood. She still gives the twins the cold shoulder but does not bully them.

"Hey, babe," Kevin smoothly says as I climb into his 2021 Red Mustang Coupe.

"Hi." I giggle and kiss him on the cheek.

It has only been a few weeks, but I am smitten. Since that day at lunch, we have spent every day together. He even liked some of my posts on Instagram, but nothing is official yet. Once we arrive at school, we kiss and head to our classes.

I am in math class when the principal enters with a new guy. And *wow!* I think Kevin is hot, but I can't help but stare when I see this guy. We make eye contact but do not speak. There is something about him that is alluring. We have several classes together that day, and by our fifth one, I decide to introduce myself, but before I get the chance to do that, he taps me on my shoulder.

"Hi, my name is Eli Powers," he says, beating me to the punch and introducing himself first. "I've noticed that we're in a few classes together. What's your name?" His voice is deep and sensual, and the words flow from his lips like melted butter.

"My name is Claudette Richardson." I smile. "Nice to meet you."

"Nice to meet you, too." And as soon as he touches my hand, I feel electric shocks vibrating up my arm and releasing through my fingers. My heart sinks into my stomach, and I gasp for air. *What was that?* His intense gaze falls on mine, and we do not speak. He looks at his hand, and his lips curve into a smirk. I know he felt the electric shock as well.

He sits beside me, and I cannot help but check him out. He is tall, and his skin is like dark chocolate that could melt in your mouth. His eyes are light brown, and he wears his hair in a short fade haircut. He is fine. But I am taken, or at least I think I am.

"So, how old are you?" He leans in as he waits for my response.

My heart is pounding at the sound of his voice. It is like his words are vibrating throughout my body. "I'm sixteen. How old are you?" I finally say.

"I'm sixteen too, turning seventeen in a few weeks."

"Oh, when is your birthday?" The mention of his seventeenth birthday approaching in a few weeks piques my interest.

"March seventeenth. When's yours?" he asks. It's like we are playing a game of twenty-one questions.

"Oh wow! My birthday is March twentieth." My eyes sparkle.

His lips upturn into a smirk. "Do you have any plans?"

"Not at the moment, but can I ask you something?" I lean closer to him and lower my voice. "What is with this town and the big deal of turning seventeen?"

His eyes widen, and for a moment, I think he will not respond.

"Once my birthday comes around, I can tell you the significance since it seems to be such a huge thing in this town. Unfortunately, I won't know what the hype is about until then." He shakes his head.

"I look forward to that." I give him a satisfied smile.

He winks and starts collecting his books right before the bell rings. It is now time for lunch.

While walking to lunch, I notice a familiar face. *Isabel.* I have not seen Isabel since the day she tried to take her life. When I get a closer look at her, she seems different, but in a good way.

"Hi, Claudette!" she exclaims, skipping toward me.

"Hey Isabel, how are you?" I ask cautiously.

"I am great!" Her mood is the opposite of our last encounter. "I wanted to say thank you so much for saving my life last month. I was so broken."

I give her a small smile. "Don't mention it. I'm happy you're okay. Where have you been since?"

"I needed time to reflect on what had happened and make my decision."

My mouth forms a small O.

"Yeah, I'll catch you later, okay? We should hang out one of these days," she says, walking away toward the West Wing. *I wonder what decision she had to make.*

I'm in the cafeteria waiting in line to get my food when Eli's handsome self appears.

"Hey Claudette, want to sit together?" he asks.

I am flattered. "Hey, Eli. I'm sitting with my friends outside in the courtyard." I point to them.

"*Those* are your friends?" His eyebrows shoot up.

"Yes, they are. Why?" Before he can answer, Kevin is behind me, snaking his arm around my waist. Eli looks unamused.

"Who is this, babe?" Kevin asks, emphasizing the word "babe."

"This is my friend Eli. Eli, this is Kevin."

"Claudette's *boyfriend*," he interjects.

Um, what? Boyfriend?

"I didn't realize you had a boyfriend, Claudette," Eli says.

I didn't realize it, either.

"Would it be okay if Eli joined us for lunch?"

Kevin gives me a look, which is enough of a response.

"It's fine; I have something to do anyway," Eli states as he scurries away from us.

Kevin places his arm around my neck, and we head outside to the courtyard. Still confused, I stop before we reach Tanya and Tristan.

"What's wrong with you?" Kevin asks.

"Um... *boyfriend*?" I look at him expectantly.

"You're my girl," he says, leaning in closer, so his lips are only inches away from mine.

"There hasn't been any discussion of titles yet, so how was I to know I'm your girlfriend?" I give him a pointed look, but on the inside, I'm swooning at the words "my girl."

He pulls me into his arms and whispers, "You have been mine since the first day you arrived here."

Shivers run down my spine, and butterflies flutter in my gut. Kevin lifts my chin and presses his lips firmly against mine. The passion I feel behind the kiss is mind-blowing. He is teasing me and making me want more, and he knows it. I feel tingling throughout my entire body; I want him badly! But I think it's best to wait a little longer before moving to the next base. He clutches my breast with his right hand and growls quietly into my ear. My mind fills with nothing but dirty thoughts. For a moment, we forgot where we were—*in school!*

"What are you doing Friday night?" he asks, pulling me from my daydream.

"I don't have any plans," I say breathlessly.

"Now you do. I am taking you out, and I've already talked it over with your dad." He smiles slyly.

My eyes widen. "You did?" A massive grin forms on my lips.

"Of course, I already know I have to be on good terms with your dad." Kevin grins.

"Interesting. Where are you taking me?" I cock my head and regard him through narrowed eyes.

"It's a surprise, babe." He taps the tip of my nose. "Be ready at six p.m."

I nod, and then we join Tanya and Tristan at the table. Hanging out with them has become a ritual I enjoy a lot. They are fun and always keep me on my toes. Tanya and Tristan are like the perfect couple; it's as if they are fated to be together—if that is a thing. *I wonder if Kevin is my mate.*

The rest of the day breezes by, and Eli does not say much to me since Kevin dropped the "girlfriend" bombshell at lunch. After the bell rings for my last class, I am at my locker, stuffing my bag with books, when I notice Eli walking past me. I catch up with him. "Hey Eli, how was your first day of school?"

"It's been okay so far." He avoids eye contact while we walk down the hallway in sync. "This school is pretty weird."

"I agree. Totally bizarre, especially the students on the west side," I reply. It is refreshing to know that someone feels the same about this school.

"But I was wondering if we could exchange numbers. I'm behind on schoolwork, and I thought... maybe... we could be science partners? Don't worry; I understand you have a boyfriend. I am not trying to overstep," he hurries to assure me.

I am taken aback by his request. Judging from how Kevin looked at Eli, I know he would not be okay with this. But I do not have a science partner yet, and besides Kevin, I don't really speak to anyone on the east side. It wouldn't hurt to make a friend. "I wasn't worried, and of course, we can."

We swap phones to exchange numbers.

"Awesome! I'll catch you later," he says, turning in the opposite direction.

"See you tomorrow, Eli." I wave before heading toward Kevin's car.

I cannot tell if Kevin is jealous or not, but when I get in the car, he gives me a look and rolls his eyes in Eli's direction.

"We're just friends." I kiss him on the cheek.

His lips curve into a sinister smirk, and he speeds off, cutting Eli off in the parking lot.

"*Kevin*!" I screech.

He does not say a word and continues driving. We sit silently for a few minutes when we arrive at my house.

"I'm sorry, babe, but I don't trust him. He gives me a bad vibe."

Does he not trust Eli, or is this jealousy? "I understand, but I don't get a bad vibe from him, and he is new here like I am. Can you try to be nice to him for me?" I plead.

He strokes his chin hair and purses his lips. "Hmm, I'll try."

I roll my eyes before getting out of the car, then walk to the driver's side, lean in, and press my lips against his.

"See you later, babe." He winks and drives off.

Walking down our driveway, I am smiling from ear to ear. I am happy for once, although my dad and Gabriella are on better terms. But because of the incident with Crissy, we no longer eat dinner as a *"family,"* for which I am incredibly thankful. I grab some takeout my father had ordered and head to my room.

After taking a shower, I eat and begin scrolling on Instagram. When I notice a follow-request from Eli, I accept it and follow back. I am Kevin's "girlfriend," but there is nothing wrong with being friends with Eli, and besides, I do not get the bad vibe from him that Kevin claims he feels.

Chapter 6

Hot Date

Today is finally Friday, and I am getting dressed for my first hot date with the sexiest guy in my school. My father gave me "the talk" and told me not to do anything he would not do. This talk with him was highly uncomfortable, but I understood where he was coming from. Besides, I am not ready for sex, no matter how much my body says otherwise. Well, at least, *not yet*.

I stand in front of the mirror wearing a long, lavender, strapless dress that clings to my curves in all the right places. This dress means a lot to me because it was the dress my mom wore to her junior high school prom she attended with my father as her date. My father was very emotional when he pulled it out of storage. Although much time has passed since my mother died, I can still see the pain in his eyes. I wish she were here so we could gossip about boys, talk about girl stuff, and discuss the best panty to wear with my dress, but she was called to be an angel. I am trying my hardest to fight back the tears because I do not want to mess up the lovely makeup I spent so much time perfecting. I feel extremely uneasy, but I don't want the sadness to overturn my mood. Our first appointment is not for a couple of weeks, but I need to speak with my therapist. I still miss my mom every day. It's a sadness I will continue to carry, but thanks to Ms. Cameau's help, I've been learning to cope. I hope my new therapist can help me deal with the move, Gabriella, and her demon twins.

The doorbell rings. "Claudette, Kevin is here," my father announces. My heart drops, and butterflies flutter around in my stomach. I am incredibly nervous because I don't know what to expect. I have never been on a date before.

I head down the stairs and walk past the kitchen to the door to meet Kevin. Gabriella and the twins are in the living room, and I can see the hatred in their eyes. *If looks could kill, I would be dead.*

"Have a nice time," Gabriella says softly, a weird smile accompanying her words. Instead of replying, I merely give her a nod.

"Have a good time, sweetheart. Your curfew is at eleven p.m. Don't be late." My dad hands me the white shawl my mother wore with her dress, and I smile and embrace him.

Kevin's eyes widen when I place my hand in his as he helps me down the steps. He opens the car door and waits for me to get in like the handsome gentleman he is. He looks rather hot in his slim-fit black tux.

"Wow!" he exclaims.

"Wow, yourself!" I imitate. His lips curve into a wide grin. I don't know where we are going, but I am excited.

We drive a short distance before pulling into his apartment parking lot, and I am confused. I thought we were going to a restaurant or something. Not wanting to appear disappointed, I keep a poker face and wait for him to explain the meaning of us being at his apartment. *I hope he doesn't think I will lose my virginity to him tonight!*

"It's not what you think," he says, looking me in the eye, and I blush. "I made you dinner."

Umm. What?

"I wanted to make you a special dinner that reminded you of home, and then we will head back to your old town for dessert." He looks at me expectedly.

I can tell he is nervous, and it is so cute. "But I have to be home b—" I say before he cuts me off.

"I spoke to your father and informed him of our dinner plans. We're going to your favorite ice cream shop, Evi."

Did I hear him correctly? "We're going to Evi's?" My eyes sparkle.

"Yeah, babe." He smiles at my eagerness; it is the reaction he was hoping for. "I spoke to the shop owner and asked if she could keep the place open a little longer, and of course, once I presented her with money, she couldn't say no."

I thought I was at a loss for words when we were in the car, but when I walk into his apartment, I am overwhelmed with emotions; Kevin has outdone himself. Adorning the dining table is a white tablecloth, ivory napkins folded in a fancy design, and long-stemmed champagne flutes. Several covered platters are on the table, and a bottle of sparkling cider is chilling in an ice bucket at one end. Oh, and did I mention he has *china* plates? Like he brought out the fine dining plates for little old me!

Kevin pulls out a chair from the table for me to sit and hands me a napkin.

"What's on the menu for tonight?" I ask, my eyes shining. *Boy, am I hungry for Kevin's fine self, but I'll be a good girl and eat first.*

"I asked your father what your favorite meal was," he says in a low, sensual tone, uncovering the platters to reveal the yummy offerings. He has prepared a filet mignon cooked medium rare, with grilled asparagus and mashed potatoes for us. *Is he a chef? What seventeen-year-old can cook this well? I mean restaurant-quality food!* It was as if Chef Gordon Ramsey had prepared the food for me. I am stunned.

Kevin sits across from me and says a quick prayer, and then we enjoy the fabulous meal he'd prepared. I am famished.

"How are you enjoying your steak?" he questions between bites.

I moan. "It's *delicious*."

His eyes darken, and he clears his throat. "Uh, how was your day today?"

I can tell he's trying to distract his mind from the gutter and suppress a smile. "Okay, seriously, Kevin. What gives?"

"What do you mean?" He quirks his eyebrow.

"Where did you learn to cook like this?" I close my eyes and sink my teeth into the tender steak, enjoying its taste.

He shakes his head, laughing at me, and then his face grows serious. "It was self-taught. After my parents kicked me out, I had to learn how to fend for myself."

I stop chewing. "I didn't know that. Why did your parents kick you out?" My voice soothes.

"That's something to discuss in a few weeks when you turn seventeen."

I am so tired of this age discussion! I make a sour face and continue eating my delicious meal. Once we finish, Kevin places the dishes in the dishwasher, and we share the sweetest kiss. Every kiss with Kevin is better than the last. My knees are weak, and my body is ready to feel him inside me. However, I am determined to wait until the right time to give myself to him. *But if he keeps this up, it will be soon.*

"Claudette, I care for you," he declares after our lips part. The seriousness in his tone does not go unnoticed. His gaze is intense, and I feel his affection for me. *Is he the one?* He places two fingers beneath my chin and tilts my head until our eyes meet. My heart is racing as he leans in and presses his lips against mine again. His hands snake around my waist, pulling my frame closer to his, and I can feel a significant bulge pressing against my thighs.

"Are you ready to leave?" he says, his voice like a low growl, and I can tell he is trying hard to restrain himself.

"For what?" I shake my head slightly, trying to pull myself from the heat and sensation I feel down there.

"To head back to your old town for dessert?" He smirks.

"Oh yeah, that's right. I'm ready." I fumble with my words, and he grabs his keys from the holder where he'd placed them earlier.

My old town is about one hour away. When we finally arrive at Evi's ice cream shop, it is closed, but because Kevin gave her extra money, Evi is waiting and lets us inside. I order my favorite butter pecan ice cream, and Kevin gets strawberry, my mother's favorite. I feel goosebumps when he orders it. *Is this a sign?*

"What's on your mind?" he says when he notices me gaping at him.

"That... that ice cream. My mom." I cannot get the words out without being overwhelmed by emotions.

He grabs a napkin, folds it, and gently dabs at a tear rolling down my cheek. I clear my throat and speak again. "I'm sorry. My mom's favorite ice cream was strawberry."

"I apologize; I didn't know."

I can see the concern in his eyes.

"Don't be silly; how could you have known? I'm fine," I reassure him. "It just took me by surprise. You know I am wearing her dress tonight?"

"You look gorgeous, Claudette." He runs his eyes over my body, and I feel like he's touched me. He leans so close to me I can feel his breath on my lips. "I am glad I met you," he whispers.

I cannot help but smile; I am glad I met him, too.

We are enjoying our ice cream and chatting when suddenly Nicolette and Spencer enter the shop.

"*Oh, my gosh*! Did you invite them here?" I jump out of the booth and smother my friends with hugs, cheesing from ear to ear.

"Yes, he did! I like this one, Claudette." Nicolette grabs me in another bear hug.

"He is certainly a keeper," Spencer agrees.

"I missed you guys so much!" I am in awe. I cannot believe it. They are supposed to visit me for my birthday, but for some weird reason, they still cannot find my town on the GPS. I will have to give them the directions. I can't believe Kevin secretly contacted my friends and invited them to meet us! This is the best first date I have ever been on, and I will remember it for the rest of my life. Of course, this is the *only* date I have ever been on, so there is that. Even so, it is undoubtedly one for the books.

Grabbing Kevin by the collar, I kiss him passionately, licking him with my tongue and stroking his torso with my fingers, wanting him to feel how grateful I am.

"Woah, Claudette, you are in public! Calm that down!" Nicolette admonishes, holding out her hand.

"Let them enjoy themselves." Spencer grins as he watches us kissing.

I am in love with Kevin, or is this lust?

"Keep this up, and you will have all of me in no time," I whisper into Kevin's ear so that only he can hear.

He gives me a smirk. "I look forward to being inside you," he teases.

I want you inside of me now!

"Would you like to be my date for the early Spring Dance in a couple of weeks?"

I am smiling from ear to ear. "It would be my pleasure."

"The pleasure is all mine, beautiful," he says, giving me one of his sexy smiles.

We spend the next thirty minutes chatting about school and everything else we can think of. My two best friends are getting along with my boyfriend, and I adore it. After we leave the ice cream shop, we hold hands the entire way home. And when he drops me off, he gives me such a fiery kiss that I think I might combust.

"I want you to know how much you mean to me, Claudette," he says as our lips part. "I really care about you."

"I really care about you too, Kevin."

He gives me one last kiss before finally sending me inside. *This has indeed been the best date night ever!*

Chapter 7

Early Spring Dance

Several weekends later, and before you know it, it's Monday morning again, and I am heading to my first-period class. I spot Isabel on my way to class and approach her. "Hey Isabel, how are you?"

"Hi Claudette, I'm feeling good. Thank you for asking."

"I haven't seen you since the last time we spoke; are you sure everything's okay?" I tilt my head to one side as I look at her.

"Yes, I'm fine. I hate to sound like a broken record, but I will explain it to you in a few days." She smiles.

"Seventeen?" I screw up my face, and she just smiles and nods.

"I wanted to ask you something." She pauses, biting her lip. "Are you friends with Tanya, Tristan, and Kevin?"

Her question is unexpected, but I answer her. "Yes, and Kevin is kind of my boyfriend."

It seems weird saying it out loud, but oddly enough, I love how it sounds. But Isabel's expression says otherwise. I am about to say something about it when Kevin walks up and kisses the back of my neck.

"I'll catch you later," she says, scurrying away like Kevin has stolen something from her.

I frown. "What was that about?"

Kevin shrugs. "I don't know. Isabel is super creepy."

"Is she now?" I purse my lips, staring after Isabel.

"Yeah, she is. Trust me, I've known her for years, and she is not right in the head." He twirls a finger beside one ear.

I nod, dismissing the subject, and we head to class.

The following five periods go by like a breeze. I am heading to the gym when I notice Eli, Isabel, another guy, and the same girl who had ushered Isabel from the bathroom on my first day, standing at a desk with sign-up sheets. *What is her name?* I intend to hurry past them, but Isabel and Eli flag me down. Eli is very handsome and welcoming, and I cannot help but feel drawn to him, but I already have an incredibly sexy boyfriend.

I stop and check out the sheet on the desk. It is a sign-up for the Early Spring Dance committee. I give them two thumbs up and walk away. I do not want to sign up for the dance committee, and who has a dance on a Tuesday, anyway? In my previous school, we always had our dances on Fridays.

"Hey Claudette, wait up," Eli calls after me. *Ugh. What does he want?* I turn to face him, my lips curving into a fake smile. *I have a boyfriend.* I repeat this mantra, trying to ignore my attraction to Eli.

"Hi Eli, how are you?" I ask through gritted teeth, swallowing a moan. *He is so sexy. Calm down, Detta!*

"I'm great." He flashes me his pearly whites. "I was wondering if you want to join the dance committee?"

"No," I reply without hesitation.

Eli laughs. I am unamused and look at him with a severe expression, which makes him laugh even harder.

"You know you're the first person to deny me like that?" He laughs so hard he is gasping for air.

I'm not surprised. I am more straightforward than most and don't want to plan the spring dance.

"Come on, Claudette, it will be fun, *and* tomorrow's my birthday," he coaxes.

Is that supposed to get me to change my mind? He grabs my hand, and I feel a jolt of electricity stream through my body, so intense I am shaken. And the way he sucks his bottom lip and glares at me lets me know he felt it too.

I jerk my hand away from his. “What was *that*?” I wrinkle my brow. It’s the second time electricity has flowed between us.

“It means you should help with the dance.” He smirks.

I really do not want to, but when he flashes me his dashing smile, I feel compelled to say yes. I reluctantly nod and follow him back to the table to sign up.

“We will meet here after school,” Eli says.

“I can’t. I have a meeting with my therapist.” I bite my lip.

“Therapist? Is everything okay?” A look of concern fills his eyes.

“Yes... well, not really,” I say. “I just have some things I need to sort out, and ah, that’s what therapy is for, isn’t it?” I swallow hard.

“I completely understand,” Isabel chimes in. “I’ve been in therapy since my parents died.”

I knew her parents had died from stalking her Instagram, but this was the first time I’d heard Isabel say it. “I am so sorry for your loss, Isabel.”

“It’s okay. I mean, it is what it is now. I am working through it.” She shrugs.

The nameless girl from the bathroom rubs Isabel’s back. “It will be okay, Izzy,” she whispers.

“How about after you meet with your therapist, you meet us back here, so we can start planning? My father didn’t leave much time for us to figure it out since the dance is tomorrow,” the girl suggests. “I’m Destiny, by the way. The principal’s daughter.” She holds her hand to shake mine.

The handsome guy beside her shakes my hand and introduces himself, too. “I’m Lin; nice to meet you.” His lips curve into a smile.

We go our separate ways, and I head to the girl’s locker room to get ready for gym class. While I’m there, Destiny enters and gestures for me to meet her by the showers.

After I get dressed and place my belongings in the locker, I meet her by the broken shower. It’s not actually broken, but we claim it is because it doesn't have hot water. It sucks when you don't get to the showers quickly enough, and it's the only one left.

"Hey Claudette, I wanted to thank you," Destiny says.

I scrunch up my face. "For...?"

"Stopping Isabel."

"Oh. I didn't really do anything. Are you and Isabel close?"

"Isabel is my girlfriend. She's been having a tough time since her parents' death. I have been trying to do everything that I can to keep her in a happy place. But it's hard to do that when people are being murdered left and right in this town."

Umm... I'm sorry; what does she mean by murdered "left and right?" I freeze, not knowing what to say, but I know she just said that. Like I heard her correctly—*didn't I?*

Not noticing my confusion, Destiny continues, "My mother was found dead three years ago, and now both of Isabel's parents are gone. I have been trying to figure out for weeks if one murder has anything to do with the other, but no luck."

I have no idea why she is telling me this or what I am supposed to do with the information, but I nod and try to keep my eyes from bugging out.

"My mom is gone too, but she wasn't murdered. She passed away from a heart attack when I was younger, so I understand losing a parent," I say. "I also understand wanting to commit suicide. There have been plenty of times when I just wanted the pain I felt to stop, and I tried to kill myself. Luckily, my father intervened. So, when I saw Isabel, I just wanted to help her, and I am glad she is doing better now."

"Oh no, I am so sorry you felt the need to want to do that." She rests her hand on my shoulder. "I can't imagine what you must have been thinking in those moments."

"All you feel is pain; that's what you're thinking about. You want the pain you feel to stop," I admit. "But people don't understand that the pain doesn't last, and better days are ahead. You just have to push forward to see them."

Destiny looks at me with complete understanding. "So many people don't see the bright light at the end of the tunnel. But thank you for helping my girlfriend when I couldn't be there. I can never thank you enough. I don't know what I would do if something ever happened to her." She wipes the tear that rolls down her cheek. "It's nice meeting you, Claudette, and I look forward to planning the dance with you later." She gives me a broad smile.

We embrace and head to the gym, where everyone sits, waiting for the activities to start.

After school, Kevin drops me off at my new therapist, Ms. Hudson's, office. It is actually her home, which I think is weird. But hey, to each his own.

Kevin kisses me and tells me he will return to pick me up after the session. I haven't told him I joined the school dance planning committee.

I enter the house through the unlocked door into a vast open area. Ms. Hudson's home is incredibly creepy, like something straight out of a haunted movie. Everything is black and gray; it's like she is unaware that an entire color palette exists with additional selections besides those two. In the waiting area are castle-like throne chairs engraved with full moons for her guests. I lower myself into one and wait for her to come out of her office to greet me.

"Hello dear, you must be Claudette," a gentle voice says.

I look up to see Ms. Hudson, a heavy-set, brown-haired woman with ocean-blue eyes, and stand to shake her hand. She wears bright red lipstick, a huge moon pendant necklace around her neck, and another dangling from a bracelet on her left arm. Aside from her creepy décor and appearance, her aura is extremely inviting.

"Let's go in here." She shows me into her office.

Along the walls are several photos of crescent moons. *What is this obsession she has with moons? Maybe she should speak to someone about this.*

She sits at a black and silver desk and reaches into the last drawer on the right side to pull out a black notebook. "Please take a seat." She points to a black two-seater sofa.

I sit and make myself comfortable, putting my bag on the floor and crossing my legs. The sofa is plush and comfy, and I want to fall asleep. I don't know what to say, so I wait for her to speak first.

She glances at me and writes in her little notebook.

I uncross my legs and shake my right leg vigorously, feeling my nerves build up.

"So, tell me about yourself?" she says finally, breaking the deafening silence.

I shift in my seat; I hate when people ask me about myself. I am not very interesting. "My name is Claudette," I state the obvious.

She gives me a soft smile and writes something down. "Yes, I know that. I would like you to tell me something new, or would you prefer I tell you about myself first?"

"How about you tell me about yourself?" *And this obsession with moons.*

"My name is Ms. Hudson. I am divorced and don't have any children. I have been a social worker for over twenty years and enjoy helping people. Now, would you like to tell me something about you?"

I gulp down the knot in my throat. "My mother died when I was younger, and my dad remarried to a woman I dislike. And I feel like she is the one that made us move here."

Ms. Hudson scribbles in her notebook quickly. "I see. First, I would like to say I am sorry for your loss. Second, how do you feel about living here?"

"Thank you." I give her a small smile. "I don't like this town much. I miss my home, but I met this awesome guy."

"Yes, Mr. Evans."

"Yes, you know him?" I watch her through narrowed eyes. *How does she know about Kevin and me?*

"This is a tiny town; I know everyone here." She chuckles.

"Oh, of course." I feel my face grow hot.

"Claudette, what do you want to gain from our sessions?" She studies me, waiting for my answer.

"Honestly, I need help dealing with this move. Sometimes, I get this overwhelming feeling that I am missing something, but I don't know or understand what. And I miss my mother; I really wish she were alive, especially at times like this, when I have a boyfriend. I wish she were here so I could have 'girl talk' with her. Before she died, we were so close. I know we would have become even closer had she lived. I envy the girls who still have their moms." The words came out of me like vomit; there it was, the one thing I could never say to Ms. Cameau. *I envy girls with mothers.*

We both knew that I was grieving for my mother, but I would spend most of my time talking about other stuff or complaining about the twins. The fact of the matter was I miss my mother, and now that I have a boyfriend, I miss her even more.

As I speak, my feelings overwhelm me, and I begin to sob, deep sobs that wrack my entire body. Ms. Hudson stands up to hand me a box of Kleenex. By the time I am done, I'm sure I have used most of the box, but when I glance at her bookshelf, I see she has a large stack of Kleenex. *I guess she is used to this.* By the time the session ends, I feel comfortable with Ms. Hudson. The session went well, and I am thankful Ms. Cameau recommended her.

After my session, Kevin picks me up, and I ask him to drop me off at school. He is unhappy about me planning the school dance with Destiny, Eli, Lin, and Isabel. I do not know what bad blood is between them, but I intend to find out.

I walk down the hallway to the gym; we have about two hours to figure out what we want to do regarding plans for the dance. We sit in a circle, bouncing ideas off one another until we finally decide on a Halloween-themed dance. I do not know how we came up with the idea, but I am all for it.

Afterward, Destiny drops me at home, and I am ready to crash when my dad knocks on my door. "Come in."

"Hey, Cheetah, how was your session today?" Dad gently tucks my baby hair behind my ear.

"It was great; I really like her." I yawn.

"That's fantastic!" he says, clapping his hands together.

"Yeah, I like her... but Dad, I am exhausted and ready for bed. Tomorrow is the school dance, and I need my beauty sleep." I push him toward the door.

He turns to kiss me on the forehead, then leaves.

I dive headfirst into my bed, not even bothering to shower or brush my teeth; I am just too drained.

The following morning, I wake refreshed; I brush my teeth, shower, and prepare for school. Because the dance is today, we only have classes until the fifth period; we have lunch at sixth and will spend the seventh period decorating the gym for the dance. I didn't know what I wanted to wear or even what I wanted to be until Eli mentioned he had an extra pair of vampire teeth that I could use. This is awesome because I can wear anything black to go with that.

I finish a few minor details on my uniform, put on some stud earrings, and head downstairs to wait for Kevin to pick me up. The best thing about Crissy smacking me in the face is since that day, Kevin vowed to pick me up and drop me off at school. I have my license but no car. And if something happens between Kevin and me, I know Destiny, Eli, or Isabel would not mind driving me to school.

As I walk to the door, Marissa and Crissy block my way with their arms folded and scowls plastered on their faces.

"Move!" I place my hands on my hips and glower at them.

When we were at our old school, where they ruled as Queen B's, I would not have dared to say that to them, but since they are not in charge at Mashal High, I feel bold. At that moment, confidence flows throughout my entire body. For years, the two have tormented me, making fun of my skin color and calling me names such as blacky, dark thunder, and shadow. Finally, they can no longer bully me and make me feel low about myself, and I know it is getting to them.

"Excuse me, who do you think you're talking to... *Dark Thunder*?" Marissa says through gritted teeth.

"I am speaking to someone who is not happy with their own life and is completely pathetic. Now, move! My *boyfriend*, which neither of you has, is waiting for me outside." Watching their mouths fall open, I give them a self-satisfied smile.

Crissy is about to smack me again, but I grab her hand. "Not this time." I use all my strength to crush her hand. Marissa pushes me, and I push her back. The next thing I know, we are fighting. My father is off work today, and he and Gabriella break us up.

"I am so sick of those demon twins! I don't understand why you had to marry that awful woman and bring them into our lives!" I screech before storming out of the house, slamming the door behind me.

Kevin approaches me quickly as I stomp down the walkway toward his car.

"What happened?" He glances at my house, then looks back at me warily.

"I don't want to talk about it!" I snap. He does not say a word after my outburst and instead opens the car door for me, and we drive off in silence.

When we arrive at school, I am still very heated over what happened and do not want to discuss it. I go to my classes, and by sixth period I am over it. My dad sends me several text messages throughout the day that I ignore. I do not see the twins for the day; from the looks of it, it does not seem like they will appear at the dance.

The bell rings, and it is time to decorate the gym. Destiny, Isabel, and Lin are already decorating when I arrive, but I don't see Eli. "Hey, where is Eli?"

"He's running late; he should be here shortly," Destiny replies.

"Did you guys get him a birthday cake?" I ask.

"We were, but then he told us he didn't want one," Isabel says.

"He isn't into those types of things," Lin adds.

We are blowing up red, black, and gold balloons and putting streamers up when Eli walks in. He does not look like himself; he seems... well, I do not know what he looks like, but it is troubling.

I place my hand gently on his arm. "Are you okay?"

"I'm fine! I just want this day to be over," he snaps.

"Wait, what?" His reaction catches me off guard.

"Don't worry about it." He waves me off.

"But—"

"Let's just get these decorations up," he hisses, cutting me off.

I cannot understand what is wrong with him, but it does not seem to faze Destiny or Isabel. They completely ignore Eli's mood, and Lin, too, acts as if nothing is happening. So, I do the same.

After we finish with the gym, I go to the girl's locker room to change my outfit. I return to find the DJ setting up his equipment and chaperones walking around as students enter. Kevin arrives, looking very handsome in gray slacks and a slim-fit, button-down black shirt.

"What are you supposed to be?" I ask, grabbing him by the waist.

"I see you're feeling better now." He smiles and kisses me on the cheek.

"Yes." I swallow, feeling my cheeks turn red. "I'm sorry for snapping at you earlier."

"Shh." He puts a finger to his lips. "Don't tell anyone, but I am a warlock." He grins, lightening the mood.

I twirl. "I am a vampire. You like?"

He waggles his eyebrows at me, then gestures to the dance floor. "Would you like to dance?"

I nod, and he leads the way.

When he places his hands on my waist and pulls me close, I can feel the entire frame of his body pressing against mine. While we dance, it's like we are the only two people in the room. It is magical until the lightbulbs shatter.

Chapter 8

Seventeenth Birthday

All the lightbulbs shatter, and the windows explode. The shattered glass levitates above us. Yeah, you read that right. *The glass is levitating.* Everyone is on the floor, screaming. Kevin shields me during the chaos and points toward a table where we can hide.

"Kevin, what is happening?" I shriek.

"I am not sure, but we must get out of here!"

"How do you suggest we do that?"

"Follow me." He crawls on the floor toward a tiny door, and I follow suit. I would not have noticed it if we were not crawling toward it. Once the glass pieces fall out of the air, everyone goes into panic mode, running for the exits. It's like a stampede of animals trying to avoid being eaten by a lion. A piece of glass slices down my arm just as Kevin yanks me through the small crawl space down a secret tunnel out of the gym. He takes my arm and checks the wound as soon as we're out. I pull away, pacing back and forth. I cannot believe what I just saw. *Did the glass levitate, or am I going crazy?*

"Kevin, I need you to explain to me *now*! What just happened? And do not tell me to wait until I am seventeen because I will be in just a few days!" I cross my arms, tapping my right foot repeatedly on the floor.

He does not respond. "Kevin, seriously?" I roll my eyes. "I will be seventeen on Friday." I tighten my jaw and glare at him.

Still not a word. *Can you believe this guy?* I shake my head and turn around, looking for a way out of whatever secret closet we're in. Finding a door behind a bunch of dusty clothes, I am about to open it when Kevin grasps my hand.

"Magic is real." His voice is so low that I'm not sure I heard him correctly. I stick my index finger into my ear, trying to clear it of whatever might be blocking my hearing. Perhaps I have some earwax I need to clean out. "I'm sorry... *what*?"

"Magic. Is. Real." He enunciates each word. He says nothing else for a long moment, and just when I'm about to freak out, he speaks again. "Listen, Claudette. Please stay calm! No one can know that I told you. I understand you will be seventeen in three days, but there are rules in this town that we cannot—*should not*—break. My telling you magic is real is against the rules. Eli has broken the rules, too." By now, Kevin is rambling.

"What?"

He places a finger to my lips, indicating I should be quiet.

"What do you mean Eli broke the rules?" I whisper.

Kevin takes a step back and exhales.

"This town is full of witches and warlocks. On your seventeenth birthday, you will receive the gift—or curse, depending on your perspective—of magic and must decide whether you want to accept it. If you do, you will become a witch. If not, you will remain human. Today is Eli's seventeenth birthday; he accepted the magic. All the chaos in the gym happened because of his choice," Kevin explains.

Have you ever watched a cartoon where something surprising happens, and your mouth drops to the floor? Well, this is no cartoon, but my mouth hangs wide open. I cock my head and place one hand on my throat, opening and closing it as if trying to ease an itch while I try to figure out the right words to say. When I open my mouth to speak, no words come out. I mean, I am mute.

"When we leave this closet, I need you to promise me you will not say a word to anyone about what I've told you." Kevin's pleading eyes fix on mine.

I stare at him blankly, still mute.

"Claudette!" He grabs my shoulders and gives me a slight shake.

"Who would believe me, anyway? I'm not even sure I believe it," I say, finally.

Which is true; I do not know what to believe. But then again, I trust what I saw with my own eyes. Glass levitated in the air, and Eli had acted weirdly. Yeah, I hardly know the guy, but going from being extremely friendly to ice-cold is a complete turnaround.

Kevin opens the door, and I see we are outside the school in the back parking lot. I can hear police cars and the fire truck coming to the rescue.

Kevin examines my arm. "You don't need stitches." He takes my hand and speed walks to his car. Once inside the vehicle, I cannot help myself. I have questions and need answers—*now*.

"Kevin, can you please pull over?" He glances at me and pulls over at the next light, parking in a fast-food lot underneath a tree.

"Did you want to make out?" he teases, trying to lighten the mood. His lips curve into a smirk when I roll my eyes.

He sighs. "Ask away, Claudette."

"What do you mean, magic is real? You said there are witches and warlocks in this town? Are you a warlock? Explain everything to me, Kevin, and please be honest."

"This town is full of witches and warlocks—" he begins, but I cut him off.

"Kevin!"

"Listen, Claudette. I will explain everything. But let me do it my way. Okay?" he scolds, and I keep my mouth shut.

"As I was saying before you so rudely interrupted." He tosses me a smile. "This town is full of witches and warlocks. There are Sun, Moon, and Earth witches. When you turn seventeen, you can keep your magic and develop it or get rid of it. When I turned seventeen, I opted to get rid of it; I felt like it was a curse. When you reach your seventeenth birthday on Friday, you will wake up not feeling like yourself. Some witches wake up angry; others are extremely sad. There is no in-between. The day you met Isabel was her seventeenth birthday, and she was tremendously sad but then decided to keep her magic, which is why she now has her classes in the West Wing. The West Wing students are 'Mags' because they practice magic, and the East Wing students are 'Norms.' We are the ones who decided we'd rather be normal than deal with the burden of possessing magic. My family are Sun witches, Eli is a Moon witch, Tristan and Tanya are Sun witches, and you, my beautiful girlfriend, are an Earth witch, which is very rare. The prophecy says I would fall in love with an Earth witch. It is why we have such a strong connection. I have felt drawn to you ever since we met. There is no doubt in my mind that we are meant to be together. As for your magic, I respect whatever decision you make. The look on your face tells me you are having difficulty believing what I'm telling you. But I want you to pay attention tomorrow. You will notice Eli is no longer in your classes; he may not even be in school. Isabel missed several days when she accepted her magic." Kevin's speech is very rapid now. I absorb every sentence, clinging to his every word.

"Are my stepsister's witches?" I ask.

"They accepted magic."

"Why haven't they tried to hurt me using their powers?"

"The rules forbid witches from using magic against norms. If they do, their power could be taken from them," he explains.

"Who would take their magic?"

"The Witch Council would conduct a ceremony using a dagger called a 'Ce-Ja' and recite a spell that takes away the power. There is a way to get the magic back, but that would require death and a lot of dark magic."

"Is my father a witch?" I cannot contain all my questions. The more Kevin tells me, the more I want to know; my curiosity increases, just like my nervousness.

"Your father rejected magic, as did your mother. That's why they could move out of town. But when two norms leave the town, they must return if they have a child, so the child can decide to remain normal or become a mag."

That made little sense to me; why go through all that trouble to move just to come back? "Does Gabriella practice magic?"

"No, she doesn't. The Witch Council took her magic away when she returned. Your father, Gabriella, and the twins had no choice but to move back to this town so that you could decide if you wanted to remain a norm or become a mag." Kevin looks me in the eye.

"I don't understand. The twins have been seventeen for two months now. Why didn't we move here before their seventeenth birthday? Or why did they leave in the first place?" I ask. There is so much I need to know, and I realize Kevin does not have all the answers.

"Honestly, I don't know. Gabriella accepted magic, so she should have never left this town," he says. "Claudette, I am sorry to tell you, but Gabriella and the twins leaving was against the rules. The twins still have their magic because they didn't have a say in leaving. But as soon as you arrived, the council summoned Gabriella and removed her magic. If you are a mag, you must stay in this town, no matter what. After the father of her children left without a word, Gabriella decided she would leave, according to what my mother said. And for years, the council searched for her; it wasn't until she married your father that she appeared on the radar again."

I honestly cannot fathom all this information. How can I go home and pretend I know nothing? *Wait? How can I go home?* With all this witch information and chaos at the dance, I completely forgot what transpired before I left home today. I am not going back to that house! I need time to digest everything about the rules, witches, and magic.

"Can I stay with you for the rest of the week?" I whisper. "I need time to process everything, and I would rather be around someone I can trust."

Kevin nods, starts the car, and we drive to his apartment. I am mentally and physically drained.

When we arrive at his apartment, I check my phone and see five missed calls from my dad. I do not want to speak to him. He is a liar. I should have known I was born a witch and would be burdened with this decision to remain a norm or become a mag. My eyes fill with tears as I think about all the times he could have told me. I do not need to wait until Friday to know I do not want to be a witch. I do not want to possess magic so powerful that I have glass levitating. *That is insane.*

"Babe, are you okay?" Kevin asks, breaking my train of thought.

"No, I am not okay," I confess. "My father has been lying to me my entire life. He could have told me before that I was a witch."

Kevin nods his head understandingly and embraces me. "Babe, they moved to the real world. They could have told you that you were a witch. But then again, would you have been able to keep that to yourself? I mean, what child can keep that a secret from their friends? Which reminds me, you can't tell Nicolette or Spencer that you are a witch." He gazes into my eyes. "I mean it."

"I won't say anything to them," I lie. Of course, I will tell my two best friends, but I doubt they will believe me, anyway. Kevin gives me one of his black t-shirts and a brand-new toothbrush, and I head to the bathroom and shower. Afterward, I shoot my father a text.

Me:

I need time to think. I am staying with Kevin for the rest of the week.

I don't wait for a response, and I'm not in the mood to eat, so I head straight to bed. Kevin, the gentleman he is, sleeps on the sofa in the living room.

The following day, I get dressed, still completely drained. It is Wednesday, and I am counting the hours until my birthday. Usually, I would be excited, but I dread the moment the magic that will soon awaken inside me. I stride toward the kitchen, where Kevin is in his boxers, cooking breakfast. *I could get used to this.* He greets me with a soft kiss and hands me a plate ladened with eggs, a biscuit, and French toast.

"You didn't eat last night, so I made you breakfast," he says. "What would you like to do for your birthday?" He wraps his arms around my waist.

"Hide in a storage facility," I blurt out.

He bursts out laughing. I am not sure what is so funny because I am completely serious.

"No, seriously, Claudette." He looms over me and looks at me with seriousness.

"Kevin, we don't know if I will be happy or sad that day. What makes you think I want to do something, especially after what happened with Eli?"

"Did you decide if you want to be a witch?" he asks.

I look at him with confidence. "Yes, I have already made my decision."

Kevin nods. "Tanya told me that when you decide before your birthday, sometimes you are sad; when you are conflicted about what you should do, you wake up angry. She is a part of the Witch Council tasked with monitoring the reactions. And so is Tristan."

"I don't want to be sad." Flashes of Isabel standing outside the window about to jump appear.

"Don't worry, I will be with you," he consoles.

"How long does it take for your magic to disappear?" I ask, pursing my lips.

"Whether you decide to become a mag or remain a norm, you will possess magic for seventeen days. Your magic will progress if you become a mag. If you decide to remain a norm, the magic will digress. If you are conflicted, then during that time, you will become angry."

A sudden thought comes to me. "Can you become evil?" I look up at him.

"Just don't let the magic consume you."

What does that even mean? "How do I prevent that from happening?"

"Let's finish getting ready for school. And please pretend you don't know any of this information," he pleads again, and I nod.

I scarf down the rest of my breakfast while Kevin gets ready for school.

When we arrive, I realize I am literally the only student in school who is unaware of magic. Also, no one discusses what happened at the dance, and all my friends avoid me throughout the day.

Isabel, Destiny, Lin, and Eli are missing in action, and when I go to lunch, Tanya and Tristan are nowhere to be found. To keep up the pretense, I go to the office and ask Principal Deanwall what happened in the gym yesterday. He tells me it was some electrical wiring and not to worry about it. It amazes me how everyone is in one accord to keep me in the dark.

After school, I listen to all my voicemails from Dad. He goes from angry to worried and back to angry. I send him a text.

I know I was not supposed to say anything, but unlike my father, I am not a liar.

Me:

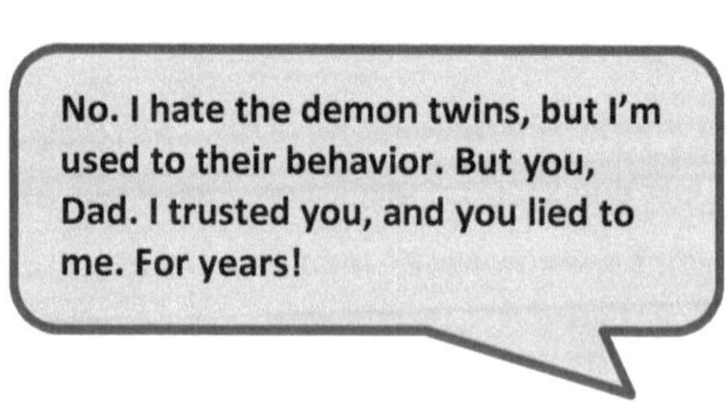

After I send him the text, I am having second thoughts. I wasn't supposed to know any of this, and now I have revealed it to my dad.

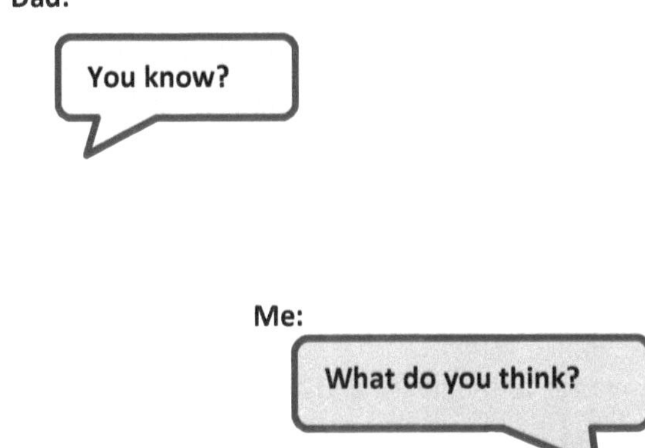

I respond without second guessing it.

Dad:

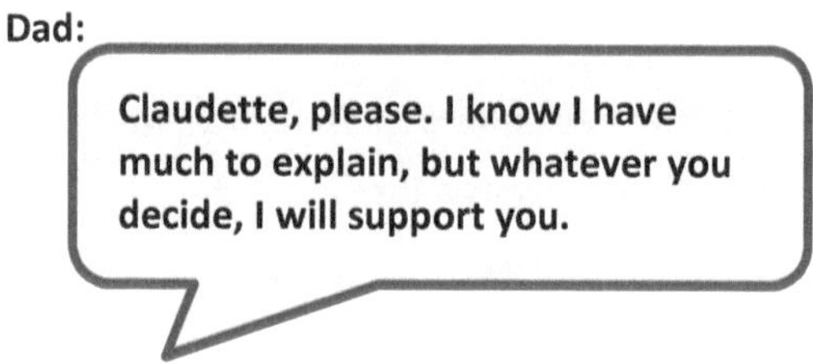

After I don't respond, he calls me. Presumably, to ensure nothing gets lost in translation. I speak to him for about twenty minutes and tell him I do not want him to choose between his wife and me, so I decided for him. I will not live at home as long as Gabriella and the demon twins are there.

I give Kevin my keys to the house and ask him to pick up my possessions because I cannot bear to look at my dad's face. When Kevin gets back with my belongings, he seems upset. He knows I revealed to my father that I have learned about witches, but I tell him I could not keep it from my father. I know my dad will say nothing to the council or Gabriella. As far as Gabriella and the others are concerned, my reason for not returning home is the fight I had with the twins. I told Dad to tell his wife I did not feel safe around the twins because they could jump me.

After Kevin and I eat dinner, we head to bed, and I set the timer on my watch until my birthday. This time, I curl up next to Kevin and fall asleep. He is so sexy, but I can't think about that now. But I know it will be perfect when I finally give myself to him.

SIXTEEN HOURS UNTIL MY BIRTHDAY...

When I awake the following morning, I feel exceedingly anxious. It is mere hours before I am seventeen years old. My friends send me text messages asking what I want to do for my birthday, but I ignore them. I do not know what to tell them.

Eli is a no-show again when we arrive at school, and so are Isabel, Destiny, Lin, Marissa, and Crissy. It's as if they purposely missed school so they would not risk me possibly asking questions. I feel like a robot attending all my classes. I am there physically but not mentally. Luckily, the day goes by quickly, and I am back at Kevin's apartment. Kevin is not at home; he told me he had to meet Tanya and Tristan and would be home later before my birthday to help me through it. I shower and wash my hair, which calms my nerves enough to eat dinner without vomiting. I look at the clock, and it is almost six pm.

SIX HOURS TO GO...

Sitting in the chair, rocking back and forth, I am petrified. I turn on the TV and flip through the channels, trying to find something to watch to take my mind off my impending doom. But nothing calms me.

When Kevin returns, he has a worried expression. I look at the time; it is almost eleven pm. He embraces me, and we watch the clock until it is midnight.

The lights begin to flicker off and on, and I feel a jolt of electricity flow through me like I am being electrocuted. I scream as I start to levitate. I have no control over what is happening. My entire body is shaking uncontrollably. I try to reach down to Kevin, but there is nothing he or I can do to stop what is happening to me.

Blue, gold, and black lights glisten along my arms and legs and finally emerge from my hands. I feel the magic awakening from deep within as my body finally descends. The room goes dark for about five minutes, and then the lights flicker on from a mere thought. *Did I do that?* When I point to a dish on the table, it falls to the floor, shattering. I cannot believe what is happening. *I have magical powers.*

Chapter 9

What Should I Do?

The next morning, I don't attend school. No one is surprised, however, because they all know it's my birthday. Kevin and I barely slept the night before; my magic seems to progress by the hour. It is as simple as thinking about what I want, and it happens. As soon as I think about butter pecan ice cream, it appears. It's my favorite flavor from Evi's ice cream shop. I sit on the sofa, trying to understand the magic growing inside me, and I can't fathom it. I never thought witches were real, let alone that I would be one.

To take my mind off what is happening, I decide to watch TV, but I can't find the remote. As soon as I think about it, it appears in my hand. *Woah!* Suddenly, I feel a rage building up inside of me. *No! I don't want to be a witch! Are you sure?* Detta, my inner voice entices me. Kevin explained that if I feel rage, it is because mentally, I want to become a mag. Even though I had decided to reject magic, I found it difficult to resist.

Kevin is in the shower, and I can feel myself getting angrier. I stand, throw the remote to the floor, storm into Kevin's room, and get dressed. The lights flicker on and off as I clench my fists. *Why is this happening?* The lights flickering upsets me even more.

"*Enough*!" I shout. The lights stop flashing, and the window explodes. Shards of glass fly around, and a piece slices my face.

Kevin rushes out of the bathroom, looking panicked, and sees the blood trickling down my face. "You're accepting the magic!" he exclaims.

"*What? No, I am not!* I don't want this." *Yes, you do!* I plummet to the floor, covering the cut on my face with one hand. "I don't want this!" I sob, grabbing Kevin by the leg. "Please make this stop!" *I don't want this magic; I don't want to be a mag. I want to be normal.*

The lights flicker again, and the bed levitates. Then everything in the room swirls around like a tornado. Chaos surrounds me, and I can't stop it. *I need to get out of here!*

I want my shoes, and they appear on my feet. Kevin is confused and asks where I am going, but I ignore him. There is only one person I want to see who will understand what I am going through right now. That's who I need to speak with—*Eli!*

When I open the front door, Eli is standing there. I get into the car with him, and we drive to his place in silence. When we arrive, neither of us speaks. I just want to get inside. I sit on the floor in a corner facing the wall as everything in his apartment shakes.

"Claudette?" he says.

Rage bursts from my body. "*What*?!"

"I need you to calm down. You can control the magic; don't let it control you. Just breathe and accept it."

"No, I don't want to accept it. I don't want to be a witch. Is that what you did? You accepted *this*?" My voice breaks, and I sob, shaking uncontrollably. I don't want to be a witch. "Please, please, Eli... help me."

He walks toward me slowly, holding his hands up as though confirming he is no threat. He reaches for my hand and helps me to my feet. My breaths slow as I calm down, and all the chaos in the room subsides. It is like someone watching this unfold hit the pause button on a remote; it is astounding.

"Did you do this?" I question.

"Yes, I used my magic to keep you calm and stopped all this." He makes a sweeping gesture around the room. "Here, drink this to calm your nerves." He hands me a cup of red juice.

I gulp it down in one sitting. “How did you do that?” I wipe my mouth with my sleeve.

“Control.”

Something has changed with Eli. He is sure of himself and his magic. I don’t know if I could be as confident as he is.

“Your body is reacting this way because you are telling yourself that you don’t want to be a mag, but it’s your fate to be one. Everything you did today before you lost control, deep down, you enjoyed it.” He smiles.

I mean, when my favorite ice cream appeared in my hands, I did like it. Magic is tempting. I can’t deny that.

He takes my hand and places it over the cut on my face. “Heal yourself.”

My eyes widen at the thought that I can actually heal myself.

He nods, assuring me I can do it.

I close my eyes, take a deep breath, and my cut disappears. “Eli! The cut... it’s gone; the pain is gone!” My eyes sparkle, and I feel in control. I wave my hand and return all the items in the room to their rightful places.

Eli’s lips curve into a warm smile, and he embraces me. As soon as he touches me, I feel a shudder of energy. I can feel our magic entwining. The electricity streams through my body and into his. Blue, gold, and brown lights encircle our fingers, and it is as if we are complete. I feel drawn to him; *I want him!*

Eli caresses my lips with his thumb. When our gazes lock, he pulls me in for a soft kiss. While he teases me, circling his tongue in my mouth, I inhale his natural musk and close my eyes. When our lips part, we stare at each other. I felt the attraction between us the day we first met, but my feelings now are different. Our magic is connected, and I feel complete and lost in its union. So much so that I totally forgot... *I have a boyfriend!*

“What’s wrong?” Eli strokes my cheek.

“Eli, we can’t do this. I have a boyfriend.” I push him back so we have some space between us.

“Do you really think Kevin is trustworthy?” His eyes darken.

"What do you mean?" I frown.

"What has Kevin told you about all this witch stuff?"

Before I can respond, he places his index finger over my lips, preventing me from speaking. "Let me tell you a story."

I slowly nod for him to proceed.

"Kevin's parents are both powerful Sun witches. Two witches of the same power uniting were unheard of until their union. It has always been Sun and Moon or Sun and Earth. In History of Magic, taught by Mr. Goatfair, two witches with the same power should not marry—Sun with Sun, Moon with Moon, Earth with Earth. When two witches with the same power bond and have a baby, that child is evil. While we all can use our magic for good or evil, you don't get to choose when born from the same coven. Kevin is not who he says he is. He didn't give up his powers. The council took his powers because he was evil. He doesn't live with his parents because they kicked him out. After that, my mom removed his parents from the witch's council. Rumors say he has been murdering the few Earth witches left in this town to regain his magic."

I can't grasp what Eli is telling me. Kevin isn't evil... he can't be. He loves me! There is no way Kevin could have been deceiving me this entire time. Kevin said he didn't want to be a mag and chose to remain a norm. If what Eli says is true, wouldn't Kevin be in jail? Or worse?

"You're just saying that!" I glare at Eli.

"Why would I make something like this up? I am sure he told you a nice little story about wanting to be a norm, but that's not true."

"How would you even know any of this? Aren't you new to this school?" Why is Eli telling me this? Kevin has been an incredible boyfriend, and I believe he cares for me. Which makes me feel even worse about the kiss Eli and I shared. The connection I feel with Eli is unimaginable, but no! This has to be a lie! *I'm an awful girlfriend!*

"Claudette! You don't attend Mashal High until you are sixteen years old. Before then, you go to a different school. I have lived in this town my entire life, and my parents are on the Witch Council."

My eyes widen at the mention of the Witch Council once again. Kevin said that Tanya and Tristan were on the council.

"Tristan and Tanya are Sun witches, and they are together. Why is that if it is forbidden?" I cross my arms and stare at Eli, waiting for an answer.

"You can't trust Kevin, Tristan, and Tanya. They are all evil, and they are planning something. Has Kevin suggested that you stay a norm or become a mag?"

I couldn't believe this; Tanya has been nothing but supportive. Tristan is funny, and Kevin is my boyfriend. I love him. But why would Eli say this? Why would he make this up? *He's jealous!*

"He told me he supported whatever decision I made. And I have decided that I want to be a witch." I stagger to the sofa and sit down. Eli has told me a lot, and I need time to process it. I cover my face with my hands, closing my eyes. *What should I do?* Kevin doesn't seem evil; he has been incredible since I met him. But there is this connection between Eli and me that I can't deny. Whenever we touch, electric shocks overwhelm me. It was as if our magic was trying to connect, and tonight, it finally did.

"I am telling you the truth." Eli ran his hands through his hair.

I take a deep breath, not looking at him. I need to ask Kevin myself. Did he lose his magic, or did he give it up as he said? I stand. I am going to find out.

"Where are you going?"

"I am going to ask my boyfriend myself!" I shout.

"You can't be serious! Claudette, he is using you!" Eli grabs me by the arm, preventing me from opening the door.

"Eli! Let go of me. I am going to ask Kevin myself. *Now let go*!" I feel my powers coming to the surface, and Eli goes flying. Rolling my eyes, I open the door to leave. I can't believe he thought he could prevent me from leaving.

Hmm... If I think about Kevin's place, will I appear there? As my thought ends, I materialize in front of Kevin's apartment, and I look around, wondering if anyone else has seen me pop up out of nowhere. But even if they did, so what? This is a town full of witches.

I knock and wait for Kevin to open it. He seems relieved when he opens the door, and our gazes meet. He leans in to embrace me. Although I feel conflicted, he came to the door with no shirt on, showing his massive abs and low-cut pants, and everything I am feeling goes away—*briefly*.

"We need to talk." I move to push past him, and he backs up with both hands in the air.

"Are both your parents Sun witches?" I demand so loudly I am sure the neighbors can hear me.

"Is that what Eli told you?"

"Umm… you don't answer a question with a question." I roll my eyes.

"Yes, my parents are both Sun witches."

I turn to leave, but he runs before me, holding his hands out to make me stop. "But please, babe, let me explain."

I tap my watch and give him the death glare. "Do not lie to me, Kevin," I say through gritted teeth. "You're walking on very thin ice."

"Okay, my parents fell in love with one another despite the rule, and when they were told that I would be evil, they took my magic away so that I would never have the burden of having to choose. I didn't make the choice. They made it for me."

So, he lied to me? What else has he lied about? "Is it true that you have murdered Earth witches to regain your magic?"

"What? No! I don't want magic and would never hurt anyone to get it. Claudette, do you really think I could murder someone?" He steps closer to me. I stare at him, not knowing whether to believe him. His eyes are clear, and he seems sincere.

"Claudette, I love you, and I know you can sense how you make me feel." He moves closer, and I notice a bulge in his pants. *Are you sure it's not just lust?* I step away from him and pace back and forth. Eli said they took away his magic because he was evil; now Kevin is telling me they took it away, but that didn't mean he was bad. I don't know what to believe.

"From what Eli told me, you don't have the choice in whether you are good or evil. You are just evil."

"I don't believe in all the old stories I've heard. I am my own person, and I choose to be good. Besides, evil cannot love, and I know I love you." Walking toward me, he leans in and kisses me on the cheek. My senses are on high alert, and I want him, but I don't feel the jolt of electricity I felt when Eli kissed me.

"Let me show you how you make me feel." He picks me up and takes me into his bedroom. Sitting me on the bed, he takes off my shoes. I am about to say something when he kisses me, using his tongue this time, teasing me with it. I lose my train of thought. I am unsure if I am ready for what will happen next. My heart is racing so fast I think it will come out of my chest and land on the floor. He unbuttons my skinny jeans, looking me in the eye as he pulls them off. The anticipation of what he will do next sends my hormones into overdrive. He licks my inner thighs, still holding my eyes with his intense gaze. Working his way up my torso, he slightly lifts my shirt to reveal my purple sports bra, kissing me as he does so. Then he pulls my shirt over my head. My body feels like jelly, yet I am stiff. I let him do what he wants to me. Eyes still locked on mine, he gets off the bed and pulls down his pants, exposing his length. I can't take my eyes off him. I am ready for what is about to happen.

After lying on the bed, he kisses and licks my neck and slides his right hand inside my underwear. I moan as he pleasures me. He stops and stares at me, a broad smile curving his sensuous lips. He slowly slides my underwear down my legs, then covers me with his body. His weight is heavy but comforting somehow. *I am ready for this.* For a moment, his mind goes elsewhere, and I wonder where his mind drifted off to. I feel his length sliding inside me, inch by inch, until his entire manhood is deep inside me.

"Does it hurt?" he whispers, peppering my face with light kisses.

Chills run up my spine, and I shake my head. He moves slowly, carefully at first, and then harder, faster, deeper. The sensations I feel overwhelm me, and my body quivers, gradually increasing until I am shaking. I throw my head back, my eyes closed, seeing stars. As I descend back to earth, I open my eyes and meet Kevin's. A sexy grin hovers on his lips as he watches me reach my pinnacle. Then he begins to move, and I feel the sensation growing within me again. When Kevin climaxes, our gazes are locked together, and I feel complete as I achieve my second orgasm. I don't want this moment to end.

Chapter 10

Depression in Session

What just happened? *I lost my virginity to the hottest guy in my school, and he said he loved me.* I am floating on Cloud 9, reminiscing about everything that transpired between Kevin and me. He had grabbed me, placed me on his bed, and kept his eyes locked on mine the entire time. My heart races as I think about it. *It is getting hot in here!* I fan myself as I think about how sexy, loving, and caring he is, not to mention he knows how to pleasure me. There is no way Kevin can be the murderer that Eli claims.

While he sleeps, I study him in awe. I am in love with Kevin Evans, and I trust him completely. What happened last night was meant to be. But although my feelings for Kevin are strong, I can't help but feel an attraction toward Eli. When he touches me, electricity vibrates throughout my entire body as if our connection goes beyond the physical, and our magic completes one another. *Perhaps we're connected on a magical level, and that's it?*

I get out of bed and head to the bathroom to shower. Today I have a session with Ms. Hudson, and afterward, I will meet with the Witch Council since I've decided to keep my magic.

I haven't seen my father since the fight with the twins; I don't trust him, and now that I know what I know, he shouldn't have married that evil woman. I don't want to be around her or the vile twins, not with my magic developing. I don't know what I would do to one of them.

By the time I finish, Kevin is awake and in the kitchen, fixing breakfast in his boxers. *Why does he do this to me?* Kevin hands me a plate of eggs with a huge smirk. I lean in for a kiss, and he lifts me off my feet and places me on the counter, and we're going at it.

"Come on; I have to go, babe," I say between kisses.

"Let me have you."

"You already did."

He kisses my neck, and I melt into his arms. I do not want to leave, but I need to get to my session.

"Babe, I have to go. I'll see you tonight," I promise.

He accepts defeat, kisses me on the forehead, and retreats to the table to eat breakfast. Kevin had offered to let me use his car, so I grab his keys and head to my appointment.

Once I get to Ms. Hudson's house, she is remarkably cheerful. She seems in great spirits, but why?

"Hi Claudette, I heard the great news!" she exclaims.

"What do you mean? What good news have you heard?" I raise an eyebrow. *I'm pretty sure my losing my virginity wouldn't be a topic of discussion.* I walk into her office, sit on the sofa, and stare at Ms. Hudson; my head cocked, brow furrowed. *What has she heard?*

"I heard you accepted your magic." She beams at me, her eyes shining.

Oh, that's what she heard. Duh, Claudette!

I glance around the room at all the moon imagery. "I am going to go out on a limb and say you are a Moon witch?" A smile plays around my lips.

"Well, yes, of course. How would you have guessed?" She chuckles. "Is it because of all of my moons?"

"I would believe so, Ms. Hudson," I reply deadpan.

She laughs, then sits and pulls out her small notebook from a desk drawer. "So, how are you feeling today?"

I feel amazing! "I am doing okay."

"Last time we were together, you discussed your mother, the move here, and your step-siblings." She flips a page, making a note. "I would like to discuss your stepsisters further if you don't mind."

"Um... sure." I shrug.

"How do you feel about them?" She studies me, eyes wide, pen poised, ready to write.

"They have been cruel to me since I first met them," I reveal.

"I see. Let me ask you this. Why do you think they have been harsh towards you?"

"Um... I don't know. Maybe because they are useless, pathetic, worthless sacks of rotten potatoes."

She scribbles in her notebook. My description of the twins might be a bit much, but I seriously can't stand them!

"Tell me about the first time you met the twins."

I huff. *I don't know why we need to discuss this.* "It was awful. I didn't know Gabriella was going to introduce them that night. It was supposed to be ice cream with just my father, but the third wheel, Gabriella, crashed our father-daughter date, and she brought the demon twins along." I scowl as I recall the memory.

Ms. Hudson nods and, of course, writes some more.

What is she writing about me in that notebook?

"Do you know the history of the twins and their father?"

"Yes, their father left them when they were babies."

"I see, and when you first met the twins, you were at an ice cream shop with your dad," she says.

"Yes, Dad and I went to Evi's three times a week. It was our ritual. You know, 'us time' until they ruined it." I fold my arms and stare out the window, my brows knitted. I never asked for a stepmother or stepsisters. My father should have asked if that was something I wanted, but then again, my mother was dead, and he was lonely. Suddenly, rage emerges from deep within me, and the room shakes.

"What is upsetting you, Claudette?" Ms. Hudson probes.

I don't respond. The lamp on her desk rocks back and forth and then plummets to the floor, shattering.

"Oh my! I'm so sorry! Please forgive me." I rush to pick up the pieces.

"It's okay. Leave it." Ms. Hudson waves her hand in a circular motion, fixing the lamp.

"Did the twins know about you and your father's ice cream dates?" she asks once the lamp is back in place.

"Yeah, they knew. I told them about it."

"I am not excusing their behavior, but you said their father left when they were babies. Then they meet a new father figure with a close relationship with his daughter. You have daddy-daughter dates, something they don't have with their father. Maybe they were cruel to you because they were jealous of your relationship with your father," she says. "And maybe you partially despise them for having a mother."

I swallow the lump forming in my throat. I never considered the twins could be jealous of my relationship with my father. But then, that's still no excuse to treat me the way they have this entire time. And okay, maybe I held something against them because their mom was still alive and mine was not.

"What you're implying is that they were jealous of my relationship with my father? What about making fun of my skin color? What was the point of that?"

"Yes, that is possible. Sometimes we must make connections to determine why people act as they do. Perhaps witnessing how close you are with your father stimulates uncomfortable feelings for them, and they don't know how to process it, so they treat you the way they do," she says. "Now, regarding your skin color. Some people are mean, or maybe they wish their skin was darker. So, they make fun of you for having something they wished they did. What you have to work on is how you respond." She closes her notebook and replaces it in the drawer. "Anytime you need to talk, I am here for you. I also spoke to your father. You should call him."

We say goodbye, and I consider her words as I leave her office and sit in the car for about fifteen minutes, processing our session. I wish the twins and I had a better relationship, but we have so much bad blood. I am at the point where I don't want to be bothered with them. Sometimes they make me feel so low that I no longer want to live. Perhaps it would be better if I left; they could have my father all to themselves. They made it clear from the first day we met they did not want me in this family.

I attempted suicide twice, and both times were unsuccessful. The first time I wanted to end it all was the day of my mom's death anniversary. I was in English class, and it was my turn to read aloud. I had been thinking about my mom, so I stuttered as I read. Marissa called me out in front of the entire class, saying I was "too stupid to read." Then at lunchtime, she stuck her foot out and tripped me, causing me to drop the tray I carried. The food ended up all over me, and Marissa laughed, pointing at me and calling me names.

I couldn't hold back my tears as she and all the other kids made fun of me, and when they saw me crying, they laughed more. I had wanted that day to be over; it was one of the worst ever.

As soon as we got home, I ran to my room and cried for hours. My dad was working late, so I snuck out and took my bike for a ride. I rode through our neighborhood and headed to the train tracks. I thought that day would be my last. My school and home life sucked, and I missed my mother. *God! I missed my mom so much!* It had only been a few months since the twins and Gabriella had moved in with us, but I wanted them to leave from the beginning. *I would not have to deal with these demons if my mother was still alive!* I got off my bike and waited for the train to come.

I planned to jump in front of it and join my beautiful mother in the afterlife. When I heard the horns signaling the train was on its way, I walked toward the track and took a deep breath. This was it; I was ready to die. I did not feel anxious as I expected; I imagined how it would feel to be at peace finally and reunited with my mother. I was sure my father would miss me, but he had his new wife, Gabriella, and two new daughters. He did not need me. I stood there waiting for my end as I watched the bright white lights approaching me at full speed. I closed my eyes. *"Mom, I am on my way,"* I whispered.

Suddenly, the tracks changed, and the train went in a different direction. I was stunned. I had thought this was it, but somehow, I was saved. I fell to the ground in tears, wanting to die and for my life to end. *Why, why, why did this happen?* I used to think that maybe my mother had saved me and that she was my guardian angel. Maybe there is a reason I am supposed to be here; perhaps there was a reason I must suffer the way I have.

Tears flow down my face as I reminisce about the first time I attempted suicide. My father materializes in my thoughts, and I dry my eyes. I take out my phone to send him a text message. He is the only family I have. There was no reason I should not be talking to him. Ms. Hudson is right; I need to speak to Dad. But there is one thing I am very sure about—I do not want to be in the same house as his wife and stepdaughters, but I want to maintain a relationship with my father.

Feeling overwhelmed with emotions, I check my reflection in the mirror. There are tear stains on my face, and I wipe the running eyeliner underneath my eyes. I suck in air, slowly exhale, start the car, and head to the Witch Council meeting.

Chapter 11

The Council

When I arrive for my meeting with the Witch Council, my first impression of the building is that it looks like an ancient castle and is very creepy. It has the school's logo, the Sun, Moon, and Earth plastered everywhere. A woman is there to greet me but does not give me her name. She nods and gestures for me to follow her. As I walk through the building, there are portraits of all the council members throughout history hanging on the walls with small, gold plates underneath indicating the type of witch they were, Sun, Moon, or… I notice there aren't any Earth witches in the mix. *Hmm. I wonder why?*

"Have a seat." The tall woman points to a foldable black chair. She is brown-skinned and looks familiar. I am unsure where I have seen her before, but I know I have. Sensing movement out of the corner of my eyes, I turn and see Ms. Hudson entering. Her face is stern as she pulls a witch-like cloak over her shoulders. Three males, followed by Tanya and Tristan, walk behind her, slipping on similar robes as they move. *What type of cult mess have I gotten myself dragged into?*

"Hello Claudette, follow us," a tall, green-eyed man commands.

I do not want to follow them into the next room, but what can I do? We walk into what seems to be a large ballroom, which is odd. *What is this place?* A large table in the middle of the room has six oversized throne-like chairs, and they all sit down. *I guess Ms. Hudson is not my therapist right now. She is some weird cult lady leader.* The tall woman takes a long sheet of paper that looks like an old document off the table.

"My name is Elizabeth Powers, Claudette. We are here today to discuss your acceptance of magic."

Powers? Eli's mother!

"This is my husband Joseph and my older son Jeremiah; I am a Sun witch, and my husband and son are Moon witches. This is Jimmy; he is a Sun witch, and I am sure you already know Tanya and Tristan are Sun witches as well," she continues.

"And you already know I am a Moon witch," Ms. Hudson says.

"We need to discuss what it means for you to have power and the rules and consequences. You are not to use your magic on norms, use magic on mags, or harm anyone. You will begin magic classes on Monday to learn how to control your powers. Humans may not know of our existence, and your out-of-town friends may not visit here. Our town is cloaked from the outside world."

Blah blah blah… I zone out as Mrs. Powers drones on. She could have emailed me the rules so I wouldn't have to stand here, listening to her squeaky voice. I haven't heard a word she says after 'our town is cloaked,' which is pretty cool and weird, but I nod. It explains why we could not locate it on Google maps.

"Would you like to join the council as our first Earth witch?" The woman's voice breaks into my reverie.

For what? I am pretty sure my response should be no. "What does a council member do?" I ask, pursing my lips together.

"We look after the magical community and make sure that no one misuses magic," Elizabeth says.

Sounds like something I don't need to be a part of. "I see. Well, this is a lot to take in, Mrs. Powers. I will have to get back to you if that's okay," I reply.

"Please respond in a reasonable time frame; the offer won't last," she hisses.

Rude much? I nod and bow because I do not know what else to do.

"You're excused." She gestures for me to leave the room like I am bothering her.

Wow, this was a bit much. Eli's mother was rude, and Mr. Powers and Eli's brother didn't even acknowledge I was in the room. Ms. Hudson was way too serious. Jimmy gave me a friendly smirk, and Tanya and Tristan nodded. I guess they are more serious at a council meeting than at school.

I get in the car and start the engine. When I am about to pull off, a pale woman with dark hair walks up to the vehicle, gesturing for me to roll down the window. I cannot make out her face.

"Hi, can I please talk to you?" she mouths, pointing to the window.

I do not want to, but I open it.

"Hello, Claudette. It's nice to meet you," she whispers.

I look to see if anyone else is around, confused, trying to figure out how she knows my name. I don't say anything.

"I'm Kevin's mother." Her voice is shaky.

Ah, now it makes sense. "Hello, nice to meet you," I say, eyeing her warily.

"You cannot trust Kevin!" she declares, then disappears into smoke.

That was vague and peculiar. But this is Kevin's *mother* saying that her own son cannot be trusted. Not knowing what to think, I sit there for a long moment, staring, unseeing, where she disappeared before finally pulling myself together and driving off.

Eli says I cannot trust Kevin. Isabel dislikes him, and now his mom says not to trust him. It does not look too good for Kevin. What am I supposed to believe?

As I drive, my mind races. It's really odd. Kevin's mom, whom I have never met, appears out of thin air, tells me her son is untrustworthy, then disappears.

I pull up at Kevin's place and sit in the car for about five minutes before heading inside. I feel like I should say something to him, but I bury the thought for now. I get out of the car and stride up the walkway. Taking a deep breath,

I insert the key into the brass keyhole and enter the apartment. Kevin, wearing slacks and a button-up shirt, is preparing dinner. *How does he have me swooning even when I'm supposed to be suspicious of him?*

"Hey babe, how was your meeting with the Witch Council?" He smiles.

"It was... interesting." I stretch out the word, placing the keys on the holder. Whatever he's cooking smells scrumptious. *I swear he spoils me.*

"What are you making?" I stand over the stove, going through the pots and pans.

"Nothing special, just steak skirts, mashed potatoes, and asparagus." He opens the pantry closet to take out a bouquet of roses and hands them to me. "Go get dressed. I got you something special for our date night." He beams.

What?! I hurry to the bedroom to find a red-lace strapless gown on the mattress. I am in awe.

Kevin is one of those trust funds kids. His parents may not be on the Witch Council anymore, but he told me his father is a judge, and his mom is one of the best plastic surgeons in this town. So they have money! If he had accepted his magic, he could conjure anything he wanted. But there are rules and limits to materialistic items.

I undress and head to the bathroom to shower for our "date night." Once out of the shower, I place my "sister locks" into a bun and apply mascara to my eyelashes, a little reddish eyeshadow, and my favorite Maybelline eyeliner. I grab my red mat lipstick and roll it onto my lips to finish my look. I stand in front of the mirror, display my best vogue poses, then head to the dining area.

I can still hear Kevin's mother telling me Kevin is untrustworthy, but I push it to the back of my mind.

"You spent one hundred years in there." He fixes our plates of food.

"To be fair, you look hot and sexy, and I wanted to match you," I retort. "And thank you, babe, for my beautiful dress."

"You look amazing in it." He grins.

"Where did you get it?"

"I asked Tanya to conjure it for me." He beams.

"Oh, and here I thought you used some of that trust fund money to buy it." I giggle.

"I use that money for the mortgage. But very funny," he replies deadpan.

We begin eating, and the food is terrific; *my man sure knows how to cook.* We chit-chat about our day. I tell him about my therapy session, and he tells me about his time at the gym and how he and his brother seem on better terms now. I want to ask him about his relationship with his mom, but I do not want to ruin the moment.

He gets up to grab my favorite ice cream, butter pecan, from the freezer and gestures for me to join him on the sofa for a movie. Before it starts, he tells me that afterward, we will meet with Tristan and Tanya to witness a shooting star, which should be magical.

Just when the movie is about to start, I receive two text messages back-to-back. Glancing at the phone, I see they are from Eli. I do not open his messages because I notice Kevin watching me intently.

I turn my phone off, push it between the sofa cushions, and snuggle into Kevin's arms to enjoy a romantic comedy he picked out.

After the movie, I dart to the bathroom to check my phone to see what Eli wanted. I need to be quick because we're heading out to meet Tanya and Tristan.

Eli:

Eli:

I can't be the only one feeling this. You had to have felt that energy between us...

I would like for us to be friends, at least.

Seriously, dude? I text him, saying I will talk to him in school on Monday; I don't want to ruin the rest of my date night with my boyfriend.

Yes, I cannot deny that I felt something special when Eli and I touched; I also felt this strange sensation when we kissed. Our magic is definitely connected. However, I am in a relationship with a charming, handsome, and thoughtful guy who even cooks for me. Kevin has been so kind to me since we met; he has not given me a reason to distrust him. Of course, I trust him, although I can't fight this nagging feeling that I might need to meet with his mother again.

Welcome to the West Side

Classes for "The mags"

· History of Magic—Taught by Mr. Goatfair
Where do Sun, Moon, and Earth witches come from?
· Potion Measurements—Taught by Ms. Caron
The right ingredients to use in a potion.
· Magical Elements—Taught by Mr. Max
How to harness your powers from the Sun, Moon, or Earth.
· Advanced Practical Magic—Taught by Ms. Billie
Spells, potions, and all things magic.

Chapter 12

Meet the Mags

When I arrive at school, I head straight to Principal Deanwall's office. Once there, he hands me a pamphlet with my classes and the instructors. I patiently wait for my first-period teacher to meet with me. I jiggle my leg and fidget in my chair. Of course, I am behind. I check my phone and see a text message from my father wishing me good luck. It is pretty much my first day all over again, except this time with magic. I text my dad to set our date for Wednesday after my therapy session, and he agrees. I have never gone this long without seeing my father, and it is time we made up. He is my only family, and it does not feel right for us to be at odds. It was against the rules for him to have told me about my magical ancestry, and I know it was not my parents' fault. They gave up their magic, and even if my mother had survived the heart attack, I don't think I should have known I was a witch.

Suddenly, a blonde-haired biker chick walks in, carrying a binder. Her eyes are blue-green, and she wears skinny black jeans and a leather jacket. A black streak running through her hair gives her a no-nonsense look. "Hi, you must be Claudette," she says, shifting her weight from one leg to the other as she aggressively chews on a piece of gum.

"Yes, nice to meet you." I extend my hand to shake hers.

She glares at my hand, then opens her binder. "My name is Ms. Billie. Do the work I give you, and we will be cool! Got it? Great!" she says, not giving me a chance to respond.

I nod, taking several sheets of paper she hands me and hurrying behind as she heads out of the office to a classroom.

There are illustrations of the Sun, Moon, and Earth on one wall. I feel awkward as all eyes are on me and keep my head down as I sit at the back of the room.

"Alright, class! Listen up; in today's lesson, we will focus on potions," Ms. Billie announces.

Most of the kids snap their fingers, and notebooks and pens appear. One kid is texting, ignoring Ms. Billie. She takes out a brown, gold, and black ancient-looking book from her black and silver bag and drops it on her desk with a resounding *thud*, which catches the kid's attention briefly. I lean in to get a closer look at the book and notice a Sun logo on the cover. It makes more sense now why our uniforms have a Sun, Moon, and Earth logo; they represent the different witch covens.

"Hey! Peanut head, get off your phone!" Ms. Billie snaps her fingers, and the student's phone turns into a flopping goldfish.

"Ms. Billie, why did you do that?" the kid whines, waving his hand to create a water bubble for the fish.

"Because I need your undivided attention!" she snaps.

The kid rolls his eyes, manifesting a notebook and pen on the desk before him.

"Okay, now that I have *everyone's* attention, let's get started! Claudette, take out your notebook unless you have a photographic memory." She gives me a grin.

Dumfounded, I pull a notebook and pen from my bag. Ms. Billie turns to the whiteboard and writes, "VANITY SPELL."

"Today, we will learn a simple vanity spell. Claudette, I will give a quick review; try to keep up! Sun witches are most powerful during the day, Moon witches are most powerful at night, and Earth witches are powerful whenever their little heart desires." She fixes her eyes on mine.

"Today, we are going to discuss healing yourself. If you were... let's say, in the middle of a battle, and your opponent inflicts pain on you, the only way you could heal yourself is if you drank *this*." She points to a small bottle of liquid. "This would heal any wound you incurred. As you all know, Ms. Caron will be the one to teach you about the ingredients needed for this potion."

I slowly raise my hand, and, of course, everyone turns to look. I do not want the spotlight on me, but I am taking this class to learn and have a question. But I immediately regret it once the question leaves my lips. "Do Earth witches have to use a potion to heal themselves?"

I feel it is a valid concern. I also want to know if I am just a typical witch or unique in some way, as Kevin and Eli seem to think.

"All witches have to use a potion to heal themselves," she says.

I must have made a face because suddenly she is standing next to me, studying me like I am some superhuman from a Marvel comic book.

"Did you heal yourself without a potion?" she asks.

"Yes," I say slowly, unsure if I should have mentioned it.

There is a resounding gasp throughout the classroom, and everyone gapes at me. Ms. Billie returns to her desk, types in a code, and pulls out a dagger. I get to my feet, frightened, and back away.

"Don't worry; if I were going to kill you, I would have done it already." She chuckles.

What kind of teacher would tell a student if they wanted to murder you, they would?

She strides toward me. "Stay calm. I am just going to cut you to see for myself."

I'm sorry, what?

"Oh, no, you're not!" I shout.

She glances toward the window, closes her eyes, and takes a deep breath. Suddenly, I freeze in place, unable to move.

"I am going to scream. You can't do this!" The only part of me I can move is my lips.

"Calm down, Claudette. I am in the middle of teaching a lesson, and I need you to cooperate!" Ms. Billie uses the dagger to pierce my right hand, and blood trickles from the cut. I try to move, but I can't.

"What is wrong with you, lady?" I yell.

The class chuckles, amused by my pain.

"Heal yourself!" she commands.

When I can move, I hold my hand in agony. I glance at my classmates, hoping and wishing I could see Eli. He was the one who had made me feel confident enough to heal myself before. I do not know if I can do it without him.

"Heal yourself," Ms. Billie repeats.

I close my eyes, inhale deeply, then breathe out slowly. A marching band stomps inside my head as my heart races to the beat of the drums. I do not know how I will do it. I can hear Eli's soothing voice telling me to heal myself, and the cut suddenly disappears. The students gasp in unison, and Ms. Billie regards me with wide eyes. She darts to the front of the class, grabs her cell phone, and exits the room. I feel like a fish out of water trying to find my way to the nearest ocean. The bell rings, and thankfully, this class is over. It is time for the next, but Ms. Billie does not return to dismiss us.

My next class is Potion Measurements, taught by Ms. Caron. As I walk there, I spot Ms. Billie whispering to another teacher. When she notices me, she turns her back. I shrug it off and enter the class, shuffling my way to the back of the room to avoid being the center of attention again. I notice Isabel and Destiny walk in, holding hands. A smile forms on my face; they are the first familiar faces I've seen today. I also notice Lin, who gives me a nod, and to sweeten the deal, I see Eli enter. *I thought he was a no-show today.* I smile and wave at him, but he does not acknowledge me. *Ouch!* I take out my phone and text him because I do not want anyone to overhear.

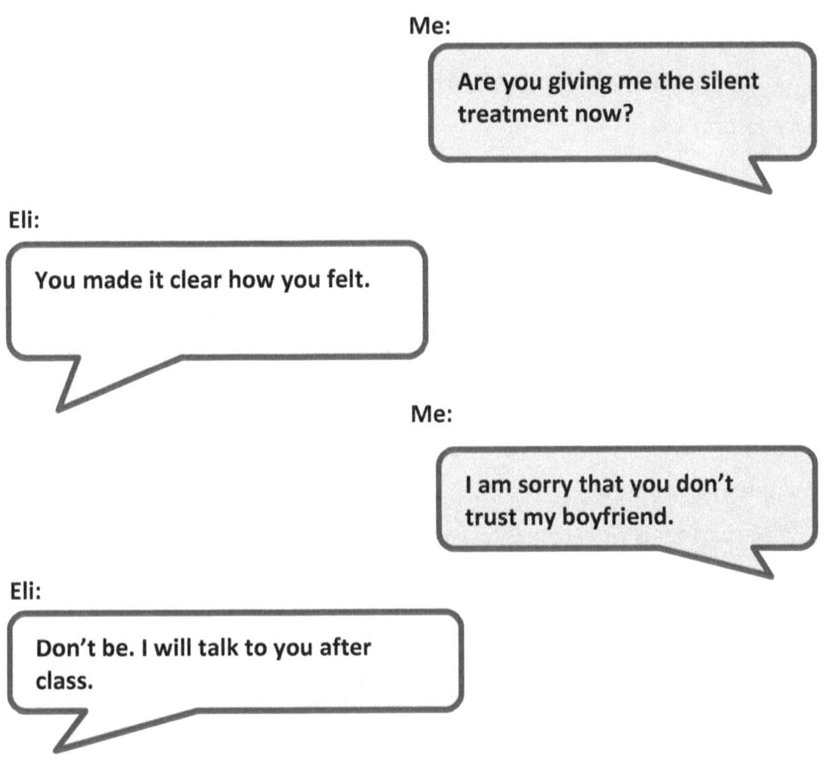

I growl and throw my phone in my bag with force. Like he did not give me any proof that my boyfriend was a murderer. When you accuse someone of murder, you should have evidence to back it up. I questioned Kevin about Eli's allegations; he said he hadn't killed anyone. I believed him. *Hmm. Didn't his mother say not to trust him?* a voice inside my head says. I am conflicted. I trust Kevin, but I also trust Eli. Maybe it's because Eli has feelings for me that he doesn't trust Kevin. *But why accuse him of murder? That is overboard.*

Ms. Caron glides into the classroom, eyes fixed on me. She is light-skinned with light brown eyes and burgundy curls. She looks familiar, but I cannot place where I have seen her before.

"Hello, class. Please take out your cauldrons. We will prepare a truth potion today," she announces in her husky voice.

Everyone's interest has peaked, and some look worried.

"Guys, please pick a partner." Ms. Caron walks to her closet and gets me a cauldron.

"Thank you," I say as she hands it to me, and she gives me a small smile.

She walks back to her closet and takes out the ingredients for the potion. I glance around at the other students as they pair up. Of course, Destiny and Isabel are partners. Eli, myself, and Lin are left. Just as I am about to ask Lin to be my partner, Eli pulls his desk next to mine.

"You're mine," he declares in a deep, husky voice.

"I'm sorry… yours?" I raise an eyebrow. "So you're not giving me the silent treatment anymore?"

"My partner is what I meant… and obviously not." A charming smile curves across his lips and makes my stomach flutter.

"Lin, please help me hand out the ingredients," Ms. Caron says.

He hands Eli and me ginger, burdock root, two cups of water, a mint leaf, and what looks like a piece of a brain. I lean in and whisper to Eli, asking him if it is a human brain, and he nods. *Gross! I wonder what poor soul they used for this!*

"Humans donate their brains for this very purpose." Eli grazes his hand over mine. *It is as if he can hear what I am thinking.* Shock waves transfer from his touch through my hand, up my arm, until I feel it in my chest. For a moment, I cannot breathe. My heart is racing so fast that I am sure I will need to see a cardiologist to regulate it again. As much as I do not want to admit it, there is something between Eli and me that Kevin and I do not have. The energy between us every time we touch is transcending.

"Eyes up front!" Ms. Caron demands, bringing us back to reality. "Please, I want you all to add one cup of water into your cauldrons, followed by two ounces of ginger, four ounces of burdock root, a mint leaf, and finally, the most important ingredient, three tablespoons of the human brain." She cackles, sounding like an evil witch. "This is my favorite part!" She stirs the ingredients together. "You guys should work on your laughs while doing this."

I glance at Destiny with a worried expression, who mouths, "She is just joking."

"Let the liquid cool for about five minutes before pouring it into your vials," Ms. Caron instructs.

I watch her before stirring mine because I want to pay close attention to what she is doing, but I cannot take my mind off the connection between Eli and me. *I wish I had met him first.*

The feelings I have are confusing. I love Kevin, and he treats me wonderfully, but Eli is just as sweet, and we have this undeniable connection.

"Now it's time to test it out on your partner; please allow five minutes for the potion to take effect. Once processed, the potion will last only five minutes," Ms. Caron announces.

While I let my potion cool, Eli pours his into the bottle. He takes out a piece of paper and scribbles.

"What are you writing?" I question, eyes wide, trying to look over his shoulder.

"I am writing questions for you to ask me," he says.

Once my potion is cool, I pour it into a small bottle and cork it.

"So, should I go first, or would you like to?" I ask, biting my lip.

He places his hand on me, sending shocks throughout my body.

"You really need to stop doing that!" I exclaim.

"I'll go first," he offers.

He opens the potion and guzzles it down. I turn the timer on and wait precisely five minutes before I ask my first question, ignoring the list he gave me.

"What is happening between us when you touch me?"

"Our energy is connecting," he replies immediately.

But how do I know if it's working? "How do I know if the potion is working on you?"

"If you look me in the eye, you will see I am not blinking," he says robotically.

I look around at everyone in the classroom, and it is as if they are all hypnotized as they answer the questions asked by their partners. I only have a few more minutes, so I want to ask a more serious question.

"What is your issue with Kevin?"

"Kevin is evil and cannot be trusted."

"Are you just saying that because you have feelings for me?" I press.

"No, I am your soulmate. Not Kevin."

"What do you mean by *soulmate*?" I arch an eyebrow.

"Sorry, you will just have to find that out later." He smirks.

The spell is over, and Eli is officially out of the trance. The bell rings, and it is time for my next class.

"Eli, seriously?" I say.

"Claudette, I get it. You're in a relationship with Kevin and trust him. But when he ultimately breaks your heart... and trust me, he will. I will be here to pick up the pieces." He hands me my books.

I do not know what to say. Yes, I feel connected to Eli, but I am in a relationship and unwilling to let that go. Even though something is spurring between Eli and me, I do not want to explore it. It is best to keep things strictly platonic—*because of Kevin*. I grab my bag and head to my next class, which I do not have with Eli. They shuffle us between the four magical classes, so Eli and I only have two subjects together. I cannot stop thinking about his words as we head in opposite directions. *We are soulmates*. I mean, I am seventeen years old. How would I know who my soulmate is?

My day continues smoothly, and I enjoy learning about magic more than I thought I would. *Becoming a mag is one of the best decisions I have ever made.*

I spend my lunch hour with Destiny, Isabel, Lin, and Eli. Usually, I have lunch with Kevin, but he left school early today because he was not feeling well. I call to check on him when school ends, and he tells me he feels worse.

Destiny gives me a ride "home"—well, to Kevin's apartment. When I get there, he does not look well. I prepare some soup for us, and after looking over a few spell books, we head to bed early.

Kevin is too sick to attend school the following day, so I ask Isabel to pick me up. Ms. Billie cancels classes for the rest of the week for some unknown reason, but I am pretty sure it has something to do with me. My other classmates gossip about me healing myself without a potion, and I am the talk of Mashal High School. The twins are avoiding me, and it is lovely. When they see me walking down the hallway, they turn around and walk in the opposite direction, avoiding me like the plague.

My classes seem to drag on for the rest of the day, and although the courses are much more interesting, there is still much information to cram for one day. I am mentally drained after school, and Kevin and I crash when I get home.

When Wednesday comes around, Kevin is still not feeling well. After school, Isabel drops me back at the apartment, so I can get Kevin's car to drive to my therapy session at six-fifteen. Our session is only twenty minutes today because I want to meet my father by six-forty. I plan to head to the house to meet him there, and then we'll drive to our old town and have ice cream at Evi's. I have not spoken to Nicolette and Spencer since before my birthday, and they stopped reaching out to me after I did not respond to a few of their text messages. I send them a text while waiting for Ms. Hudson to arrive.

Me:

Hey guys, I am so sorry I have been MIA. I learned a lot about my history, and I can't tell you until it is safe. I want you both to know I love you and will fill you in soon.

Spencer:

CLAUDETTE! It's great to hear from you finally. Please tell us what's going on!

Nicolette:

You have some explaining to do!

Me:

I promise I will explain everything to you guys. When I can.

It is against the rules to inform humans about magic, but I must tell them. They are my two best friends. I know they won't tell anyone.

I glance at my watch when I realize that Ms. Hudson is still not here. Looking at my phone again, I notice I had somehow missed a voicemail from her saying she was running late. I call Kevin to check on him, and he does not answer. Perhaps he is sleeping. While sitting in the throne-like chair, waiting for Ms. Hudson to arrive, I text Eli to see what he is doing. But he does not respond either.

"Hi, Claudette. I apologize for my tardiness," Ms. Hudson says as she rushes in.

"No worries," I reply, following her into the office.

As I sit down, I look at her closely. She seems flushed, like she has been doing something. She stares out the window. I follow her gaze and see an older gentleman outside. He winks at Ms. Hudson, and she blushes.

Was she late because she was getting some? Eww. Ms. Hudson smiles and waves at the man.

"Today's session will be short, and I apologize for being late. It is very unprofessional of me," she says.

"Is that your guy?" I incline my chin toward the window. She smiles but does not respond.

"Claudette, how was your day?" she asks instead.

"It was great. I'm managing my magic better, with fewer outbursts, and who knew witches were so fascinating? My relationship with Kevin is great. The twins are avoiding me. Gabriella doesn't bother me anymore, and I am supposed to meet my father today after this session for an ice cream date." I grin from ear to ear.

"Oh, that is awesome! So, let me ask, when do you plan to return home for good?"

"I don't think living there is best for me; I will be cordial, but living under the same roof as my stepmother and stepsisters is a huge no."

"Okay, I get that. And there is nothing wrong with not wanting to be around them. And it's great that you are going out with your father later. You guys need your daddy-daughter one-on-one time." Ms. Hudson scribbles down a few words in her notebook and tells me to work on gradually getting in one-on-one time with my father every week. I agree, and we part ways. Then I head to my dad's house.

After so long, I am looking forward to seeing him again. I give Kevin another call, but he still doesn't answer. *I hope he is okay.* I arrive at my father's house and ring the doorbell. When he does not answer, I get the spare key underneath the mat and let myself in. My dad informed me about the spare key underneath the rug when Kevin gave my key back for me. I open the door and enter, checking the kitchen first, but Dad's not there, so I run upstairs.

"Dad, are you here?"

There's still no sign of him. I go to check the den next and find my father lying on the floor in a pool of blood.

Chapter 13

Why?

Dispatcher: 911, what's your emergency?

Me: My father! My father is not breathing!

Dispatcher: Okay, I need you to calm down. Please tell me your name.

Me: My name is Claudette. Please help me!

Dispatcher: Okay, Claudette. I will help you. Where are you located?

Me: 1103 TK Avenue.

Dispatcher: Claudette, put the phone on speaker and listen carefully.

Me: Okay.

Dispatcher: Seal your mouth over your father's and blow steadily and firmly into his mouth for about one second. Can you do that for me?

Me: Uh-huh.

Dispatcher: Check to see if his chest is rising. If so, continue with cycles of thirty chest compressions and two rescue breaths until help arrives.

Me: Mm-hmm.

Dispatcher: Alright, Claudette, help will be there soon. Keep it steady... okay?

Me: Mm-hmm.

Dispatcher: I will stay on the line until help arrives.

So many thoughts reel through my mind as I try to bring my father back. *What happened? Where are Gabriella and the twins? Why is this happening?*

"Please, daddy, come back to me," I plead, tears flowing. *Wait, I am a witch!*

With my hands on his chest, I channel my energy into him, chanting, "Please wake up, please wake up, please wake up!"

But nothing happens. My heart is breaking; my face soaked with tears. What could have happened for my father to end up in a pool of blood? Did he fall and hit his head? I don't understand why this is happening. *He is the only family I have left!*

The paramedics bust through the door, and one pulls me to the side. I watch them work on my father for over twenty minutes, trying to bring him back. I stand there, wringing my hands, watching the chaotic scene unfold. It's as if I'm watching from afar. My heart squeezes in my chest, and my legs tremble. They can barely hold my weight, and I lean against the wall, not taking my eyes from my father, lying unconscious on the floor. When the paramedic announces, *"Call it... time of death,"* my legs give out, and I collapse. A loud wail fills the air, and after a moment, I realize the animalistic sound is coming from me.

My father is dead, and I am officially an orphan. Before the paramedics can place my father in a body bag, I lay my head on his chest, no longer hearing his thumping heart. My vision blurs, and I whimper silently. Clutching my father for one last hug, I stare at his beloved face through my tear-blurred eyes. That's when I notice he has something clenched in his fist.

One paramedic steps forward, ready to take my father away.

"Please let me say goodbye to my father," I plead. The woman moves away, and I discreetly open Dad's fist to remove the object and slip it into my pocket. I kiss his forehead. "Goodbye, daddy," I whisper before getting up from the floor.

I call Kevin once more, but he still does not answer. My heart sinks. I need him so much right now. *Where is he?* I call Gabriella next, and then the twins, but no one answers my calls.

The paramedics roll the stretcher with my father out of the room. I cannot call Nicolette or Spencer because they will want to come here, but how could I explain to them it's against the rules? I scroll down my contact list, calling everyone I can think of, needing to talk to someone. I try Eli first, but the call goes straight to voicemail. Neither Destiny nor Isabel answer their phones. I know it's their date night, but I hoped they would pick up if they saw my back-to-back calls, getting the hint it's urgent.

The detectives walk in right after the paramedics and begin asking me questions. *Why are they here?* My mind spirals, and my throat is dry from all the crying, so my voice comes out hoarse when I speak. I do not know how to respond to the detectives' questions. They ask if anything is missing, and I recall noticing that my father wasn't wearing his Earth ring and necklace. The Earth ring makes sense now that I know about my magical heritage. Dad never took it off. When I tell the police about the missing jewelry, they immediately conclude this was a robbery "gone bad," in their words. They ask about my stepfamily, and I tell them I've been calling but have not gotten an answer. From what the detectives say, I realize they think Gabriella and the twins are suspects. *Suspects? Do they think someone killed my father?* Mashalville is a small town. Surely they will find the person who murdered my father if that's what happened. But then I remember the police have still not solved the murders of Destiny's mother and Isabel's parents.

I shudder and wrap my arms around myself. There is no way I am staying in this house, so I leave after checking with one detective that I am free to go. I do not know where to go; no one answers my calls. As I sit in the car, thinking, loneliness implements the worst ideas in my head. *Why is no one answering my calls? Where is everybody?* I punch the steering wheel, my jaw set, a fire blazing in my eyes. A burning fury swells inside me as my mind flips through potential suspects. Right now, I *can* trust no one. Not until I check alibis that prove they couldn't have killed my father. I decide on my next destination, start the engine, and head directly to Kevin's parents' house. *It's time to get to the truth.*

When I arrive at the house, I see Kevin's mother immediately—all the confidence I had while on the way here dissipates at the sight of her. I am about to pull away when his mother appears in the passenger's seat, making me gasp.

"Why are you here?" she whispers.

I grip the steering wheel until my knuckles turn white and take a few seconds to even my breathing before I can answer her. *It is now or never.* "I need to know why I can't trust your son," I say, my voice giving away none of the turmoil I feel.

"What has he told you?" She cocks her head to the side, fixing me with her eyes.

Kevin told me his parents are Sun witches, and their union is against the rules. Because they did not want to take the chance of him being evil, they took away his magic, preventing him from making a choice.

"He hasn't told me anything," I lie, and my head feels heavy. I just need answers without having questions shot at me.

"My son..." Her voice trails off, and she suddenly looks like she is in a daze.

I shift in my seat to face her. "What's wrong with you?"

"I am an empath, and your pain overwhelms me. I am so sorry for your loss."

"Thank you." I wave a hand dismissively, avoiding eye contact. I do not want her pity. What I want are answers. "What about Kevin? Please tell me why I can't trust your son! I am living with him!"

Someone has murdered my father, and even though I do not want to think about it, my boyfriend is a potential suspect. I want to clear his name to get rid of this disgusting thought.

"I am sorry I gave you that impression. Kevin is a fine man who loves you," she replies, her voice a monotone.

I notice her eyes are blank and watch in disbelief as she opens the door and walks away.

My phone rings, snapping my attention away from Kevin's mother, and I see Eli calling me back. I don't answer. Eli will have to wait until later when my mind is in a suitable space.

I head straight to Kevin's, intending to confront him. I need to know his mother's deal. *First, she tells me I can't trust Kevin, and now she says I can. I'm so confused.*

I hop out of the car, not even locking the door behind me, and storm inside. Before I can unleash my wrath, I see Kevin scrunched up in one corner of the kitchen floor, beaten. Immediately, concern replaces my anger.

"Oh, my God!" I rush to him. "Kevin! What happened to you?" I kneel on the floor beside him, stroking his face. Flashes of cradling my father in my arms earlier materialize as I hold Kevin, and I suck in air.

"Eli!" he whispers, bringing me back to the present.

"No, no, no, this is not true. He couldn't have done this to you. He wouldn't," I say. *Who am I trying to convince, him or myself?*

"He did this to me, Claudette. Why would I lie?" he weakly protests.

When I do not respond, Kevin struggles, trying to get up, but falls back down, and I steady him. "Stay away from Eli, Claudette. He is dangerous," he urges, pleading with his eyes.

I swallow hard and shake my head. "Eli is not dangerous," I say and help Kevin to his feet and into the bedroom. *Kevin can't be right about Eli, but why would he lie?* I bite my lip. This back-and-forth between us about Eli is an ongoing argument. Kevin is tired of me always defending Eli, taking Eli's side over his. And I am tired of the friction between the two of them. *But Kevin wouldn't lie.* I shake my head again. Whether in disagreement with the thought or to clear my mind, I don't know.

My phone rings as we enter the bedroom, and I help Kevin to the bed before answering. It's Gabriella, finally returning my call. I hear her screaming on the other end that someone has murdered my father. Kevin overhears, and I see his eyes widen, his mouth falling open.

Gabriella's reaction sounds sincere; I can hear the pain in her voice. She could not have murdered my father. She may hate me, but her love for my father is genuine.

When I hang up, Kevin is waiting for me to talk to him, but I rummage through the dresser, looking for something to wear, not saying anything. I am antsy and cannot stay still. My mind is running a mile a minute, and my body is trying to keep up. I am determined to find my father's killer, and, most importantly, I want to know *why. Why would someone kill Dad?* This town is so small. Whoever murdered my father could not have gone far—magic or no magic.

"Claudette, come here." Kevin pats the mattress beside him, breaking the silence.

I whirl around and glare at him. "No, Kevin! My father is dead. Somebody killed him. I am going to find out who."

My limbs feel weak, and my heart races. This is a nightmare I need to escape. "I can't right now. I just... can't."

He gets up, grunting from the pain, and shuffles toward me. He pulls me into his muscular frame, and I bury my face in his chest and sob uncontrollably as he rubs my back.

"I love you," Kevin whispers, and I weep even more. I feel broken and lost, completely and utterly devastated by my father's death. *Why did this happen?*

Kevin guides us to the bed, and we lie down. I cry for hours while he holds me, chanting sweet nothings in my ear until sleep claims me.

I wake up in the middle of the night in a panic from a nightmare. I glance at Kevin, but he is still asleep, so I pull on my robe and head to the kitchen to get a glass of water.

When I return to the bedroom, I grab my phone from the nightstand and see a few missed calls and a text message from Eli. By now, the news about my father's murder has spread. Kevin accusing Eli of beating him up resurfaces, and I step out of the bedroom to call Eli back to question him about what happened between them. He answers almost immediately, his voice sounding sleepy. When interrogating him, he tells me he has reason to believe Kevin is behind my father's death, and I hang up on him.

I feel sick to my stomach at his allegations against my boyfriend. I had doubted Kevin for a brief moment, but I could not have been more wrong. He has been nothing but supportive the entire time he has known me. Rage builds inside me, and I march to the bedroom to get dressed, inadvertently waking Kevin.

"Claudette, where are you going?" He sits up, rubbing his eyes.

"I need to clear my mind," I whisper. "Go back to sleep."

"Let the detectives do their job, baby. They will find out who killed your father," he assures me.

He gets out of bed and treads toward me, grasping my waist and running his fingers along my thigh. He presses his lips softly on my forehead, and I inhale his natural musk, temporarily feeling at ease.

I peer up at him, seeing his cut lip and swollen eye. I place my hand over his wounds and heal them.

He takes my hand and kisses it. By the look on his face, I can tell how thankful he is that I healed him.

"I love you, Claudette," he says.

"I love you, too," I say.

His lips touch mine, and the rage I feel fades away. I want to feel something other than this pain. I no longer wish to think about never seeing my father again. I wrap my arms around Kevin's neck, turning our passionate kiss into something more.

Kevin catches my drift and palms my breast softly, teasing me. "Babe, come back to bed."

I remove my pants and shirt and sit on the bed. Eyes fixed on mine, Kevin slips off my underwear and removes my bra, leaving me naked. Pushing me into the middle of the bed, he climbs on top of me. I can hear his heart racing.

"I wish I could take your pain away," he whispers. His warm breath on my earlobe sends my body into overdrive, and he knows it. I can feel his affection for me, and I do not want this moment to end. He removes his boxers, exposing himself to me, then inserts his hard length deep inside me. I moan.

This was what I need to distract myself from my sorrow.

The following morning, I stagger to the bathroom. I awoke feeling refreshed after my night with Kevin, momentarily forgetting about yesterday's events, but reality slapped me in the face as soon as I regained consciousness.

I glance at myself in the mirror; my eyes are puffy and red from crying. I look like a blowfish. I put my hair in a bun, slip on sweatpants, leaving the apartment as quietly as possible. Kevin is sound asleep, so I use this opportunity to finally get to the bottom of the altercation between Eli and him.

Once outside, I three-way call Nicolette and Spencer and tell them everything, not only about Dad's murder but also about being a witch. I swear them to secrecy, telling them I will come to see them. I am sure Nicolette is questioning my sanity about my claims of being a witch, but I will prove it once I am with them. They need to know what happened, and I no longer care about the rules. The rules did not save my father.

I look up from my phone and see Eli's car pulling up. Parking, he quickly hops out of the car and approaches me. I cannot deny our magical connection because he appears with a mere thought.

"What did you do to Kevin?!" I demand.

He grasps me by the shirt and places his index finger over my lips. "Shh! Not here."

He snaps his fingers, and suddenly we are atop a mountain in the middle of nowhere. I break away from him, my heart slamming in my chest as I have no idea where we are. I inch away from him and look over the edge of the cliff. It's a long way down. Lifting my eyes, I survey the scenery. It's beautiful; the sunrise is stunning, and a cascading waterfall is a sight to behold. My eyes widen. *Why would Eli bring me here?*

"Claudette?" Eli whispers.

"*What*?" I yell, and my voice echoes.

"Kevin is up to some—"

I raise a hand, gesturing for him to stop.

"Wait, please hear me out. I brought you here because I made a truth potion for you. I need you to sneak and give it to Kevin. Ask him if he killed your father."

"You think Kevin murdered my dad?" I stare at him in disbelief. *Why am I surprised? Eli hates Kevin.* I roll my eyes. I do not have the energy for this.

"I am pretty certain he did," he says.

"*Pretty certain* and certain are two entirely different things, Eli! Pretty certain leaves room for innocence. Do you understand what you're insinuating?" I ground my jaw, seething.

Eli sighs. He places both hands on my shoulders and looks directly into my eyes. "Listen to me, Claudette. Kevin is close with Tristan and Tanya. They are from the same coven, are romantically involved, *and* are part of the Witch Council. The three of them are evil. Furthermore, there has been no sign of an Earth witch until *you*. Destiny told me that Kevin suddenly signed up to be an escort for new students when he found out that *you* were coming to this school. Why would I make this up?!" Eli gives me a little shake. "And before you answer, I know you think, or I'm assuming you think, I am not a fan of Kevin because I have feelings for you, but that's not it. He has something to do with your father's death, and I need you to trust me on this." He lets go of my shoulder and extends the potion to me. "Take this and ask him if he killed your father. I know you don't have feelings for me in that way, but I can't sit back and let you be lied to by the likes of him. If I'm wrong, I'll let it go."

I'm silent for a long moment, absorbing everything he says. "Eli, I'm sorry, but I trust Kevin," I say gently, choosing my words carefully. "And if we are to continue a friendship, I need you to stop this—*especially* now. I can't handle any more disappointments. I need you to be a friend." My voice quivers. I do not have the strength to continue this fight.

"Please, Claudette, take the potion. If he is telling the truth, I promise it will be the last you hear from me about it."

I sigh and take the potion, putting it in my pocket. Eli takes my hand, and instantly we are back at Kevin's apartment.

"Ask him," Eli mouths before heading back to his car.

I trudge back inside, my heart heavy, my mind drained. I do not want to believe my boyfriend could have committed such a heinous crime. There is no way he killed my father. He wasn't even feeling well. I would believe it was Gabriella, or even the twins, who murdered Dad before I thought Kevin had. But they were just as surprised as I was. When I spoke to Gabriella, I could tell she was genuine. My heart is pounding so hard I can feel it in my head. The air feels thinner, and the room spins. I feel weak and lightheaded like I'm ready to pass out. Kevin is charming, loving, sexy, and kind. *He couldn't have done this. Could he?* I take out the potion and stand there, staring at the bottle for a moment. Then, almost zombie-like, I move to the stove and put the teapot to boil. I don't feel like myself. I am about to break Kevin's trust, and it feels wrong. Yet, I continue.

Once the water boils, I take Kevin's favorite red mug and another one for me from the cupboard. Removing the stopper from the potion bottle, I stare at it again before pouring the contents into the red mug. I wait five minutes before heading into the room. Kevin is still asleep.

I shake him gently. "Babe, I made you some tea. Here, drink it."

Rubbing his eyes, he smiles sleepily. "Thank you, babe."

I blow on my tea and take a sip, studying Kevin from the corner of my eye. Knowing that the potion effects only last five minutes, I try to think of my questions and word them correctly.

"Why would Eli beat you up?" I ask.

"Because he hates me," he replies in a robotic tone.

The potion is working! "Did you kill my father?"

"No, I didn't," he says, tone still robotic. "Why are you asking me that?"

"Because Eli told me to ask you," I blurt out. I am not under the potion's effects, but it does not sit right with me lying to him.

Kevin eyes me warily. It is as if he knows he is under a spell.

The silence stretches between us, and I say, "Do you know who murdered my father?"

He hesitates for about two seconds before saying, "No."

When he hesitated, I was unsure if I could believe his response. I glance at my watch and see that over five minutes have passed. The potion's effects have worn off.

"Did you use magic on me?" Kevin stares at me. His voice sounds broken. I can tell it hurt him that I would use magic on him, knowing it is against the rules.

"I am sorry, Eli—"

Kevin cuts me off mid-sentence. "No, you don't need to explain. You lost your father. As far as I am concerned, everyone in this town is a suspect. We will get to the bottom of his murder," he promises, taking me into his muscular arms, and I could not have been more content with his response.

I snuggle deeper into Kevin's arms, drawing comfort from his warm embrace. Remembering my earlier conversation with Eli, a sudden thought hits me. Eli said he attacked Kevin because he thought Kevin had something to do with Dad's murder. But... *how did Eli know about my father's murder before we spoke?* I clench my jaw, my hands curling into fists. *I will find out who killed you, Dad. There are no lengths I will not go to, even if it means losing myself in the process. Your death will not go unavenged.*

EARTH

MAGIC
is REAL

Chapter 14

Confessions of a Teenage Witch

Dear Diary,

I am writing in this diary because Ms. Hudson advised that I use this as a coping mechanism to eliminate my aggression. I am debating whether transferring my thoughts onto paper will work, but I'll try. What do I have to lose?

It has been eight weeks since someone murdered my father, and the police still have not caught the person who did it.

Just like they swept Destiny's mother's and Isabel's parents' deaths under the rug, the police seem to have given up on solving my father's murder. I haven't attended school in over a week and don't eat or sleep. I keep thinking about who could have murdered my father and why? On that dreadful day my father died, he had something clenched in his fist. I retrieved it from his hand when the paramedics weren't looking and hid it in my pocket. It was a flash drive. I haven't looked at it yet because I am not ready to see what is on it, but I have it in a safe place. I don't care about anything other than finding out who murdered my father. But here's a turn of events. Gabriella calls me daily, and Kevin and I aren't on good terms.

The Witch Council summoned me for a meeting tomorrow because I told my friends about magic. What they don't know is my magic has grown over the weeks, so if they think I'll let them remove it, they can think again.

"Good morning, Claudette," Kevin greets me as I walk to the sofa. "Do you plan on eating breakfast today—or ever?"

I don't look at him as I pick up the remote and flip through the channels. A few days after the funeral and my first phone call from Eli's irritating mother, I overheard Tanya and Tristan discussing the Witch Council's plan to remove my magic with Kevin, and he agreed with them. I know that telling my friends about magic was against the rules, but I hoped my *boyfriend* would support me no matter what. But apparently, he doesn't think I can control my emotions and believes I shouldn't possess such powers as a new witch. Since overhearing that conversation, our relationship has been on the rocks. The council, including Ms. Hudson, didn't approve of my two best friends accompanying me to the funeral, and now they want to take my magic away using a spell and a ceremonial knife known as a *"Ce-Ja."* All because I took Kevin's car, drove to my old hometown to pick up my friends, and brought them to Mashalville for the funeral. I didn't care about the rules then, and I don't care about them now. I trust Nicolette and Spencer with my life—about the only two people I do trust—and I know they would never betray me.

"How long are you going to give me the silent treatment?" Kevin presses.

I snort. "Why should I talk to you?"

"What is your issue, Claudette?" He walks towards me cautiously.

"My issue? What. Is. My. Issue?" I spit out slowly through gritted teeth.

His lips twist into a frown, and I can tell he chooses his words carefully when he speaks. "Claudette, I know you miss your father. But this is not the way to act. I haven't done anything to you, and I can't help but think you're blaming me for something."

I throw my head back and descend into uncontrollable laughter. *Is he serious? He really doesn't know?*

"Really, Kevin? Are we going to pretend you don't know why I am upset? I know you were angry about my friends being here. Am I supposed to act as if I am okay with you siding with the Witch Council?" I hiss.

"Claudette, humans aren't supposed to know about magic! If that's why you're upset, I suggest you get over it! Because I am not changing my stance on it."

"Noted!" I jump to my feet, rushing out of the room. I get my already-packed bag from the closet and use my magic to take me to Eli's house. That argument was all I needed to solidify my decision to leave.

I understand the rules are there for a reason, and I get that just because I trust Nicolette and Spencer doesn't mean everyone else will or can. But how could they think I wouldn't want my two best friends from childhood to be by my side as I said goodbye to my father? I didn't tell them that the town was full of magic; I told them I had magic and that my mother had it. I also told them someone murdered my father, and no one in this god-forsaken town knows who! Yes, I revealed some secrets, but not all, and the fact my "*boyfriend*" can't be on my side is a deal breaker for me.

(A text message between Kevin and Tanya)

Kevin:

Hey, you need to locate Claudette. NOW!

She just left, and I have no idea where she went.

Tanya:

Are you serious? You were to watch her.
What are we supposed to do now?
The Witch Council wants to see her tomorrow.

Kevin:

What do you expect me to do with no magic?
She's powerful.
You need to conduct the ceremony ASAP.

Tanya:

You best pull out your charm and reel her back in.

Kevin:

It's too late!

She knows I've sided with the Witch Council to take her magic away.

And I am tired of keeping up this façade.

Tanya:

Stick to the plan, Kevin!

We almost have what we want.

Chapter 15

Earth Witches

Appearing in the middle of Eli's living room with no official warning, he jumps to his feet from the sofa, startled by my sudden intrusion.

He holds a blanket in front of his lower half to cover himself. "Claudette, what are you doing here?" he asks, snapping his fingers as sweatpants appear on his legs.

My cheeks grow hot, and I shake away the sudden dirty thoughts that threaten to invade my mind. "Where are we with pinpointing who killed my father?"

He glances at my bag. "Why are you here with a duffle bag? And we don't answer a question with another question, Claudette." His lips curve into one of his dashing smiles, but his eyes remain serious.

"Oh. I was just in the neighborhood and thought I'd stop by to see how the investigation was going." He sees right through my lousy excuse. "Um... can I stay here?" I ask softly.

"Why do you want to stay here?" He presses. "Did something happen between you and Kevin?"

Lowering my eyes to the floor, my heart descends to the pit of my stomach.

Kevin had been caring until he wasn't. He became distant and cold after I invited my friends to be my support system for my dad's funeral. From that moment on, our relationship deteriorated. Even the sex felt strained and forced—something to keep me craving him—but he did not want me. I guess telling my friends about my magic was a "deal breaker" for him. Still, my gut tells me that he got what he desired from me, and now he's done, especially now that I'm damaged goods. However, if it was that easy for him to withdraw from me, perhaps he never truly loved me in the first place. Maybe he was only telling me what I wanted to hear to get what was precious to me!

The day after my father's funeral, I had dinner with Nicolette, Spencer, and Eli. We discussed the truth spell and deliberated Kevin's reactions. Nicolette still believed he was the perfect guy for me until she spoke to him at the funeral, and he gave her the cold shoulder. He was nothing like the caring and loving person who took me to my hometown for ice cream with my friends. Spencer was skeptical, and I was sure he thought I had lost my mind until I showed him my magic. They asked Eli if he had powers, too, but he shrugged them off and said that only I had them. I did not blame him for lying. Just because I disclosed my magic to them does not mean he had to. Eli wasn't pleased with me for telling my friends about magic. Still, he did not turn on me like Kevin did. Eli still shows his unwavering support, and according to him, the prophecy foretold that he and I were meant to be together, not Kevin and me.

"Claudette?" Eli calls out my name, taking me away from my inner thoughts.

He walks toward me, arms open, and I fall into his embrace, letting his strong arms wrap around me while I sob. It's easy to be vulnerable with Eli. He hasn't judged me unless it was about Kevin, and even then, he did it out of concern for my well-being. I inhale his familiar scent, feeling safe and protected in his arms, until waves of electricity flow from his body to mine, our magic uniting.

"Will you stop doing that?" I say, pushing him away.

His lips curl into a sexy smile. "I'm not doing it on purpose. Our magic is connecting."

Heat rises to my face, and I look away immediately with guilt.

Eli regards me through narrowed eyes. "Are you going to tell me what happened between you and Kevin?" he asks, his tone gentle but firm.

My eyes fill with water again, and tears stream down my cheeks before I can stop them. "Kevin and I broke up. I have nowhere else to go."

Eli's stern expression softens, and he doesn't press further. "You can stay with me for as long as you need. We can be roommates."

"Thank you." I wipe away my tears and manage a small smile before masking my feelings. "How close are we to finding out who killed my father?"

Eli has grown used to my shift in emotions, so he thinks nothing of it and disappears to his room to retrieve a notebook and pen.

He flips through the pages. "Honestly, Claudette, I don't know where to start. We don't have any solid leads."

Observing his notes closer, I notice he still has Kevin's name circled as the murderer.

Screwing up my face, I place my hands on my hips. "Why is Kevin still a suspect if we have no leads, Eli?"

Eli sucks in the air and exhales slowly, choosing his words carefully. "Because, Claudette, he hesitated when you asked him if he knew who killed your father. The potion had timed out, so that means he knows more than he's letting on. His hesitation wouldn't have happened if he were still under the spell."

"You don't think he killed my father? But he knows who did?"

"It's a possibility we can't ignore."

The mystery of my father's death is becoming more complex by the minute. I don't want to believe that my boy–*ex-boyfriend* could be involved. Was Eli right all along about Kevin?

The people crossed off my list of suspects are the ones whose alibis were accounted for during my father's murder. The twins and Gabriella were at the movies; they knew my father, and I had a date planned. Lin was taking piano lessons. Ms. Hudson was late to our therapy session because she was with Mr. Handsome. Kevin didn't feel well and was fighting with Eli. And Destiny and Isabel were on a date.

I have half a mind to create more truth potion, administer it to everyone, and directly ask if they killed my father, but Eli advised against it. He warned that although the potion forces the truth out of people, there is a spell that can be cast to counteract its effects. *Go figure! Magic has its limits.* What else can I do? It has been weeks, and I am not any closer to finding the murderer, or rather, the detectives aren't any closer. They are likely to write it off as a cold case soon, like Isabel's parents and Destiny's mom. I don't know much about the law or how it works in a town of witches cloaked in the real world. *Nothing here seems realistic!*

Eli meets my gaze with a solemn expression, pondering before finally speaking. "My mother was alerted when you made the 911 call."

My brows snap together. "What?"

"She listens in on all the 911 calls made in town," he admits.

Folding my arms across my chest, I ask, "Is that even legal?"

Eli shrugs. "It's supposed to be against the law, but are you going to tell her that? In a town like this, who knows what's legal and what's not?"

This town doesn't follow the basic rules of life!

"When I heard the call, I left to confront Kevin about it," Eli continues.

Rolling my eyes. "We know how that turned out," I mutter under my breath.

My phone vibrates in my pocket, interrupting our conversation.

Tanya is calling me. *What does she want?*

"Are you going to answer that?" Eli raises an eyebrow.

Shaking my head, I ignore the call. "We need to figure out who killed my fa–"

My phone vibrates again, and this time, I answer it while Eli draws a new circle with my dad's name in the center. He adds arrows to a question mark as a suspect.

Tanya demands I attend tomorrow's council meeting, or they will drag me there kicking and screaming! I hang up on her so fast that I almost break the screen.

Who does she think she is, ordering me around like that?

Eli's brows shoot up, overhearing Tanya. "I guess there's a meeting tomorrow that demands our attendance."

Shaking my head. "No. You should go to school. I'll handle it."

"*Both* of us should be in school," he reasons, grabbing my shoulders. "I'm going with you, Claudette. I'm not going to let you face this alone, and I'll be there as a friend and nothing more."

"Thank you." I sigh under his steady gaze.

Eli is a really great guy, and I wish I met him first.

"Unless..." He smirks suggestively.

"Unless *what*?" I raise an eyebrow.

"Unless you want something more between us."

"Are you flirting with me during a time of crisis, Elijah Powers?" I crack a smile.

"Of course not, Claudette Richardson," he chuckles. "Just making sure you know all your options."

Rolling my eyes playfully, I nudge him. "Let's focus on the task at hand before we start discussing anything else," I say, trying to keep our priorities straight. "You should probably add Kevin's parents as suspects as well."

As great as Eli is, I am not ready to dive into anything more than a friendship with him just yet. And I don't want him to be a rebound. He is too special of a guy for that.

"Will do," he responds with a nod, scribbling down their names and catching my gaze with a reassuring smile. He understands and respects my feelings, which only makes me appreciate him more.

He motions for me to follow him down the hallway.

With my bag in hand, I swiftly trail behind, eager to discover my new bedroom. Eli and his brother Jeremiah shared the two-bedroom, two-bath apartment until Jeremiah got his own place and moved out. This is convenient for me because I need a place to stay. Gabriella made it clear I couldn't live with them, although I'm sure my father left the house for me. However, I am still a minor, but even if the law were enforced in Mashalville, I wouldn't want to live there anyway. I hate all of them! *Hate* is a strong word, but you've been following along, haven't you?

Gabriella agrees that the twins and I shouldn't live under the same roof. *There is no argument there.* Also, that's the last place my father was alive.

Eli opens the door for me, and I exhale slowly, studying the space before me. The room is painted royal blue with a bunch of Marvel characters plastered on the walls and a significant crescent moon engraved with the letters JP. A twin-size bed with no sheets and covers sits in the center, although a full-size bed could be a better fit for the room.

"I'll leave you to get settled in," he says, giving me a small smile.

I thank him again before he closes the door behind him.

Standing in the room, I close my eyes. The room smells of lavender, giving it a relaxing feel. Snapping my fingers, leopard bedding appears on the bed. Did I mention I love being a witch? Because I do! I envision a brown wall to complement the bedding, and the walls transform from royal blue to a warm chocolate brown. Thinking about a small desk, it appears in the corner of the room. I put my bag on the bed to unpack my Dell laptop and place it on the newly manifested desk. Unfortunately, magic has its limits, so I have to manually remove the posters from the walls.

Two hours later, the room is starting to feel like mine, and I'm settling in nicely.

Sitting on my new bed, I decide to finally look through the flash drive my dad left me; my answers may very well be on there. Between dwelling on who murdered my father and silently battling with Kevin, I have put this off long enough. It is time.

Unzipping the side pocket of my blue and black duffel bag, I grab my jewelry box and place it on the desk. Holding my breath for a moment, I sigh before opening and pulling out the flash drive. I contemplate whether I should plug it into my laptop or not. *Do it!* My inner voice, Detta, urges me, so I open my computer, turn it on, and insert the flash drive into the USB port. Here goes nothing!

The contents of the device load onto my screen, displaying a series of files. Tapping my fingers nervously on the desk, I wait for the files to fully load. This drive has my father's entire life condensed into folders of information, and it's going to take me hours to go through it all. Maybe even days. There are folders labeled with dates, names, and places. The one that catches my eye is labeled *Chance,* my father's name.

Double-clicking on the folder with his name, I begin reading through the files. His mother was an Earth witch, and his father was a Moon witch. According to this document, the parent with the stronger heart determines the magic their child inherits. My grandmother was an Earth witch, and so was my father. And I was lucky enough, depending on how you look at it, to become an Earth witch as well. After my dad's seventeenth birthday, his parents were murdered, and he fled from this town. *Why are everyone's parents being murdered?* I don't get it!

Earth witches were feared, but the council did not come after him because he chose to be a norm. Back then, Earth witches were viewed as a threat. For decades, they were hunted and murdered by a secret cult of evil witches. *How could they let this go on for all these years?*

Scrolling through all the pictures of the Earth witches that were slain, I fight to hold back tears. Taking a deep breath and exhaling slowly, I continue reading. The witches were murdered with a Ce-Ja dagger.

Used to eliminate magic from Sun, Moon, and Earth witches.

There is a subfolder labeled *The Daggers*. Clicking on it, there are pictures and descriptions of a few different daggers with names I cannot pronounce, each with a distinct purpose—all for me to study. A Ne-aik-eart was used to murder Earth witches and absorb their magic. The dagger is gold, black, green, and brown.

Used to absorb Earth magic.

Although my father did not practice magic, he was born an Earth witch, which made him a target. The monster who murdered him used the Ne-aik-eart on him and absorbed his magical essence, and it is a matter of time before I am the next victim. Except I'll be ready! The magical autopsy Destiny illegally performed on my father revealed that his wounds were inflicted by this dagger. However, whoever did it masked his stab wounds with magic to cover their tracks. *Jerk!*

Exiting out of the *Chance* folder altogether, I scroll down until I see *Claudia,* my mother's name. My mom was born a Moon witch; so was her father, and her mother was a Sun witch. I recall my dad telling me that her parents died in a car accident, but this file indicates that they were also murdered for a ritual. Ne-aik-oon is the name of the dagger that was used on my grandmother, and it is black and white.

Used to absorb Moon magic.

The gold and yellow dagger used to remove Sun witches' powers is called Ne-aik-un.

Used to absorb Sun magic.

Browsing through unsettling photos of my grandparents and the other brutally murdered witches, my heart breaks. Their hearts were ripped out of their chests, their eyes carved out, and the blood drained from their bodies. Only the witches who accepted their magic were murdered in this gruesome manner. Since my father wanted to remain a norm, he did not succumb to the same awful fate. *Or did he?*

He is dead. Holding my chest, I choke back the rising panic. Yet Destiny assured me that his body was not completely drained of blood and did not have any open wounds that were visible to the naked eye. I really don't know what happened to my father, and after reading through his files, I'm more confused than before.

My heart shatters for all the witches who suffered at the hands of the secret cult, especially for my grandparents, whom I never got to know. It is beyond me that these *monsters* haven't been brought to justice yet.

I remove the flash drive from my laptop, put it back in my jewelry box, and hide it underneath my mattress. I need time to process all of the information I uncovered.

Pools of tears well up in my eyes, and I want to run to Eli for comfort. Unfortunately, he is in bed, so I opt for a shower instead and hop into bed after letting the warm water wash away some of the pain. With my brain reeling with all the information I have learned, hopefully, I will be able to rest.

Chapter 16

Take my Magic Away, I Think Not!

The next morning, my stomach is in knots as I prepare for the impending doom with the council. It is foolish for them to think they can take my magic away. Of course, this is the Witch Council I'm going up against. They are seasoned in their magic, and I have only been practicing for a couple of months. However, working with Eli has prepared me for any challenges they may throw my way.

Mrs. Powers withdrew her offer to add me to the council, which is fine because I never wanted to be a part of their stuffy group anyway. Eli's choice to go against his parents scores him major points in my book; he has shown me his loyalty, no matter the repercussions. He disagrees with my decision, but he is still standing by me. Kevin, on the other hand, has not reached out to me since I left. It has only been a day, but his silence speaks volumes. He is my supposed soulmate, according to his version of the prophecy, yet my decision has made him distant from me.

While Eli gets dressed for the council meeting, I wait in the kitchen. Toying with my phone in my hand, I debate whether to text Kevin or not. *Just do it!* Detta urges. I ultimately decide to send him a quick message in an attempt to bridge the gap between us. I am still upset with him, but did my feelings for him disappear overnight? Of course not.

A few uneasy minutes pass before I double-text him.

Tapping my foot anxiously, I wait for his response, but it never comes. *Excellent!* Now, I am coming off as desperate. I sigh in frustration, sending one final message. *Fine!* Our relationship is clearly over.

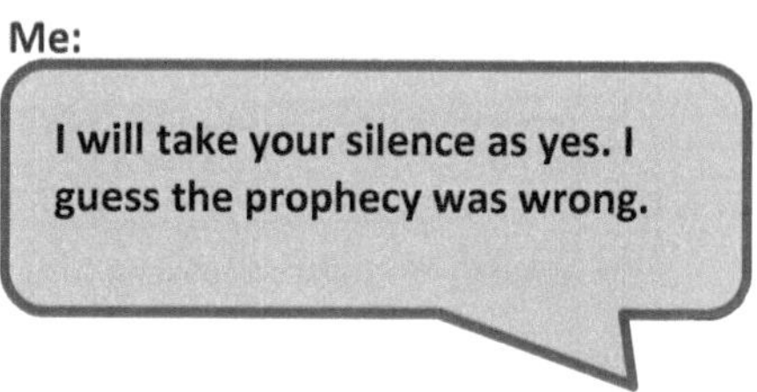

No response. I toss my phone in my bag and shrug my shoulders. It is what it is!

Eli walks into the kitchen, smiling from ear to ear. "Good morning, Sunshine."

I give him a half-hearted smile. "Why are you in a great mood for 'doomsday?'" I gesture air quotes around the word doomsday.

Folding his arms across his chest, Eli chuckles. "Why are you being so dramatic this early in the morning?"

Rolling my eyes, I tie my locs in a bun. "I'm just not in the mood for sunshine and rainbows today. The Witch Council wants to take my magic!"

His smile fades. "You're not alone in this. Destiny, Lin, and I will help fight the cause with you. There is no way they will take your magic away without casting a vote first."

It is sweet that he is hopeful, but let's be honest, I'm not going to win.

Screwing up my face. "I need a plan, Eli, not blind optimism. Most of the council wants to rid me of my magic. I am not sure how voting will help me when the majority is against me!" I shout, throwing my hands in the air. "Tanya, Tristan, your parents, and your brother are all in favor of team *no magic*. I don't know Ms. Hudson's stance, and the other guy goes with the flow."

"You mean Jimmy?"

"Who cares about his name?!" I shout, "He's just another vote against me!"

Eli puts a comforting hand on my shoulders. "Don't worry, Claudette. It is my birthright to be a part of the Witch Council, and I have formally accepted my role as a member to vote against them. I have also recruited Destiny and Lin. My parents offered them positions on the council months ago, but they declined until now. They have taken their rightful place alongside me to vote in your favor." He gives me a reassuring smile, optimistic that his plan will actually work. "You are the only Earth witch in town that we know of, which naturally deems you a member by default. I know the rules like the back of my hand. Trust me, Claudette. I will not let you down."

His eyes are so sincere that I am in awe. Yet, I am still doubtful. Nonetheless, I entwine my fingers with his. "Let's kick some Witch Council butt!" I am standing my ground against those who seek to suppress my magic.

He squeezes my hand gently, and we head to his car to drive to our impending doom.

Kevin catches my eye, and I can't help but take a sharp breath once we arrive at the town hall. His face is stern, in stark contrast to that usual sexy smile. He's standing in front of the building with his guard dogs, Tanya and Tristan. I guess this is his reason for not texting me back; he was with his trusted minions. Tanya lightly brushes her hand against Kevin's. She whispers something into his ear, changing his facial expression from stern to soft in a matter of seconds. *That is odd.*

A slight pang of jealousy surfaces in my chest. Pushing the feeling aside, I march behind Eli to the entrance of the building, walking past Kevin and avoiding his direction. He grasps my arm before I can fully pass by.

Jerking my arm away, I shoot him a questioning look.

"Can we talk?" he asks.

"No." My answer is firm and final. "I tried talking to you before, but you ignored me. Keep that same energy!"

Tanya's eyes are wide at our exchange. Kevin tries again to grab my arm, but I step back out of his reach. "I have nothing to say to you," I state firmly, turning to walk inside for what I believe will be a showdown.

When I enter the room, a bustling sea of whispers and stares surrounds me. It seems like the entire town of Mashalville is here, waiting for a decision to be made. *Shouldn't they be in school? Or working?*

The ballroom is a grand spectacle where the council members conduct ceremonies and rituals. Tanya and Tristan lower into their seats with the rest of the council. Mrs. Elizabeth Powers takes the stage front and center.

"We are gathered here today to address Miss Richardson's insubordinate actions." She announces from the podium through gritted teeth. Her eyes zero in on Eli. "I see my son is in attendance. For what purpose, I wonder?"

"I am here to advocate for Claudette, mother!" He spits out defiantly.

The room gasps in unison.

Her lips curl into a scowl as she fixes her gaze on Eli. Dismissing his words, she retrieves a large book with a crescent moon engraved on the front cover. The book is black and white, and I watch closely as she flips through the pages. She eyes me warily, reaching into her bag and pulling out a dagger—the Ce-Ja dagger—and sitting it on top of the book.

She builds momentum by pacing back and forth, her eyes never leaving mine. "We–"

"We should cast a vote!" Eli interjects, cutting his mother off.

Mrs. Powers laughs dryly in Eli's direction. "*Now* you are on the Witch Council?"

Eli nods.

"Cast a vote on *what*?" Mrs. Powers sneers with annoyance laced in her tone.

Eli carefully approaches her, taking the dagger away. He gives his mother a stern look, and she reluctantly stands down. *What was that about?*

"Claudette Richardson is innocent," Eli asserts. "Her father was murdered, and she reached out to the two people she trusts the most. As a town, we should sympathize with her, not condemn her. She did not disclose to her friends that this is a town full of witches; she only disclosed her magic to them. And, of course, as it is wrong and against the rules, she needed her two best friends to mourn."

Eli's announcement did not seem to sit well with everyone in the room.

Mr. Powers whispers into his wife's ear, and she exhales before speaking. "Fine. All in favor of eliminating Claudette's magic because she broke our number one rule. Raise your left hand."

Everyone in the crowd raises their left hand, including Kevin.

Jimmy, Ms. Hudson, Eli, Destiny, and Lin are the only ones who keep their hands down. Eli did not expect this. But I did.

It is flattering that Eli wanted to represent me; however, it is time I show this town what I am capable of. Clearing my throat, I shake off the nerves and turn my stern gaze toward the crowd as I take the stage to plead my case.

"Excuse me, the town of Mashalville; I would like to speak for myself regarding the matter."

Mrs. Powers is about to intervene, but I wave my hand, and she plunges to the floor. The crowd gasps. *No more playing nice.*

"The focus of this town is futile! My father was murdered eight weeks ago, and instead of focusing on who killed him, the town wants to remove my magic. How does that make any sense?" I shout, not expecting anyone to answer.

My eyes lock with Ms. Hudson's. "I strongly advise you to leave the room, as this may be a conflict of interest if you wish to remain my therapist," I say, my voice steady.

Ms. Hudson covers her mouth in shock. I have the undivided attention of the room. Even Eli is looking at me with wide eyes. Mrs. Powers is now standing, and she retaliates by using her magic to aim a knife at my heart. I effortlessly catch the knife, an ominous grin spreading on my face. *Too slow.*

There's a switch in my emotions. A weight of guilt lifts off my heavy heart, and I no longer care about the consequences. My brown eyes darken, and my energy shifts into something sinister and more powerful. I feel empowered. All I care about is finding my father's killer and why he was murdered in cold blood.

With a flick of my wrist, I send the knife flying back towards Mrs. Powers, stopping just short of making contact. The room falls silent as Mrs. Powers stares at me with widened eyes.

"I will not hesitate to kill you if you do that again!" I shout, my voice echoing through the room.

"Who do you think you are talking to like that?" Mrs. Powers demands, clenching her fists, but she appears visibly shaken.

Laughing dryly in response to her idiotic question, I snap my fingers, and the knife disappears from sight. And while all eyes are on me, Eli shoves the

Ce-Ja dagger in his pocket.

Clearing my throat. "Listen up, townspeople of Mashalville! No one will be taking away my magic! And if you try, I *will* kill you. You have been warned."

Ms. Hudson intervenes, her eyes filled with concern. "Claudette, perhaps we should speak in private?"

"No. That won't be necessary." My expression remains neutral, dismissing her request.

Eli confronts me with a worried expression. "Are you okay, Claudette? You just threatened the entire town. They could rebel against you."

"I'm aware. And I've never been better, my friend," I assure him gleefully, nudging his broad shoulder.

"Are you sure?"

Rolling my eyes. "I know what I'm doing, Eli."

"She broke the rules!" Crissy shouts from the crowd, pointing an accusing finger at me. "The council needs to strip her magic away!"

Did I hear Crissy talk? *She never speaks.*

Her outburst takes me by surprise, and my eyes narrow as I focus on her. Perhaps she doesn't realize how serious I am about my warning to this ridiculous town.

"My mother's magic was removed! Claudette's magic should be stripped, too. People outside of this town are not supposed to know about magic! She broke the rules!" Marissa yells, backing up her twin and charging towards me.

Soaring through the herd of people, I meet her head-on.

This is the last time I will allow her and her demon twin to speak to me without consequence.

My mind focuses on her knee, calculating the exact angle and force needed to incapacitate her without causing permanent damage and with just a thought.

Crack.

Marissa collapses to the ground, clutching her knee in agony. "What did you do to me?!" she screams, glaring up at me with pure hatred in her eyes.

I smile, knowing that she will think twice before crossing me again.

Crissy charges at me, her chest heaving with anger as she lunges forward. I sidestep her attack.

Ankles.

Crissy falls to the ground, writhing in pain as she clutches her broken ankles. "You're crazy!" she cries out, tears streaming down her face.

It's a lesson they won't soon forget. With a mere thought, I broke Marissa's knee and both of Crissy's ankles.

"That is my last and final warning!" I declare loudly, my voice cold and unwavering.

Storming out of the room, Destiny, Eli, and Lin scurry behind me. I am livid. This town had the audacity to try to take away my magic. *Mine!* And no one seems to care about the murder of my father, not even the detectives. It is up to me to get to the bottom of it, and once I do, I will kill him or her—*or them!*

"What happened in there, Claudette?" Destiny asks, a crease forming between her eyebrows. "Your anger will eventually consume you into darkness if you don't find a way to channel it."

Choosing not to reply, I walk toward Eli's car and climb into the passenger seat.

"Is she not going to respond to me?" Destiny looks between Eli and Lin, who both shrug.

The rage I am feeling is unfathomable. I never thought about killing anyone—until *now*. I need to get back to Eli's place to unravel more information from the flash drive. The file has so many folders, and I must go through them all.

Eli says bye to Lin and Destiny and gets into the driver's seat. He doesn't start the car right away; instead, he places his hand on top of mine and squeezes it gently. Electric shockwaves surge through his touch into me, and the rage settles inside me for just a moment. We drive off in silence. Eli is my calm in the severe storm that is brewing.

Once we get back to his place—well, *our* place—I head to my room to start sifting through the folders on the flash drive. Inserting the drive into my laptop, I exhale. Scrolling through the different folders, my eyes land on the one labeled *Gabriella*.

Chapter 17

Beloved Wife

One week before the death of Chance Richardson...

C*hance's point of view:*

Next Wednesday, I am taking Claudette on a father-daughter date in our old town. I made arrangements with Evi to save our favorite booth. Evi's is a special place for us; it's where I took Claudette after Claudia was called to be with the angels. I can't wait to spend time with my baby girl, my Cheetah. I have missed her so much these past few weeks. It's the longest we've been apart.

My friend Adam is coming over today to conduct a spell so I can speak to my beloved wife while Gabriella and the girls are out shopping. It's time Claudette learned the truth about her heritage and the dangers lurking in the shadows. Mashalville is my home, but the evil that has taken root here must be stopped. Unfortunately, it will be up to Claudette to face this darkness head-on. No teenager should have to carry the burden of the entire town on their shoulders. Still, this is the fate we have been dealt.

There is a knock on the door. I open it, and Adam pushes past me.

"Chance, my man, we have to do this quick. I have a date tonight!" he says, pulling out a candle from his bag.

"Well, we better hurry then. Let's get this done so you can go sweep your lady off her feet."

"Appreciate it, man," Adam chuckles, dashing around the living room and setting everything in place for the spell.

"How has your day been so far?" I ask, making small talk as he prepares for the ritual.

"Today was a nightmare!" Adam screws up his face. "Next week, we have another batch of kids turning seventeen who still need to decide whether they want to become mags or remain a norm. I also need to plan my lessons. And once I leave here, I have to pick up Lin."

Nodding in understanding. "Sounds like a lot on your plate."

Adam half smirks. "You have no idea. It's one thing to deal with teenage hormones. It's another when they choose to keep their magic."

Slapping him on the back. "You handle it like a pro, man. I don't know how you do it, I have three teenage girls, and that's challenging enough."

"No offense, man, but I would never trade places with you."

"None taken. Teenage daughters are a different ball game." I chuckle.

"No arguments there." He says, waving his hand back and forth.

"Also, I wanted to tell you taking in Lin was very noble of you."

He nods. "Yeah, it was the right thing to do after his parents were killed."

"Speaking of that, we need to figure out what happened to all the witches who were murdered."

"I agree." Adam retrieves a piece of paper from his pocket. "Chase, are you ready to get started?"

Nodding my head.

"Recite this spell word for word three times," he instructs, handing me the paper.

Silently reciting the incantation in my head, I nod once more, and Adam lights the candle.

"I am going to fall asleep, and when I do, Claudia will cross over."

"Got it," I reply. "Let's do this."

Adam pauses. "I have one question before we begin: why haven't you tried talking to Claudia before?"

That's a significant question. I was severely depressed after losing the love of my life, and I made the hardest decision to move on for my daughter. I figured it was best to never cross that path of bringing Claudia back. She is no longer in the realm of the living, and I have accepted that. However, our daughter is in danger.

I choose my words carefully. "There is a war brewing amongst the witches, and I need to speak with Claudia."

A crease forms between Adam's brows, and he nods slowly. "I can smell war in the air. There is some deep-rooted dark magic going amuck."

"Agreed," I reply.

"Ready?"

Nodding my head, I recite the spell. "In this sacred hour, I call upon the leader of the Light World to allow me time with Claudia, the one I love and honor," I repeat the spell three times, and Adam falls into a deep slumber.

The lights flicker off and on as a beaming white light fills the room. A brisk wind swirls around, causing goosebumps on my skin, and the air in the room turns cold. I exhale, and I see my breath form a mist. A cloud of smoke appears in front of me, taking the shape of a slim and curvy silhouette. Claudia walks through the smoke, a small smile on her beautiful brown-skinned face. Tears form in my eyes, and I reach for her hand.

"Claudia," I whisper, my voice trembling with emotion.

She squeezes my hand gently. "I'm here," she says, and she falls into my embrace. I hold her as tight as I can, never wanting to let go again. When we finally pull away, I squeeze her shoulders, forearms, and wrists, making sure she is real and not just a figment of my imagination.

Claudia's eyes meet mine. "I'm real, my love."

With her words, I press my lips to hers, savoring the taste of her sweet kiss. She feels cold, but my heart warms at her touch. I have missed my wife, my one true love.

Our lips part, and her brown eyes suddenly turn black before turning brown again.

"What is it?" I ask, running my fingers along her arms and grasping her hands, pulling her close to me.

"We don't have much time, Chance," she says. "And this is a serious matter."

"What do you mean, Claudia? What's going on?"

"There's something I need to tell you. It's about our daughter." Claudia pauses before scolding me. "How could you allow her to move out, Chance?"

Scratching the back of my neck, I look everywhere but at her.

She grabs my chin, forcing me to meet her gaze.

My shoulders slump. "How did you know?"

"Sometimes, I peek through the veil. Imagine my surprise when I saw that she wasn't living with you anymore."

I swallow hard. "Kevin is a fine young man, Claudia. I thought Claudette would be happier living with him instead of living under the same roof with..." I trail off, suddenly feeling awkward discussing my current wife with my dead wife.

Claudia grasps my hands in hers. "I just want you to be happy, Chance. That's all I ever wanted," she says softly. "I am not upset you moved on. I am upset at what it has done to our daughter." There's sadness in her eyes as she speaks. "Kevin is up to no good, Chance. He's not who he says he is. And those twins are not much better. However..." She briefly looks away before continuing. "Gabriella does love you."

Her words hit me like a ton of bricks. "I thought if I kept Claudette here, she would try to—"

"I know," she says, cutting me off. "I was there when she stepped in front of the train." Her voice breaks slightly. "I saved her just in time. But she's hurting, Chance. I will continue to watch over her and protect her, but you need to do your part, too. Which brings me to my next purpose: There has been talking in the Light World that evil is brewing—a much more powerful darkness than what's been going on in this town. This greater evil stems from the Dark World, and our daughter is the key to stopping it. You must get her away from Kevin. He is not right for her, and he is not the one–"

The lights begin flickering off and on, and our eyes lock.

"My time is up, my love." Her body begins to dissolve into a mist, and I reach out to grab her hand one last time. "Please protect our daughter at all costs. Kevin is not her soulmate, Chance. Her soulmate is E–"

She disappears through a cloud of smoke, and Adam wakes up.

"No!" I shout. "Go back under, Adam! I need more time with her!"

But it's too late.

Adam regards me with a solemn expression. "I can't, Chance."

"What do you mean you *can't*?"

"I can't just bring people back from the Light World whenever I want. That's not how it works."

Running my fingers through my hair. "What do we do then?"

Adam pulls out a gold pendant from his bag. There is a small line on the pendant that is drifting in a circle. I survey it closely, however, I can't tell what I am looking at.

"Well?" I ask expectantly.

Adam explains, "I can only bring someone back from the Light World when the veil is open."

"When will the veil be open again?"

Adam sighs. "According to this," he jiggles the pendant, "the next time the veil will be open is next month."

Feeling impatient, I pace back and forth in frustration.

Adam looks at me with a furrowed brow. "What did Claudia say that has you so worried?"

I stop pacing to meet his gaze. "She said not to trust Kevin."

Adam's mouth forms a silent O.

"Claudia mentioned she peeks through the veil sometimes. How does she do that?"

"Chance, peeking through the veil, and stepping through are different things," Adam explains. "Peeking through the veil allows her to see glimpses of the other side without being seen or heard."

Pinching my bottom lip between my index finger and thumb. "How was Claudia able to save Claudette if she couldn't be seen or heard?"

Adam pauses, his brow furrowing in thought. "Have you ever experienced a haunting?"

"No," I reply, folding my arms across my chest.

"It is possible that Claudia blew cold air onto Claudette to give her a sign that she was there, but I don't know, Chance. You would have to ask her."

That is the problem; I can't speak to her again until next month.

"How do you expect to get your love-struck daughter away from Kevin?" Adam raises an eyebrow.

If I push too hard, Claudette will only rebel, and if I'm not careful, I could very well force her into his arms forever. What do I do?

Adam waves his hands in front of my face, taking me out of my inner musing. "Chance, my man, are you okay?"

"No, Adam. I'm not. If Kevin is indeed evil, then that could mean he's caused Earth witches to die. My daughter is in danger."

Adam looks at me with concern, his brow furrowed. "But this has been going on for decades. Kevin hasn't been alive that long."

"True." I need to find a way to subtly guide Claudette without being too forceful. "I am going to compose documents for Claudette and save them on a secure drive. She will have access to the information she needs about this town: magic, her family history, and the dangers."

Adam agrees, nodding silently with approval.

Next week, when Claudette and I meet for our father-daughter date, I will present her with this flash drive, and we will handle the next steps together.

Chapter 18

Claudette's Father

The day of Chance Richardson's death...

E*li's point of view:*

"Kevin and his minions are planning something big!" Jeremiah shouts, walking into my bedroom.

My fists clench at my brother's disclosure. "What are you talking about, Jere? What do you know?"

A crease forms between Jeremiah's eyebrows. "I overheard Kevin telling Tanya and Tristan that a plan involving Claudette's father is going down tonight! This is serious, Eli. Kevin has been murdering Earth witches for some time now."

I throw on a jacket and grab my car keys so I can head over to Claudette's father's house to warn him about the danger he may be in. Claudette doesn't believe me when I tell her Kevin can't be trusted; maybe I can convince her father to believe me instead before it's too late.

"Where are you going?" Jeremiah asks.

"To warn Mr. Richardson."

Jeremiah frowns. "What are you going to say to him, Eli? That his daughter's boyfriend is a murderer? He will ask for proof."

My shoulders sag. "Jere, I don't know, but I have to try. I can't just sit back and do nothing. Mr. Richardson is the only family Claudette has left."

Jeremiah's frown deepens. "I don't want Kevin and his minions coming after me next."

"Dude!" I shout, "What do you expect me to do? I love this girl! I can't sit back and let something happen to her father. I promise no one will know I found out from you."

"She is not your girl or your responsibility, Eli. Stay out of it!" Jeremiah retorts, rubbing his temples.

He is right. Claudette is not my girlfriend, and she doesn't feel the same way about me. However, she is my mate, and we are fated to be together. I can't ignore the danger her father is in. I have to do something to help. Until she realizes that she is my destiny, I will love and protect her from the sidelines.

"I have to do something," I tell him firmly.

"Why can't you just let it go?"

Exhaling slowly, I continue, "I can't stand by and do nothing when someone I care about is in trouble. She is my mate."

Jeremiah eyes me warily. "Are you sure she is your soulmate?"

"Yes!" I reply with conviction. "Electric shocks ricocheted from my fingertips to my toes the first time I touched her. We were connected."

Jeremiah looks skeptical, but I can see the wheels turning in his head.

"I will use the moon bracelet to be sure she is my mate."

"Fine," he finally concedes, "the bracelet will confirm your bond." He lets out an exasperated sigh. "Just be careful."

"I will."

"I will text you on my way to the house. Our mother knows that Kevin and his minions are up to something," Jeremiah says.

I nod before leaving the room to head to my car.

Sweat is dripping down my temples when I park up in front of Mr. Richardson's house. I grip the steering wheel tight. How do you properly tell a father that his daughter's boyfriend is not who he seems to be? There is no easy way! I will come off as jealous or paranoid, and I am far from either. *This is a messy situation!*

Slouching lower in the driver's seat, I watch Gabriella and the twins leave the house. I wait in my car for them to drive away before mustering up the courage to approach Mr. Richardson. Steadying my breathing, I inhale and exhale once more before finally getting out of the car and walking towards the front door. *Here goes nothing.*

Knocking on the door, I wait for what feels like an eternity before Mr. Richardson answers.

"Hello, Eli," he greets me. "What brings you here today?"

"Hello, Mr. Richardson," I reply nervously. "I wanted to talk to you about something important."

Mr. Richardson nods and gestures for me to trail him inside the house.

Following him into the house to the kitchen, he offers me something to drink, but I politely decline. Kevin and his minions will be here at any moment, and I need to get this off my chest before they arrive.

"What's on your mind, Eli? Claudette should be here soon, so we should make this quick," Mr. Richardson says, looking at his watch.

I get straight to the point.

"I have to talk to you about Kevin," I reply.

Mr. Richardson's eyebrows knit together. "Eli, I do not want to get in the middle of you and Kevin's teenage love quarrel over my daughter."

How did he know?

"Sir, it's not about that; it's about something entirely different," I assure him, swallowing hard before continuing. "I know you are an Earth witch. *Kevin* has been murdering Earth witches to regain his magic."

Mr. Richardson runs a hand through his hair. "That's a serious accusation, Eli. What proof do you have, young man?"

Gulping back the lump in my throat, I answer him truthfully. "I can't give away my source, sir, but this person is credible. I believe Kevin, Tanya, and Tristan are planning something as we speak."

I am interrupted by Mr. Richardson's phone ringing. He raises his index finger to signal for me to wait as he answers the call.

"Hello, Kevin. How are you feeling? Claudette told me you weren't feeling well." Mr. Richardson listens intently, his expression changing as he speaks with Kevin.

Speak of the devil himself!

I start pacing back and forth in the kitchen, waiting for him to finish his call.

He hangs up and turns to me, a serious look on his face, and I immediately stop pacing. "Kevin is on his way here."

My face pales. "Kevin cannot be trusted! Sir! Perhaps I should stay here with you." I try to convince him.

Mr. Richardson shakes his head. "Eli, Kevin doesn't have magic. What can he do to hurt me?"

"You don't have any magic either. Please let me stay." I insist, hoping he will reconsider, but he doesn't.

He reaches for something, a flash drive, from underneath a vase and slides it into his pocket. "I appreciate your concerns, Eli, but I will be fine. Thank you." He looks out of the window and sees Kevin approaching. "Kevin is here to discuss important matters."

That was fast!

I reluctantly turn to leave, heading towards the back door before stopping myself. "Do you believe me?"

He turns back to me, his expression grave. "I believe you, Eli. But we will need credible proof for Claudette to believe us. Trust your instincts to keep her safe, and keep yourself safe as well."

"I will do whatever it takes to protect her." I exit from the back to avoid being seen by Kevin and the two people with him.

Surveying them from my car, I have a clear visual of Kevin and Mr. Richardson talking in the living room. I'm trying to get a closer look at the heavy-set man, or maybe it's a woman, but I can't quite make out their features from this distance. There's another person right behind the robust individual, but their face is obscured by the angle of the window. *I need a closer look!* The only significant thing I can see is something shiny reflecting on the person's left arm. *Maybe a bracelet?* Perhaps it's a woman? I can't really tell from here.

My phone vibrates, and I quickly glance down at the screen to see Claudette calling. I ignore the call and continue to watch Mr. Richardson through the window. I'm on a mission to obtain hard evidence, and I don't want to speak to her until I have concrete proof in hand.

Beep. Who is it now?

Jeremiah:

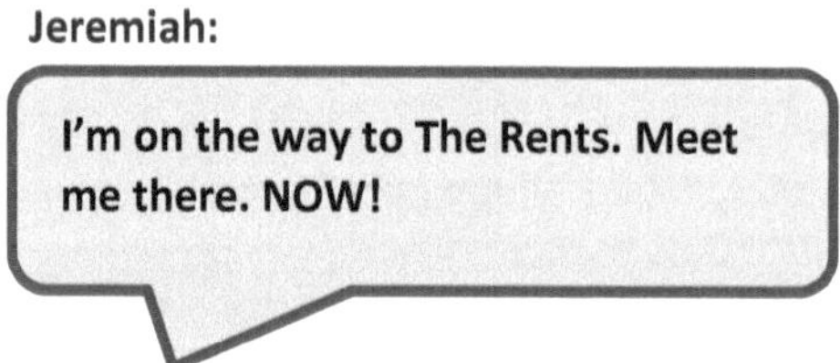

Jeremiah sometimes refers to our parents as *The Rents* because they do not care about us.

I quickly text back and start the ignition. The engine roars and comes to life. Glancing back at the window again, I see Mr. Richardson, Kevin, and the two individuals standing in a circle, talking. With a sigh escaping my lips, I press down on the accelerator and race towards The Rent's house.

It's a twenty-minute drive. Pulling up to the house, I storm into my mother's office. She and my father fear Earth witches and want nothing to do with them. They also knew Kevin had been murdering Earth witches to reclaim his magic all along, and they did nothing about it.

My mother jumps in her seat when I enter. "Eli, what are you doing here?"

"What is Kevin planning?" I shout.

Fidgeting with her 911 machine, my mother rolls her eyes and says nothing.

Slamming my clenched fist on her brown wooden desk. "Answer me!"

"I don't know what he is planning," she shrugs.

Closing my eyes, I focus on my breathing. Because she is my mother, I have a slight respect for her. Still, she is evil, and if it comes down to it, the little respect I have for her will be gone. I stand to my full height and back away from her desk, eyeing her with suspicion.

She hits the top of her machine. "Darn thing work!"

Turning my back to her, I clench my jaw. *What am I going to do?*

Suddenly, a 911 call echoes throughout the room.

"911 What's your emergency?"

Rushing to my mother's desk, I lean in to hear better. "Turn it up a bit!" I shout.

My mother gives me a sharp look before adjusting the volume.

"My father! My father is not breathing!"

A chill slithers up my spine—the sound of the voice is Claudette's!

"Okay, I need you to calm down. Please tell me your name."

No! This is what I was afraid of. Glancing at my watch, it's only been about forty-five minutes since I left Mr. Richardson's house. How could this have happened so soon?

Fists clenched, I march out of my mother's office. This cannot be happening. I just saw Mr. Richardson alive and well with Kevin and two others. Claudette's shrieks echo in my ears, and my heart shatters for her. If her father does not recover, she will be devastated. *If he is not breathing, then he must be dead!* I knew Kevin could not be trusted! *I should have stayed there!*

"Where are you going, Eli?" my mother calls out, following me out of her office.

"I am going to Kevin's house!" I shout back.

"For *what*?"

I freeze in place, my eyes narrowing as I take a moment to observe her carefully. "Kevin killed Mr. Richardson!" *Is she delirious?*

"Eli, you're jumping to conclusions. The dispatcher told Claudette to conduct CPR on her father. You don't know if he is dead." She replies, playing stupid.

"Mother! I know Kevin has been killing Earth witches to regain his magic!"

She appears to be stunned. Jeremiah and my father enter the living room.

Jeremiah shakes his head. "I don't think that's a good idea, Eli." He must keep up pretenses by siding with our parents. As far as they know, we do not get along, which is true in some cases. He is the worst roommate.

"I don't care," I spit through gritted teeth, slamming the door behind me.

I pull up to Kevin's house, overwhelmed with a wrath of fury that has been building inside me for weeks.

Balling up my fist, I bang on the door. Kevin opens it, and I punch him square in the nose, using my magic to close the door behind me.

He stumbles back, grabbing his bloody nose. "What is wrong with you?"

Motioning my hand in a circle, I levitate him off the floor. "You know exactly what you did!" I seethe, hurling him against the ceiling and then throwing him into the wall.

"I know you killed him!" I growl, my eyes glowing with anger, as I watch Kevin struggle to stand up.

He charges at me, and we go blow for blow. He uppercuts me in the chin, causing my teeth to collide painfully. I shake it off and counter with a right hook to his jaw and a left jab to his ribs. He staggers back but then regains his footing and retaliates with a swift punch to my stomach. The pain shoots through me, but I refuse to back down. Pushing forward, I tackle him to the floor, pinning him beneath me and throwing a series of punches to his face until he is bleeding profusely.

"I know you killed Claudette's father!"

He spits out blood and smirks, confirming my suspicions with a sinister laugh. "Oh, is he dead?"

This sick demon is proud!

"You're a monster," I growl, tightening my grip on him. "You'll pay for what you've done." I shove him back on the floor and stand up.

"Dude, are you upset because I got the girl and you didn't?" Kevin taunts, trying to get under my skin. He gets up and wipes the blood from his face, a cocky grin on his lips.

Taking a deep breath, I try to control my rage before doing something I'll regret.

He walks towards me, poking me in the chest with his finger. "Is it because Claudette trusts me more than she trusts you? Looks like you never had a chance."

Trying to maintain my composure, I feel my fists tighten.

"Or is it because I got to be inside her?" He scoffs, a smug expression on his face. "Grinding my length into her uncharted territory until she screamed my name, her body writhing beneath me in pleasure. You'll never know that feeling, will you?"

My vision blurs with rage. The thought of him touching her makes my blood run cold, and I resist the urge to lunge at him as he licks his lips, reminiscing about taking her innocence.

"You're disgusting!" I spit out.

Kevin blows on his fingernails and rubs them against his shirt, a sadistic smirk playing on his lips. "Jealousy is an ugly look on you, Eli. But hey, I can't blame you for wanting what I have." His words cut through me like a knife. "The little slut was worth it. Especially because I had her first!"

Clenching my jaw, the urge to make him pay for his words grows stronger with each passing moment.

"Imagine if I had trapped her!" he laughs.

Balling my fist, I bite back on the urge to punch him in the face for his callous words.

Kevin laughs again when he sees my clenched fist. "Don't worry, I will use protection when I have fun with her again," he says with a smirk. "You know I can have her anytime I want. I have her wrapped around my finger."

His arrogance and disrespect for her make the anger inside me boil over, and I can't hold back any longer as I lunge towards him in a fit of rage.

Grabbing him by his shirt. "You're a disgusting excuse for a human being," I seethe. "She deserves better than you."

I was supposed to be her first. Not him! She fell in love with his charm and manipulation.

Despite my outburst, he maintains a smug smirk on his face. "You wish you had her first, but I beat you to it." He laughs in my face, sealing the nail in his own coffin.

His words only fuel my fury. I don't know how Claudette trusted this demon of a man, and she still doesn't see his true colors. I need solid proof.

Letting my temper consume me, I knock him unconscious with a swift punch to the jaw. That was for taking my soulmate from me.

I will prove to Claudette that he is not the man she thinks he is, no matter what it takes!

Chapter 19

The Gabriella Files

Clicking on the folder labeled *Gabriella*, I scroll through the contents. She was born and raised in Mashalville as a Moon witch. On her seventeenth birthday, she decided to keep her magic, but she fell for a guy who chose to be a norm. She thought they were in love until he knocked her up with the demon twins after her seventeenth birthday. He disappeared from town shortly after, leaving Gabriella pregnant and alone. Embarrassed and devastated, she fled Mashalville the day after the twins' first birthday to find him. *Interesting.*

Scrolling further, I continue reading about the twins' father and when Gabriella tracked him down, only to discover that he had a new family. I stop at a picture of the twin's father with his other family, smiling and happy. There are multiple pictures of him with his new wife and children, clearly showing the life he chose over Gabriella and their twins. *Wow! What a prick!* Zooming in on the photo of his daughter, I find it uncanny how much she and I favor one another. *Perhaps this is why the twins hate me so much.* Resting my forehead on my palm, I shake my head. I wonder if the twins know about their half-siblings. *They have to, right?* Because why else would they be so cruel to me? I look just like their half-sister! Still, it doesn't excuse their behavior toward me. It's not my fault their father chose to start a new family.

Exiting the folder, I click on Gabriella's parents' folder. Her mother passed away after she gave birth to her, leaving her father to raise her alone. She had no siblings, and her father died from an aneurysm a few years after she left town. *What a life! I actually feel sorry for her.*

She clearly had no intentions of moving back to Mashalville; there was nothing left for her here. Perhaps she does–*did* love my father.

Exiting out of Gabriella's folder, I go back into my dad's; he has the most subfolders under his name. The one that sparks my interest is labeled *Claudette*. Clicking on it, a letter from him pops up, dating back to the last week he was alive.

Dear Claudette,

If you are reading this, it means I am no longer with you, and I am so sorry for leaving you alone, Cheetah. I love you more than words can express, and I hope you can find happiness without me. Please know that I did the best I could and did what I thought was best for you. I am sorry I fell in love with Gabriella, but she fulfilled something in me that I couldn't explain to you at the time. I was lonely when your mother died, and I felt overwhelmed with depression. Your mother was my one true love, and I wanted nothing more than to be with her again. Still, I knew I couldn't leave you behind.

When you were a little girl, you asked me what happened to your mom. I didn't know how to explain it to you in a way that wouldn't hurt you, so I hid in my office and avoided the conversation. My pain was something I carried alone, but I shouldn't have hidden it from you. I knew you were grieving, too, and we should have been mourning together. It was selfish of me to keep my pain from you. Please forgive me.

When I met Gabriella, she made me feel complete again, and I fell for her. I am sorry she didn't treat you the way your mom would have, and there is nothing I can say that would make any of this better. I was a fool. Although you and Gabriella didn't get along, if there was one thing I knew, she did love me and care for you. Because of that love, she moved back to Mashalville to face the council. They wouldn't have found her as long as she didn't practice magic, and she forbade the twins from using their magic as well. Still, she chose to come back for me. I was the one who wanted to come back to this town so you could learn about your magical heritage and make your decision on your seventeenth birthday. I never imagined it would lead to this. There is so much more I wish I could have told you, guided you, and prepared you for. But I left this flash drive with all the information you need to navigate this world on your own.

You will need our family's Earth book. It is hidden in a locked box under the floorboard underneath your bed in your room. The combination is 3-2-1-7, and the key you will need is in my Earth necklace. Ask Gabriella for it; she knows I left it for you. If, by chance, the box has been removed from the floorboard underneath your bed, you can use my ring to locate it. Please be safe, and remember that you are never truly alone. You can seek help from Jimmy from the council and Adam Goatfair. They will have more information on keeping you safe!

Your mother and I will always be watching over you, no matter where you are.

I love you, Cheetah.

Love, Dad.

My eyes swell with tears as I read my father's final words. I sob, clutching my chest at the weight of his absence. My father was stupid and in love, but he always cared deeply for my safety and loved me unconditionally. *His necklace?* I wipe the tears from my eyes and the snot from my nose. *My father's necklace and ring are missing!* Thinking back to the day my dad died, I remember he wasn't wearing either. *Did someone take them?*

My phone rings, and Kevin's name flashes across my screen. *What does he want?* Nevertheless, I answer anyway.

Me: Hello.

Kevin: Hey, babe.

Me: I'm sorry. Babe?

Kevin: Claudette, I don't want to fight with you anymore. I think we should make up.

Me: Funny. I think we should break up. What do you want, Kevin?

Kevin: We're just going through a rough patch—nothing serious. Or are you already with Eli?

Me: What? I am not with Eli. We are just friends.

Kevin: Sure, sure. I thought you should know that you can't trust your friend.

Me: What is it with you and Eli singing the same tune?

Kevin: Trust me, this is not fun for me either. Eli's parents are plotting to kill you. I thought maybe you should know.

Me: Trust you? Not anymore. Thank you for warning me of my planned demise, though.

Hanging up on him, I sigh, tossing my phone onto the bed. Eli's parents are plotting to kill me? That's a new one. I'll have to confront Eli about this and get to the bottom of it. Storming out of my room, I stomp down the hallway to Eli's room. I barge in without knocking first and find Eli walking out of the bathroom, a towel wrapped around his waist.

We both freeze, our eyes locking in surprise, and his towel drops to the floor, exposing his length to me.

Woah!

Eli pulls his towel back up quickly, his cheeks flushing, and I cover my eyes with my hands.

"Have you heard of knocking, Claudette?"

My face grows hot. *I'm so embarrassed.*

"I am so sorry for barging in like that, Eli. I just wanted to talk to you about something important." I peek through my fingers to check if he is decent before continuing the conversation.

"What is so important that you couldn't knock first?" Eli presses with a hint of teasing in his voice.

"I promise I'll knock next time," I say sheepishly.

Eli cocks an eyebrow, looking at me.

"Kevin called me."

His jaw clenches. "Let me get dressed. I'll meet you in the living room."

With a nod, I quickly sprint out of his room, a small smile playing on my lips as I savor the memory of what I had just witnessed.

I wait for Eli on the sofa and daydream about him throwing me over his shoulder and carrying me back to his r–

"What did Kevin want?" Eli appears, sitting beside me, his expression unreadable.

I bite my bottom lip. He looks so handsome and distracting that I almost forget about Kevin's call.

"Hello, Claudette," he says, snapping his fingers in front of my face.

He can–

"Claudette!" He raises his voice a little louder this time, snapping me out of my inappropriate daydreaming.

I jump, a blush creeping up on my cheeks. "Sorry, Eli, something... distracted me for a moment."

He gives me a strange look before turning his attention back to the conversation at hand. "What did Kevin want?"

He probably thinks I am crazy. *Maybe I am!*

Shaking my head, I try to focus on Eli's question. "He said your parents want to kill me."

Eli's face is grim. "I see. Kevin should tell my parents they will have to go through me first if they want to get to you."

Wow! Eli would go against his parents for me? *Is it hot in here, or is it just me?*

My cheeks flush as I meet his intense gaze. "Thank you, Eli. That means a lot to me."

He stands up, scratching the back of his neck. *What did I say to make him so nervous?*

Clearing his throat. "I have to show you something."

He disappears from the room, leaving me with a million questions swirling in my head. When he returns, he's holding a candle and a royal blue and gold book with a crescent engraving on the cover. He flips through the pages and stops on a page with a crescent and an Earth symbol overlapping one another. He lights the candle and closes his eyes.

His facial expression is stern and focused. "I call upon the Moon and Earth to access their power, combine our magic, and give us what my heart desires." He repeats this incantation two times.

"What are you doing, Eli?"

"Do you trust me?"

I nod without hesitation.

He shoves his hand in his pocket and pulls out a moon bracelet. "May I?" He asks, holding out the bracelet to my left wrist.

I extend my arm, allowing him to clasp it on.

"Let's see if this works," he says with a determined look in his eyes, and he recites the spell two more times.

"Don't resist, Claudette," he urges.

I do not understand what he is trying to do.

He grabs my hands, and electricity flows between us. I feel complete. Eli recites the spell once more, and we spin in a circle, levitating to the ceiling.

Blue, gold, and brown swirls of light circle us. The papers in the living room fly around us like a tornado, and visions—or perhaps memories, *Eli's memories*—flash before my eyes. *I can see everything he has seen!*

Eli was at my house the day my father died, and so was Kevin. Two other people came with Kevin. Eli confronts Kevin at his house. His reaction to Eli's accusation is suspicious. He may not have killed my father, but he knows who did! The boys fight. Kevin taunts Eli; he calls me a *slut!* Eli knocks him out.

How could I be so stupid?

Kevin doesn't love me!

He never loved me.

He used me. And he acted as an accomplice to my father's murder.

He lied to me.

Manipulated me.

I trusted him.

My heart shatters into a million pieces, equivalent to Kevin piercing his hand through my chest and ripping out my heart, squeezing it until it's nothing but a bloody mess.

Letting go of Eli's hands, we drop to the floor abruptly.

"Kevin knows who killed my father?" It comes out as a question, but I already know the answer, and the look on Eli's face confirms it.

Kevin's betrayal cuts deeper than I ever thought possible. He was so good at lying and pretending to care. He strung me along, toying with my feelings, all while plotting behind my back. He is so deceitful. A master manipulator. A wolf in sheep's clothing. I never saw it coming. But Eli did, and he tried to warn me so many times. I should have listened to him. He has been there for me since the beginning, trying to get me to see the truth about Kevin. He even beat Kevin up for me. He was right about him the whole time.

I cup Eli's face in my hands, pulling him close to me. "Thank you for always looking out for me," I whisper before pressing my lips against his in a long, overdue kiss. I try to express my gratitude for his loyalty and protection in a way that words cannot fully convey in this kiss. He responds by wrapping his arms around me tight, pulling me even closer as if to say that he will always be there for me no matter what.

The worst kinds of people are the ones who pretend to care about you but then turn around and stab you in the back. Their loyalty is shallow and self-serving, and they only support you when it's beneficial for them. As soon as you no longer serve their interests, they will abandon you. Kevin is the epitome of betrayal and selfishness—he got what he wanted from me and then discarded me like I was nothing.

Eli and I reluctantly pull away. The pain in his eyes is evident, mirroring the hurt I feel in my own heart.

"Did you see the two people who came with Kevin?"

Replaying Eli's memories in my head, it's hard to distinguish who they were. One of them had curves, implicating she was a woman, while the other had none, suggesting he was a man. *Who are they?*

"Yes, it was a man and a woman." Recalling the truth serum I used on Kevin, I say, "I asked Kevin if he knew who killed my father. He said no. But he hesitated when he responded."

"Yes, Claudette! He hesitated because he was lying. He's been lying to you the entire time. You finally believe me now."

Nodding my head, I finally believe Eli for the first time about Kevin's deceitful nature. Turning away from him, I walk to my room, with Eli following closely behind me. I grab my phone to block and delete Kevin's number; I want nothing to do with him anymore! Falling to the floor—I had been blind for too long—sobbing as I think back to the night I lost my virginity to Kevin.

With Eli, my knight in shining armor, kneeling beside me, his embrace envelops me, making me feel loved and cherished.

"Kevin told me we were fated to be together." I sniffle in between sobs.

Eli wipes my tears away, but despite his best efforts, more tears continue to fall.

"It's going to be okay, Claudette." Eli soothes. "Kevin was wrong about a lot of things. *We're* fated to be together, not you and him. I love you. I have loved you from the first day we touched, and the shockwaves flowed through us. Trust the magic, Claudette. The spell wouldn't have worked if we weren't destined to be together." With tears blurring my vision, I lock eyes with Eli, and his sincere gaze pierces through me. Since the very first day we met, I have felt an undeniable connection with Eli, as if our souls were meant to intertwine.

How could I be so blind not to see the truth in front of me all along?

It was always Eli. *Not* Kevin.

Still, am I ready to admit that out loud to him?

Chapter 20

Back to School

Eli stayed the entire night in my room, comforting me while I sobbed. My father's death broke me, but this was something different, almost sinister.

I trusted Kevin.

I thought he cared for me.

I thought he loved me.

How could I have been so wrong? He tarnished my virtue and broke my heart into tiny pieces. This pain is different. Is this what it feels like to have your heart broken by love? I wouldn't say I like it. I'm only seventeen, yet I thought what Kevin and I had was real and that we would last *forever*. He was my boyfriend, pretending to care for me when, in reality, he didn't. How could anyone be so cruel–so *evil*?

Eli rolls over to face me and flashes me a warm smile. *I wish I had met him first!*

Meeting his gaze, I try to smile back, but the pain in my heart is still fresh. Pools of tears spill down my cheeks again, and Eli gently wipes them away with his thumb.

We have school today, and I am supposed to be getting ready. How do I face Kevin, or anyone else, for that matter? I threatened the entire town, so I'm not the most likable person right now. And Kevin is living his best life as if nothing happened while I am left to pick up the pieces of my shattered heart.

The thought of seeing him again makes me sick to my stomach.

You will get through this! My inner voice assures me.

Sucking in a sharp breath, I wave my hand at the lamp on my nightstand, tossing it to the floor—the shards of glass scatter across the surface.

"Ahh!"

Eli pulls me into his arms, holding me tight. "It's okay to be angry."

I bury my face in his chest, letting out a muffled sob.

How didn't I see this before? The entire time Eli's been in my life, he's been the one holding me together. We had a connection before and after we accepted our magic, and our attraction is undeniable. I should have trusted him sooner, but this was a lesson I needed to learn. I don't know why my life is filled with so much chaos, but there has to be a reason for it all—a silver lining to all this mess, right?

Eli plants a soft kiss on my forehead. "Let's get ready for school. We can face the madness together."

He is right. No matter how much I don't want to go to school today because of the possibility of running into Kevin, I have to rip off the band-aid.

The first two periods go smoothly. I manage to avoid Kevin altogether. Despite not seeing him, my stomach remains twisted in knots as I anticipate the unavoidable confrontation with him. I want to punch him square in the face for what he did. I should tell him I thought about Eli when we were having sex, to see the look on his arrogant face! It probably wouldn't bother him, seeing how he never cared about me in the first place. I roll my eyes at the thought of his indifference. I really need to get rid of this hatred toward him, but he knows who killed my father, and I can't let that go. *I hate him!*

Walking into class, I attempt to turn my frown upside down with a slight smile. Today, we are learning the history of the Sun, Moon, and Earth witches. This should be interesting. In a hurry, Mr. Goatfair strides into the classroom and drops all of his papers on the floor when our gazes meet. He rushes to pick them up. My father mentioned him in his letter. *I should reach out to him soon.*

"Do you need any help with that, Mr. Goatfair?" Isabel offers.

"Yes, thank you, Isabel."

When Mr. Goatfair settles in, he faces us to begin his lesson. "Alright, class, today we will discuss the first two witches." He turns to the board and draws two stick figures to represent the witches.

Leaning toward Isabel, I whisper to her. "Is he seriously drawing stick figures?"

She snorts, trying to stifle a laugh, which causes me to giggle as well.

Mr. Goatfair turns around, shooting us disapproving glances. "Pay attention, you two!"

He faces the board again, continuing his lesson by drawing another stick figure and naming it Mother. Mr. Goatfair walks over to his desk and takes out his pointer.

Clearing his throat. "One thousand years ago, there were two brothers who were gravely ill." He says, pointing to each stick figure on the board. "Their mother cast a dark spell to heal them and granted them gifts. They soon became powerful brothers who couldn't have been more different from one another." He clears his throat once again and looks at each of us. "As they grew older, one turned toward evil, and the other turned toward good. Antus was the evil brother and wanted to become a god to all and rule the world, whereas Jaju just wanted to live in peace. The two disagreed on their purpose. Jaju desired a world for witches to reside in, while Antus aimed to live in the real world and dominate it. After years of resentment, fights, and exposure to humans, Jaju created Jajuville, the Magical Realm, and he gifted his people magic from Fire and Ice. In doing so, he trapped Antus and his followers in a town cloaked by magic and named it Mashalville. Antus became a problem and wanted to perform rituals to sacrifice witches for his personal needs." Mr. Goatfair has the class's undivided attention as he recounts the origin of our magic. He pauses for dramatic effect and then continues. "The witches grew tired of his behavior and stood together, killing him once and for all and banishing him to the Shadow World. Antus was angry and cursed the Sun, Moon, and Earth witches so that every child born from the same coven would be evil and bound to him." He pauses once again and meets my gaze. "When Antus placed his curse on the witches that stood against him, every child born from the same coven was forced to serve him, carrying out his tasks and granting him the ability to reach not only this realm but the Magical Realm."

Listening to Mr. Goatfair's lecture, I find myself leaning into my desk, fully engrossed in his words.

"It is said that Antus created a Shadow King—unbeknownst to Jaju—that is currently wreaking havoc on Jajuville. They will need help preventing an all-out magical war. Only the most powerful witches will prevent this," he says, glancing in my direction.

Why is he looking at me? The bell rings, and shuffling fills the room as everyone gathers their things to leave.

Mr. Goatfair's eyes bore into mine with an intense gaze. "Please read over chapters one through five for tomorrow." He says, still holding my gaze.

I break eye contact first and quickly pack up my things.

"Why was Mr. Goatfair looking at you like that?" Isabel asks as we exit the classroom.

Shrugging my shoulders. "I have no idea."

"That was so weird. It's like he was only talking to you."

Nodding. "I agree, it was weird."

I wonder why he was looking at me when he mentioned Jajuville? My dad left me a lot of helpful information on that flash drive. I'm sure there is something about Jajuville on there. Suddenly, my mind falls on Kevin, and I think about how he was born from the same coven. Eli was right about this, as well. *Kevin probably serves Antus.*

I practically jog down the opposite hallway to my next class in an attempt to avoid running into Kevin. Heading to the back of the classroom, I take my seat.

Mr. Max walks in on high alert. "Hello, class. We are going to discuss magical elements today."

Everyone settles into their seats, and I quickly pull out my notebook and pen to take notes.

"As you know, there are Sun, Moon, and Earth witches," Mr. Max begins. "Sun witches harness power from the sun, Moon from the moon, and Earth witches are the most powerful, as they can draw power from all elements of nature on Earth. Today, we are going to focus on Earth magic." He explains, glaring in my direction.

Swallowing the knot forming in my throat, I let out a loud gulp.

"Claudette, would you like to help me teach this lesson?" he asks, his eyes fixed on me.

Why are all my teachers picking on me today?

Not really! "Sure, Mr. Max," I say instead.

He claps his hands together. "Excellent! Earth is an important magical element. There are a few others, such as fire, ice, and water, but our focus today is on Earth and how it pertains to Earth witches."

He gives me a small smile. "Claudette, as an Earth witch, you can use your gift at any time of the day; you can focus on grass, dirt, and trees and let them consume you to harness your power. But if you don't know what you're doing, the magic can drain you. Let me show you."

The classroom illuminates as he opens and closes his hands, causing his eyes to glow a vibrant yellow. Through the window, the sun's rays pour in, creating a fleeting burst of light in his hand before disappearing in an instant.

My face lights up with excitement, and my heart races. *Wow!*

He gives me a reassuring nod. "Go ahead and try it."

Taking a deep breath, I close my eyes and let my senses take over. The floor beneath my feet vibrates, and a warm sensation overrides my body.

Flashes of Kevin seize my mind, and I lose control, causing the classroom to shake.

Mr. Max grabs my arm, trying to prevent me from causing destruction. "Claudette, you need to channel the good, not the bad."

My heart beats rapidly beneath my chest as though I were running a marathon, resulting in my abrupt collapse onto the floor.

Mr. Max and the rest of the class gather around me, their faces showing signs of distress.

"Claudette, are you okay?" Mr. Max asks.

"Y–yes, I think so. What happened?" I ask, sitting up and scratching the top of my head.

Mr. Max helps me up. "Claudette, may I ask what you were thinking about?"

Sighing heavily. "I really don't want to talk about it, Mr. Max."

He lowers his gaze. "Maybe we can go over accessing your power in a more positive way. Whatever you were thinking about caused your powers to overload."

Nodding in understanding, I smile. "Yes, of course."

"Try again," he suggests.

Inhaling deeply, I concentrate on channeling my magic. As I sway my hand back and forth over my feet, I feel the floor trembling beneath me and the tiles gradually unfolding, revealing a gaping hole that descends into the ground. The dirt emerges from the depths of the hole, swirling in the palm of my hand. A smile forms on Mr. Max's lips as the class collectively gasps.

"See what you can do when you focus on the good?"

Smiling from ear to ear, I hold the dirt in my hand and use my other hand to spin it in a circle–like a mini tornado. The class watches as I push forward, returning the dirt back to the Earth and closing the hole in the middle of the classroom floor. The bell rings, and Mr. Max shouts over his shoulder to read over chapter ten for tomorrow's quiz. Nodding, I grab my bag and pack up my books before hurrying out of the classroom. My next class is my favorite,

Potion Measurements. Today, we are learning how to create a healing potion.

Chapter 21

Rage

Once again, I make my way to class avoiding a certain *someone*. Entering the classroom, I proceed to my desk in the middle of the room, next to Eli. A charming smile crosses his face when our eyes meet.

"Hey," he greets, nudging my hip with his elbow. "How has your day been so far?"

Removing my bag from my shoulder, I hang it on the back of my chair. A sigh escapes my lips when I lower myself in my seat, shooting him a disapproving glare.

Eli chuckles. "What's all that for?"

"I have been trying to avoid you know who, like my life depends on it all day."

He briefly looks away, his jaw clenching and unclenching, before meeting my gaze again. "Claudette, you're eventually going to have to face him, and when you do, I will be there for you."

Rising from my seat, I throw my arms around his neck to hug him tight. "Thank you," I whisper.

"Of course," he murmurs.

I pull away and settle back into my chair when Ms. Caron strides into the classroom.

"Hello, class! Are you all ready for today's lesson?" She asks with a wide grin on her face.

The class nods with enthusiasm.

"Okay, let's get started. Who would like to help me hand out the tools and ingredients for today's lesson?" she asks, glancing around the classroom.

Raising my hand. "I would like to help," I volunteer.

Ms. Caron gives me a wink, and I head to the front of the room.

"We are going to hand out vials for the potions, mini cauldrons, hot plates, a needle, and measuring cups." She meticulously hands me each object, making sure they are transferred to me with the utmost care.

I carefully take each item and distribute it to my classmates.

After depositing the tools required for the potion, she hands me the necessary ingredients: a cup of water, ginger powder, and elderberry juice.

Taking my seat, I place the items in front of me. Ms. Caron, in an effort to capture our attention, clears her throat and proceeds to provide step-by-step instructions.

She walks to the board and writes *Healing Potion*.

"I need everyone's undivided attention because we will be using hot plates today. Please place your cauldrons on the hot plate." She waits until everyone has followed her instructions before continuing. "Next, I want you to open the package that has a needle in it and poke yourself."

Everyone exchanges uneasy glances, and whispers fill the classroom.

She claps her hands together. "Settle down, settle down. The needle is just for pricking your finger to add droplets of your blood to the potion. It's completely safe and necessary for the Healing Potion to work." Ms. Caron waits for the chitter chat to simmer down, and then she continues. "Use the needle to prick your finger and add three drops of blood to the cauldron. When you are finished, please pour one cup of water and one-third cup of ginger powder." She pauses for a moment, eyeing the class warily. "If you were making this potion at home, you would use fresh ginger and grind it into powder. However, we have limited time. Do you guys know what ginger is good for in terms of healing properties?" She asks.

"Ginger has potent anti-inflammatory and antioxidant properties." A student answers from the front of the classroom.

"Correct, and it's also good for relieving nausea, improving the immune system, brain function, cholesterol, and weight loss, amongst other things." She says with a smile. "See how it is bubbling? Now add two-thirds cup of elderberry juice. Elderberry is important for its health-promoting properties. Get to stirring." She instructs, letting out one of her usual loud cackles. Ms. Caron enjoys mixing and stirring together potions. "Let it cool for about three minutes, and then I need a volunteer," she says.

"I'll do it," Destiny says, walking to the front of the class.

"Excellent!" Ms. Caron exclaims. She gestures her hand forward and back, and a dagger appears.

Destiny bravely places her hand in Ms. Caron's hand. Ms. Caron slices it. She then pours the potion on the wound, and within five minutes, the gash disappears.

Gasps echo throughout the room.

Ms. Caron grins from ear to ear, showcasing Destiny's healed hand before us. "Voilà," she beams. "Now you all try it."

Leaning over to Eli, I whisper, "I am not cutting myself to see if this potion works."

Eli lets out a small chuckle, shaking his head. He materializes a dagger and slices his hand.

My eyes are as wide as a saucer. "What are you doing?"

"She told us to try it out for ourselves. I want to see if the potion works." He raises an eyebrow at me to follow suit as he pours his potion into the wound.

I watch in horror as Eli's cut miraculously heals before my eyes.

Ms. Caron walks by each desk, observing everyone's progress and nodding her head in approval. When she reaches my desk, she folds her arms across her chest.

Understanding the hint, I materialize a dagger from thin air and slice my hand. "Ouch!" I wince in pain as blood starts pooling on the desk. *Perhaps I cut myself too deeply.*

Ms. Caron's and Eli's eyes are wide.

"Hurry and pour the potion on your hand," Eli urges me.

"Oh, right!" I reply, pouring it on my cut.

The wound heals, and Ms. Caron regards me with a satisfied grin.

Examining the front and back of my hand in awe, I'm amazed. The cut is gone, with not even a scar left behind. *Magic is amazing!*

The bell rings and we gather our things to head to our next class. Isabel, Destiny, and Lin join Eli and me as we stride down the hallway. My anxiety resurfaces from the anticipation of running into Kevin, and Eli notices the look of distress on my face. He pulls me to the side, and Isabel, Destiny, and Lin exchange concerned glances.

Isabel stands beside me, her long lashes fluttering. "Are you okay?"

My mind spirals. Everything Eli said to me was the truth, and Kevin has been lying to me for months.

How can I trust my own judgment?

"Everything Eli said about Kevin is true," I reply.

Isabel glances between Eli and me. "I'm sorry, Claudette. I wanted to tell you," she says.

A slight sense of guilt reflects in Destiny and Lin's eyes as they both turn their gaze elsewhere.

Leaning against the locker. "I don't understand. If everyone knows Kevin is evil, why is he allowed in school? In this town?"

Eli shakes his head, and Isabel replies. "The Witch Council."

My brows pull together, and I screw up my face. "How can a town full of powerful witches allow a teenager to be in control? It makes no sense to me."

Nothing in this town does!

"We don't have solid proof that Kevin is evil," Eli explains. "He appears to be a normal teenager with no magic. His parents told the council that his powers were taken away from him, so he didn't have to make the choice. It was made for him."

"And because he didn't choose, he is not deemed evil," Destiny adds.

"Mr. Goatfair said in class today that Antus cursed the witches of this town," I retort, confused by the town's decision-making process.

"Yes, that is true, according to the history book. However, Kevin's parents believe they found a loophole by taking his magic away before he could make the decision. They thought this would prevent him from becoming evil." Lin chimes in.

Rolling my eyes so far back in my head. "This town is full of idiots!" I mutter under my breath.

The next bell rings and we continue on our way down the hall. Before I get a chance to walk through the doors, I freeze, and an uneasy feeling settles in the pit of my stomach. *Kevin.* He is standing in front of us with his trusted minions behind him, wearing a smug smirk on his face.

He cocks his head to the side. "Hello, Claudette. You haven't returned any of my calls or texts."

Isabel attempts to grab my hand, but I pull away from her.

"I blocked and deleted your number," I say, meeting his gaze head-on.

He takes a step closer to me, feigning innocence. "I'm heartbroken."

"Quit the act, Kevin. You need to have a heart to be heartbroken," I retort.

Kevin's smirk widens.

My stomach churns in disgust. Who is this person before me?

I do not know him anymore.

I guess I never did.

Eli steps in between us, blocking Kevin from getting any closer. "That's enough, Kevin. Leave her alone," he says.

Kevin chuckles. "Are you her knight in shining armor now, Eli?"

Eli's jaw tightens, his eyes narrowing. "I'm just a friend who knows when to step in."

Rolling my eyes. "That's enough." Pushing past Eli to confront Kevin face-to-face. "Who killed my father?"

He grins, crossing his arms and not bothering to respond.

The look on his face is familiar. It has been there all along. I was just too blinded by his good looks and charm–until now. I see the truth in his cold, calculating eyes. *He is pure evil.*

Blackness clouds my vision as anger takes over. I levitate, opening and closing my fist. Kevin falls to his knees and holds his head in agony. I'm causing the veins in his brain to rupture.

"Tell me who killed my father!"

Eli, Isabel, Destiny, and Lin stand frozen in shock. Tanya, Tristan, and the demon twins rush to Kevin's rescue as I give him an aneurysm. *I see the twins have healed themselves.* They attack me with their magic, but it has no effect on me. Opening and closing my fist, they fall to their knees, grabbing their heads. I give them aneurysms as well.

"Claudette, please stop!" Isabel pleads over their agonizing screams.

"Please, Claudette! This isn't you!" Eli shouts.

Ignoring them both, I will not stop until all of them are dead. My rage is consuming me, and the school is shaking, sending everyone panicking and scrambling for safety.

My friends are desperately calling out to me, begging me to take control of my emotions, but I ignore their feeble pleas. My mind is focused on killing those who have caused me so much pain. My magic is powerful, but it is draining me.

Just hold on a little longer until all of them are dead!

Suddenly, Mr. Goatfair, Mr. Max, and Lin hold out an unfamiliar object before me, and they recite a spell that knocks me to the floor. Kevin and his minions collapse as well, relieved. The moment Eli holds my hand, his magic courses through me, easing my anxiety and restoring a sense of peace.

How did they stop me? What was that object they were holding? *Mr. Goatfair must be an Earth witch!* Why else would my father tell me to reach out to him for help? As our eyes meet, he nods with a knowing look as if he can read my thoughts.

Principal Deanwall charges at me, brows knitted together. “My office. Now!” He roars. “Everyone else, go to your next class immediately!”

He storms off in the direction of his office while Eli helps me up. “I’m coming with you.”

I hold Eli’s arm as we follow Principal Deanwall to his office.

Slamming his door shut behind us, Principal Deanwall whirls around to face me with a look of pure fury. “Miss Richardson, no killing is allowed in this school! Your behavior is unacceptable and will not be tolerated. I am going to have to expel you.”

I blink. Once. Twice. Three times. “You can’t be serious. Kevin knows who murdered my father. He is evil. And I’m getting expelled? What is wrong with this town?” I spit out.

“Violence is never the answer, Miss Richardson. You need to leave the premises immediately.”

“With pleasure,” I retort, grabbing my backpack and storming out of the office.

Eli catches up to me in the hallway, and we walk in silence to my locker. I practice my breathing, counting to ten in my head, and swing my hands in circles, bringing my hands together for a single *clap*. All the lockers burst open simultaneously, and books and papers fly out, scattering across the hallway.

Feeling faint and lightheaded, I slightly lose my balance. Eli catches me, a look of concern etched in his deep brown eyes.

“Are you okay?” he asks, steadying me.

Nodding, I glance around the hallway. It looks like a category-three hurricane named St. Claudette has hit Mashal High.

Chapter 22

Hometown

Blinking twice, I see Eli standing tall with his arms crossed over his chest, looking down at me. His expression is unreadable. I have been cooped up in my room since yesterday's incident.

"Get dressed," he instructs, leaving me alone in the room.

Sitting up and rubbing my eyes, I furrow my brows. Why is he telling me to get dressed? The school expelled me. Where is he taking me? Nonetheless, I quickly shower and change into denim high-waisted skinny jeans and a leopard crop top, finishing my look with red slides. I give myself a quick once-over in the mirror and apply my L'Oréal Infallible matte lipstick before heading out to meet Eli in the kitchen.

Eli looks at me, his lips twisting into a sexy smile, and my stomach flips a little. He hands me an everything bagel with cream cheese. *My favorite.*

"We are going to visit your friends today," he says while I bite into the bagel.

"What do you mean?" I ask in between bites.

Eli wipes the cream cheese off the corner of my mouth with his thumb and licks it off. *That was so sexy.*

"I thought it would be nice for you to spend some time with Nicolette, Spencer, and Mitch, so Lin and I are taking you to your old town."

What?

A huge, goofy grin spreads across my face. "Are you serious?!"

He smiles and nods. "I thought it would be a nice surprise for you."

Excitement bubbles up inside me. "What about Destiny and Isabel?"

Eli chuckles before saying, "Unfortunately, being the principal's daughter has its downsides, and being the girlfriend of the principal's daughter means Isabel has to stay behind for this one."

I am not Principal Deanwall's favorite student at the moment, so it's probably best if they stay put. Eli and Lin are cutting school to take me; Principal Deanwall wouldn't be too pleased if he found out about Destiny and Isabel joining us.

Suddenly, images of yesterday flash through my mind, and I quickly excuse myself to the bathroom before Eli notices my sudden change in mood. Needing a moment to collect myself, I splash some cold water on my face, staring at my reflection in the mirror. I don't recognize the person looking back at me. I never in my life wanted to hurt anyone, let alone *murder* someone. I was so angry yesterday that I was about to do something irreversible. *This is not me.* I threatened people at the council meeting and inflicted physical pain on the twins. What I did is nothing compared to the pain they put me through over the years. Still, it's no excuse to become the same monsters that I despise. I have to figure out how to channel the anger and hurt Kevin has caused me before I lose myself completely.

Here come the waterworks. Tears fall down my cheeks. I am so sick of crying all the time. Is this my life now? Just a constant cycle of pain and tears. How do I move on from what Kevin did to me?

He looked at me like I was the only person in the world. Our dates, our conversations, our memories—it was all a lie. And to top it off, he knows who killed my father, and he's been keeping it from me. *How could he do this to me?*

"Claudette, are you ready to go?" Eli knocks on the other side of the door.

I want to stay in this bathroom and continue wallowing in my pain, but Eli is waiting for me. And I appreciate his effort in taking me to my hometown to see my best friends.

"Yeah, give me a minute," I call out, wiping away my tears with toilet paper. I apply some concealer and more eyeliner, exaggerating my angel wings to conceal any traces of my emotional breakdown.

Opening the door, I force a smile for Eli, which I'm sure he sees right through. However, he doesn't say anything. He offers me his hand and leads me to the car where Lin is waiting for us.

We arrive at Spencer's house and pull into his driveway. I jump out of the car, instantly forgetting about all of my troubles.

Spencer runs toward us, wrapping his arms around me in a tight hug. "Kevin is a jerk, and you deserve so much better," he says, meeting my gaze.

Looking away, I playfully punch him in the arm. "Thanks, Spence. Let's not discuss it; I just want to enjoy spending time with you, Nicolette, and Mitch."

"Of course, honey. Come on inside. Nicolette is waiting with snacks and games, and Mitch will stop by later."

Spencer greets Eli and Lin and leads us into the house. Nicolette meets us at the door with a slight frown on her face, walking toward me for a hug. "Hey, girl," she says, squeezing me. "We planned a game day to cheer you up."

Smiling back at her. "That sounds perfect."

"Gather around," Spencer calls out, ushering us into the den.

It's enormous and cozy, with a cabin feel to it. The wooden floors are coated with a burgundy throw rug, and a fireplace crackles straight ahead.

Eli sits next to me in a two-seater black recliner. Spencer pushes three of the single recliners in a circle around the marble table. Nicolette greets Eli and Lin, discreetly checking Lin out. *Hmm... I bet she thinks I don't notice.*

"What lie did you guys tell your parents to skip school today?" I ask, looking between Spencer and Nicolette. I'll ask her later about what she thinks of Lin.

"I told my mom I wasn't feeling well, so she might call to check on me," Nicolette says. "She's working late tonight, so it won't be a long call. And my dad has back-to-back meetings today."

Nodding, I turn to Spencer. "What about you, Spence? What did you tell your parents?"

Spencer shrugs with an over-the-top eye roll. "My father is away on business, and my mother is way too involved in my cousin's relationship drama to notice if I'm home or not." He shuffles a deck of UNO cards and adds, "Let's play UNO."

"Are we playing by the rules or house rules?" Lin, who has been quiet, pipes up.

Spencer eyes me warily. He likes to play every game by the rules.

"Let's play a round by the rules," I suggest, knowing it will make Spencer happy.

Nicolette's phone rings, and she excuses herself for a moment.

Spencer beams, dealing out the cards.

"After we play UNO, I have another game in mind that I think you'll enjoy." Nicolette winks at me when she returns, and she and Lin exchange flirty glances.

I raise an eyebrow in response.

Spencer deals out seven cards to each of us and places the rest of the deck in the center of the table. I collect my cards and group them by color.

"Who wants to go first?" Lin asks.

"Nicolette goes first. She is to the left of the dealer," Spencer says deadpan.

Eli leans in and whispers to me, "Spencer takes the rules seriously, huh?" He chuckles, and I snort.

Spencer shoots us a glare, and we quiet down.

Nicolette flips a card over from the top of the deck. It's a green four. She goes through her cards with her nose scrunched up in concentration. Sucking her teeth, she takes a card from the deck and places down a yellow four. Lin goes next and lays down a draw-four, grinning at me.

Just my luck. I groan and draw four cards from the deck, cursing under my breath. I thought this was supposed to cheer me up, not make things worse.

"What's the color, Lin?" Eli asks, holding his cards to his chest.

"Blue."

Eli grins and puts down four cards with the same number *two* on them, leaving him with only three cards left in his hand. *Seriously?*

"Excuse me." Spencer rolls his eyes. "This is not how we play UNO."

Eli's grin grows wider, stretching from ear to ear. "Well, it's how we play." He says, pointing from Lin to himself.

Nicolette looks the other way, giggling, and Lin tries his best not to burst into laughter, his cheeks turning red.

Spencer gives me a pointed look and then leans back in his chair, muttering something under his breath as he studies his hand. He puts down a blue skip card, skipping Nicolette. It's Lin's turn again, and he puts down another draw four.

Rolling my eyes. This is ridiculous! I am not having fun. *You're being a sore loser!* Detta scolds.

"The color is red," Lin announces.

Here goes Eli again, grinning. He notices my face and seems hesitant to put down his card.

"Put a card down, dude," Spencer says impatiently.

Eli looks at us and puts down all three of his cards. "UNO out."

"What? How did you–let me see your cards?" Spencer demands as I sigh and hasten to the bathroom.

I know what you're thinking. I'm acting like a sore loser, but my life sucks right now, and I just can't handle losing at UNO on top of everything else. *I have already lost so much!*

We are supposed to be having fun, yet thoughts of Kevin keep creeping into my mind. Pushing the door shut, I sink to the floor with my back pressed against it, massaging the sides of my temple. *Ugh!* My brain feels like it's going to explode! I wish I could forget him. *How could he do this to me?*

"Claudette, open up." Nicolette knocks on the door.

"Just give me a minute." I sniffle, pulling myself off the floor.

Cracking the door open, Nicolette pushes her way in and wraps me in a tight hug. "I know you don't want to talk about it, but I'm worried about you."

I bury my face in her shoulder, tears streaming down my cheeks. "I'm a sore loser. I'm so stupid. I should have seen it coming. I can't believe I fell for his lies. I feel so betrayed and humiliated." Nicolette listens, rubbing my back and letting me cry it out. "And on top of all that, I'm an orphan!"

She forces me to look up at her. "You're not stupid, Claudette. You might be a bit of a sore loser, though," she jokes, nudging me playfully. "But you're strong and resilient. You trusted someone who didn't deserve it; that doesn't make you stupid. It just means you have a big heart. And as for being an orphan, remember that family isn't just blood. You have people who care about you, like me."

"I should have been smarter about who I trusted," I argue, wiping away my tears. "Why didn't I see it sooner?"

"Sometimes it's hard to see the truth when you're looking for the good in people." She gives me a small smile and continues. "Kevin fooled all of us. I thought he was so charming, especially when he reached out to us to meet him. I thought, *wow*, this guy is amazing for Claudette."

Clenching my fist, my breathing becomes heavy, and the bathroom lights flicker.

Nicolette grabs my hand and squeezes it. "Claudette, I need you to calm down. I know it is easier said than done, but I need you to focus on the present moment and take deep breaths."

Closing my eyes, I try to steady my racing heart. Breathing in and out slowly, again and again, I assert my control over my magic. With each breath, I feel the tension in my body slowly dissipating.

Opening my eyes, I notice the lights have stopped flickering. *I did it!* "I think we should start referring to him as *the demon* from now on."

Nicolette laughs. "The demon it is."

There is still so much on my mind. My dad was murdered. I still haven't gotten over my mom's death, and she died years ago. The demon shattered my heart. I'm depressed. I need to find a way to heal. And to make things more complicated, I have feelings for Eli. Unable to contain the weight of my emotions any longer, I sink down the wall and find solace on the floor.

Nicolette joins me, using her index finger to lift my chin to meet her gaze. "What's on your mind?"

"It's nothing," I reply.

Nicolette's eyes search mine. "It's not just your dad's death that's bothering you. Or the demon. I know you, Detta! Talk to me."

Squinting my eyes at her. "You always see right through me."

She elbows me. "Yes! So, spill it!"

Throwing my hands up in surrender. "Fine! It's... Eli. I have feelings for him."

A smirk plays on Nicolette's lips. "I knew it! Aren't you guys fated to be together or something?"

"Yes. And that's the problem. I don't know if my feelings for him are real or just part of some prophecy." I furrow my brow in uncertainty. "Does that make sense?"

She places her hands on my shoulders and looks me straight in the eye. "Listen to me, Claudette. You and Eli had a *real* connection before you knew about magic or any prophecy. Your feelings for him are genuine, and you know it. Don't let that demon spawn fella deter you from trusting your gut. Magic or not, you and Eli have something special that goes beyond fate or prophecy from the very first day you met. This is what you told me. Was that not true?"

Nodding slowly. "Yes, it is true. Still, my heart is too broken right now, and I don't want Eli to feel like a rebound because he is not."

"Girl, he knows he is not a rebound. He sees the real connection between you two because he told you from the get-go that you two were meant to be together," she says, narrowing her eyes. "What else is bothering you?"

"Okay, okay. We are meant to be together; I get it. I know it. It's just..." My voice trails off, and I look down at my hands.

"Claudette!" she snaps. "What is really bothering you? Don't hold back."

"Okay, fine, calm down. Sheesh! What if we start dating and then... and you know... sex comes up?"

Nicolette's brows knit together, forming a deep crease on her forehead. "I am not following."

"I lost my virginity to that demon. I'm damaged goods now," I admit, hugging my knees to my chest and pouting. "I don't want to be a h–"

"Claudette!" she cuts me off. "You can't be serious?" She lets out a soft chuckle.

My cheeks burn with embarrassment. "Yes! I am serious." I reply, rolling my eyes.

Nicolette's laughter fades, and she rolls her shoulders back. "Claudette, I didn't mean to laugh at you. I was laughing at your statement," she continues, her voice softening. "I'm going to tell you what my mother told me when she found out I lost my virginity: you may think you are in love right now, and you might be. Use this experience as a lesson, and when you find your true love, you will know it. You will feel it in your soul. He will love you and appreciate you for who you are, and he will accept you completely, flaws and all. In other words, just because you lost it to you know who, that means nothing. At the time, you were in love with him, and you felt it was right. If you and Eli decide to date and take things to the next level, then so be it. It will be because you are in love, and the timing feels right. This is not a fairy tale, and unfortunately, you didn't lose it to a prince charming and lived happily ever after. It doesn't always happen that way in real life. Still, Eli may not have been your first, but perhaps he will be your last."

My eyes widen. I'm taken aback by her words of wisdom.

She laughs, seeing my reaction. "Why are you looking at me like I have three heads?"

"When did you become so wise? We are the same age."

"Life experiences, my friend." She taps my nose playfully. "I lost my virginity before you did. And my mom had the 'birds and the bees' talk with me at a young age, sugarcoating nothing. She told me she had been with a few guys before she met my dad, but none of them compared to him. Their first time—I didn't ask to know this," she defends, her face contorting into a grimace. "Their first time was even more special because she knew that he was the one she wanted to be with forever." She rolls her eyes at the image of her parents, and I shake my head to dismiss the mental picture. "It was a beautiful story, really. Minus the visuals."

In times like this, I'm reminded of how much I miss my mom. I never got the chance to have these talks with her.

Nicolette shoots me a knowing glance, jolting me back to reality, and we both share a bittersweet smile.

"My point is that you're not damaged goods."

"You said all that to get to this as a point." I tease, nudging her.

Nicolette chuckles. "Everything I said you needed to hear."

"I did not need that image of your parents in my head," I giggle, and we burst into a fit of laughter.

"I've been living with that image since I was twelve years old. It feels good to scar you with it, too."

"Oh wow. Thanks, friend, thanks."

We continue to laugh, and I rest my head on her shoulder. "I love you."

"I love you too," she says, resting her head on mine. "You're stuck with me forever."

A comfortable silence settles between us.

"I have a question." Nicolette breaks the silence.

"Yes, Lin is single." I laugh, knowing exactly where she is going with her question.

"How did you know I was going to ask about Lin?"

"Because I know you, too."

Nicolette chuckles. "Well, you're not wrong."

We eventually stand up from the floor, still laughing and joking with each other.

"Are you going to be okay, Claudette?" She asks.

"I will be."

Nicolette gives me a reassuring smile, and we head back to the boys in the den.

Eli catches my eye from across the room when we walk in.

"Are you okay?" He mouths to me.

I smile and nod.

"Hey, Claudette!" Mitch calls out from the single recliner, waving me over.

"Aww, Mitch! I am so happy to see you!" I beam, making my way over to give him a hug.

"Let's play ten minutes in heaven," Nicolette wriggles her eyebrows.

Everyone exchanges confused glances. Then it clicks. It's supposed to be seven minutes in heaven, not ten. *This girl.*

"I am pretty sure it's seven minutes, not ten," Mitch corrects her.

"Babe, clearly she wants an extra three minutes of lip-locking." Spencer chuckles.

Nicolette winks at Spencer. "Well, who's going to be my lucky partner for those extra three minutes?"

"Lin volunteers as tribute!" I not so subtly point to Lin, who doesn't look disappointed in the slightest.

"I guess I'm the lucky one," he jokes, causing everyone to laugh along with him.

"I will set the timer for ten minutes," I announce. "Go into the other room and make it count!"

Nicolette thanks me with a wink before taking Lin's hand and leading him away.

When the timer goes off, and they don't come out, we exchange knowing glances, laughing.

"I guess they wanted to smooch a little longer, huh?" Spencer jokes, making kissing noises.

The rest of us chuckle, and we all agree that Lin and Nicolette would make a cute couple.

Mitch sits next to me, extending his arm around my shoulders. "How are you doing, Claudette?"

"I'm okay, mostly."

He squeezes my shoulder gently.

Mitch doesn't know about my magic. Spencer, Nicolette, and I agreed to leave him out of it. He knows about my father's death, and I'm sure Spencer told him about Kevin and me breaking up.

We catch up and enjoy each other's company. It feels good to be around my friends.

Nicolette and Lin finally return after twenty-something minutes, both of them looking a bit flustered.

"It's about time!" Spencer rolls his eyes teasingly.

Nicolette gives him a playful shove before tying her braids back in a bun, and Eli fist-pounds Lin. I meet Nicolette's gaze, and we share a knowing smile.

Mitch laughs and scolds Spencer to play nice, and then they share a long kiss while Nicolette and I pretend to gag, causing everyone to burst into laughter. *I needed this!*

"It's Claudette and Eli's turn," Nicolette announces when our amusement dies down.

Eli and I exchange a glance, and I bite my lip.

He extends his arm like the gentleman he is. "Shall we?"

Linking arms with him, we head to the other room.

"Ten minutes," Nicolette calls after us.

The nerve of her to shout ten minutes. Meanwhile, she and Lin were gone for twenty thousand minutes.

Eli closes the door behind us. My heart is pounding so fast, the thudding sound reverberating in my ears. We have kissed before, but this is different. This kiss will mean something more to us. I am single. He is single. We are attracted to one another, not to mention the fated lover's thing.

"We don't have to do this if you don't want to," Eli says, breaking the silence between us.

I want to kiss him. I want Eli to heal my broken heart and make me forget I was ever with that demon. But he would be a rebound. I can't do this! I don't want to do this to him.

I'm ready to bolt out of the room, but before I can make a move, Eli gently takes my hand and looks into my eyes. "Claudette, what are you thinking?"

Taking a deep breath, I feel the weight of my emotions pressing down on me. "I'm just scared, Eli. Scared of hurting you," I admit. "I'm broken. I don't deserve you. You don't deserve to be a rebound! You deserve better."

Eli digests my words before responding, "Claudette, you're not broken. You're scared, and that's okay. We can take things slow until you're ready, no matter how long it takes."

My breath catches in my throat, and a wave of anticipation washes over me, making my stomach churn.

"I wouldn't be a rebound, Claudette. I would finally be yours, as you have been mine since the day electricity flowed throughout our bodies."

His words wrap around me like a warm blanket. He feels like home, like safety.

"I will wait for you until you are ready to be loved by a real man. Because that's what you deserve." He grasps my waist, pulling me closer to him in one quick motion. I gasp at his sudden proximity, feeling his heartbeat against my chest. He kisses me slowly, his lips soft and gentle against mine, before picking up the pace and knocking the air out of my lungs. This kiss is different from the others we've shared. He has been holding back. As electric shocks ricochet between our bodies, blue, brown, and gold lights circle around us. My back presses against the door as our kiss deepens, and I feel his length pressing against me. I can tell he is trying hard to control himself, which causes butterflies to flutter in my stomach.

When our lips part, he brushes his thumb over my cheek. “Baby, you’re worth waiting for, and I will mend your heart with every beat of mine until it is no longer broken.”

Chapter 23

The Dark Plan

K*evin's point of view:*

It has been two weeks since that little slut tried to murder me. *Unbelievable!* I wasted all those weeks pretending to be interested in her just so she could try to kill me. *Once I regain my magic, I will make sure she never sees the light of day again!* I am glad her father is dead because he won't be able to protect her from what's coming next. Too bad I wasn't the one to end his life. However, I believe in the saying that revenge is best served cold, and I am determined to make her pay for what she did to me.

I anticipated that Claudette would use the truth potion on me, so I kept my involvement in her father's murder to a minimum. Still, the satisfaction of watching the fear in his eyes as he grasped his fate was sealed was sweeter than anything I could have imagined. A slight smirk tugs at the corners of my lips as I remember the look in his eyes. Rubbing my hands together, I realize that my plan is succeeding. Claudette's reunion with her father in the afterlife is imminent.

Glancing at my watch, I notice the time. Malcolm should be on his way over with the Earth necklace and ring that Claudette's father was wearing on the day of his death. He has been holding onto it for safekeeping until this very moment. Tonight, when the Sun, Moon, and Earth align, I will call upon Antus, the leader of the Shadow World. I have devoted myself to him in exchange for my magic, and tonight is the night it will rightfully return to me.

In my dreams, Antus revealed a startling revelation about the town. There is a covert presence of Earth witches posing as Sun or Moon witches. The necklace will reveal the truth, and the ring will guide me to the Earth's spell book, a tome known for its formidable magic.

All of my pursuits have been dedicated to Antus's name to restore my magic. In an attempt to prevent my malevolence, my parents—both Sun witches—believed that removing my magic would be effective in saving me from the darkness. They couldn't have been more wrong. They thought removing my magic would stop the dreams from Antus, but it didn't. I enjoy killing people—especially those who aren't supposed to occupy this realm. There is nothing wrong with me, and if my parents had never revoked my magic, I wouldn't have suffered the torment of being powerless. For far too long, I have concealed my true self, feigning to care and be kind like the other witches in this town. Pretending to be someone I am not has been draining me. Finally, I will regain my magic and embrace the essence of who I truly am! *My parents should be proud!*

All children born into the same coven are bound to Antus, and it is time for us to grow in numbers. We will force Sun and Moon witches to breed with their own kind to create an army of children born to serve Antus as king. We will completely obliterate the remaining Earth witches and anyone who opposes us, once and for all.

Antus has visited me in my dreams for years with instructions to reclaim my power. Every dream is akin to a blazing furnace, consuming me from the inside out. Still, the pain of the dreams is nothing compared to the power I will wield once I complete his bidding. Antus instructed me to slaughter seventeen Earth witches in his honor, and I have carried out his orders without hesitation. Earth witches are targeted because their magic surpasses all the other witches, making them formidable opponents. My mother has assisted me in killing sixteen of them. Although Chance never accepted his magic, he was born an Earth witch, and that served as a sacrifice in Antus's name. His death was also necessary to obtain his Earth necklace and ring, and the only way to acquire them was through his demise. Now, I have one more witch to kill before I can restore my magic and defeat Claudette with Antus by my side!

Three weeks prior to Claudette and her family's arrival in Mashalville, Tanya and I concocted a scheme for me to cozy up to Claudette to gain her trust. I initially hoped for a platonic friendship with her. However, her subtle flirtations made it clear that she would be more receptive to a romantic relationship. In one of my dreams, Antus disclosed that I wouldn't be able to kill Claudette without my magic. I needed to use her attraction to me to my advantage and keep her away from her fated lover because once they admit their love to one another and perform a spell, they would be a powerful force to be reckoned with. This required me to walk a fine line between gaining her trust and keeping her at arm's length.

Pretending to reciprocate her feelings was insufferable. It felt like I was walking through a maze of thorny roses, the vibrant red petals masking the prickly reality of our lives. The sound of her voice was like nails on a chalkboard grating against my eardrums. The scent of her perfume was suffocating with its sickly sweetness that clung to my skin long after she had left the room. Each interaction with her brought a sense of dread and discomfort. Tanya had to coach me the entire time I was with her. Sex was the worst part. I found solace by visualizing Tanya in Claudette's place; she was the only one who could genuinely arouse me. Every time we had sex, my mind would drift to thoughts of Tanya, her touch, her scent, and her voice. It allowed me to perform with Claudette, albeit reluctantly. Tanya is my true mate. She would send me naughty texts right before I saw Claudette, which helped me get through those revolting moments. *Thank you, Antus!* I am finally free from the burden of Claudette Richardson's presence.

Knock, knock.

I open the door, expecting to see Malcolm standing there, but instead, I am met with Tanya's radiant beauty.

My lips curl into a delightful smirk at the sight of her. She is wearing a short skirt and a low-cut top that highlights her ample breasts perfectly.

"Where is Tristan?"

"He will be here soon." Tanya steps inside, closing the door behind her. "We have about thirty minutes." She says suggestively, stripping down to her lacy lingerie.

Licking my lips, I observe her body intently. She is a sensual sight to behold, and being inside her is a welcome distraction. Tristan does not know about Tanya and me, and I like to keep it that way. So, we have to be quick.

"Come here," I growl, gripping her by the neck and closing the distance between us with a hungry kiss.

Her scent is intoxicating, and I lose myself at the moment as we quickly make our way to the sofa. Clothes are discarded in a frenzy, and she straddles my lap, her body moving in sync with mine.

Twenty minutes later, our pleasurable escapade concludes, and we quickly dress before Tristan arrives.

I grab my phone to call Malcolm and make sure he's still on schedule. He is currently with Libby, but he assures me he will be here in ten minutes. Libby has been keeping up pretenses with Claudette; she does not know that Libby was the one who killed her father.

"Malcolm will be here soon," I say to Tanya as we finish getting dressed.

Tanya nods, adjusting her hair. "Where are we with the plan?"

Gripping her neck once more, I press my lips against hers, bruising her skin. "Everything is going according to plan," I whisper, a sinister smile playing on my lips. "I just need to locate the imposters in this town before finally regaining my power."

"Excellent!" she replies, a wide grin spreading across her face.

Casting a wink at her, I turn and head to my room to fetch the Shadow World book from my drawer. The book is black, with Antus's name engraved on the front and coated with his dry blood. I grab my dagger and walk over to the snake cage in the corner of my room. It hisses, but I quickly silence it with a swift strike to its head with the dagger and discard its body in a bag.

I meet Tanya in the living room, and she welcomes Tristan at the door with a kiss. Tristan acknowledges me with a nod before following Tanya inside.

When Malcolm arrives, it's showtime. Tanya hands me a dark brown bowl with the snake head, three ounces of burdock root, and one pound of dead grass. I throw the Earth necklace into the bowl and light the contents with a match. Flipping through the ancient book of Antus, my eyes quickly scan the pages in search of the precise spell that I must recite. The spell is in the language of Antuson.

"Ah nu ja ka. Si ra ka. Ah, nu fig tu. Sap kai ru." I chant four times.

The lights flicker erratically, and a cloud of black smoke billows out of the bowl. Antus has granted me his blessing.

The black smoke swirls around my phone, and its purpose is to find Earth witches hiding in plain sight. I open the GPS app on my phone and watch as the map pinpoints five separate locations of the hidden witches.

"This looks like Jimmy's house," Tanya says, pointing to one of the locations.

"Some are our teachers' homes," Tristan adds, looking at the other pins on the map.

Mr. Goatfair and Mr. Max are Earth witches. Lin, *Eli's best friend,* is also on the list. *Two Earth warlocks living under the same roof!* The fourth location is Jimmy's house, and the fifth location is *Claudette*.

These parasites have been living right under our noses this whole time, completely unnoticed. I will derive immense pleasure from ending all of their pathetic lives. However, right now, I only need one of them to sacrifice to tap into my power.

"Who will it be?" Tanya muses.

Jessie Max and Adam Goatfair have been practicing magic for years. Successfully concealing their status as Earth warlocks for such a prolonged duration is beyond my comprehension.

"Either Lin or Jimmy," I reply, my mind racing with delight.

"You have to make the final call, Kevin," Tanya says, her voice filled with uncertainty.

They look at me expectantly, awaiting my decision.

As much as I want to execute Lin to see the look on Eli's face, it makes more sense to kill Jimmy. He wouldn't see it coming.

"Jimmy," I decide.

The group nods in agreement.

"I will call him to meet us here," Tanya says, walking away to dial his number.

"My work here is done," Malcolm states, packing up his things. "I will take the ring back to Libby's and update her on what's happening."

"Good idea," I nod. "We don't want the ring and necklace to sit in the same place for too long."

Malcolm looks at me with a knowing expression and leaves my apartment.

Tanya returns, saying that Jimmy will be arriving in twenty minutes.

"What did you tell him?"

Tanya shrugs. "I just told him we were having game night."

Twenty minutes later...

"Jimmy is here!" Tanya shouts from the living room.

Rummaging through my dresser, I search for the Ne-aik-eart dagger Tanya procured for me. Changing into a long-sleeved black shirt, I slip the dagger up my sleeve. Before leaving my room, I gather a rat's tail and spider legs from my collection of ingredients for the spell.

"Hey Jimmy, ready for game night?" I ask casually, walking into the living room.

"Uh, yeah." He scratches the back of his neck, his eyes flitting between the three of us. "I am surprised you invited me."

I give him a reassuring smile, reaching for an apple cider. The sound of the can opening fills the air. I offer him a drink in an effort to put him at ease. "Of course, we're all friends here."

Tristan stifles a chuckle, and Tanya nudges him with her elbow.

Jimmy's shoulders relax, and a smile forms on his face as he accepts the drink. "Thanks," he says, taking a sip.

After a few minutes of small talk, his defenses begin to lower, permitting me to make the swift and fatal move of slitting his neck with the dagger.

Jimmy's body slumps to the ground, and his eyes open in shock as his magic drains away. Tanya throws me a kitchen knife, and I relentlessly stab the blade into his chest, snuffing out his life while Tristan and Tanya rejoice in the success of our plan.

With a calm demeanor, I meticulously clean the blade and then turn towards them, a sinister smile forming on my face as I utter, "It's finally come to fruition. I will have my magic back!"

Tristan and Tanya exchange a knowing look, their excitement palpable.

Adding the rat tail and spider legs to the bowl with the other ingredients, I thumb through the pages to find the spell that will restore my magic. The final component required is the vital life force coursing through Jimmy's veins.

With a wave of his hand, Tristan harnesses his magic to draw Jimmy's blood into the bowl.

"Ready?" Tanya asks gleefully.

Nodding, I begin to chant the incantation two times. "In this witch's hour, I call upon my master's power. Give me back what my heart desires. Give me back my divine power."

As the incantation ends, an eerie ambiance fills the room, causing the air to grow cold. A surge of energy courses through me and sets my skin ablaze, emanating a searing heat from deep within. I bite back on my screams. A thick, black liquid swivels around my forearms, trickling down my fingertips. The lights flicker, and electric crackling fills the room. It's as if gravity has disappeared, and I feel weightless. Hovering in mid-air, I feel a surge of electricity as bolts of lightning dance across my skin. The pain is excruciating, but I push through, each breath feeling like fire in my lungs. My magic is finding its way back to me.

After what feels like an eternity, my body descends slowly back to the floor, the black liquid dissipating into my skin. I stand tall, feeling my awakened power coursing through my veins, marking the completion of the spell.

My magic has returned.

Chapter 24

Family Reunion

As the morning sun rises, its radiant rays pass through the fabric of my brown curtains, casting a spellbinding glow that fills the entire room. Eli's words live rent-free in my mind: *"Baby, you're worth waiting for, and I will mend your heart with every beat of mine until it is no longer broken."* The mere thought of it makes my heart race with excitement. Rolling over on my back, I stare at the ceiling. I want to be with Eli. However, the events involving that demon have left me feeling torn and uncertain. Can I trust Eli? Should I even be thinking about another relationship? Or should I focus on who killed my father? *Who murdered your father?* My inner voice shouts. When considering the available alternatives, it becomes evident that the last option is the most logical and rational choice.

Rolling my eyes at Detta's nagging voice in my head, I know she is right. Finding my father's killer is my top priority before anything else. That doesn't stop my mind from wandering back to Eli and the feelings he stirs within me. Will he break my heart like Kevin did?

Finding out about Kevin's betrayal broke me. I can't let myself be hurt like that again. My heart is still healing from the devastating loss of my mother and the tragic murder of my father. Their deaths shattered me into countless pieces, each shard serving as a painful reminder of their absence. And Kevin only added to that pain. On top of the relentless bullying and torment I endured from the demon twins and at school, I need to protect myself from any more heartbreak. The emotional scars are still fresh and raw. *Why was I put on this Earth to suffer so much pain and heartache? What is my purpose? Why am I here? I mean, seriously, why do I even exist?*

Tears start to well up in my eyes and then cascade down my cheeks. "God, if you're listening, please tell me your plan for me. Show me a sign—anything to let me know that there's a reason for all this suffering."

No response.

"Jaju or... Antus, why gift me with magic?"

No response.

Each question I hurl into the air is met with silence, leaving the empty sound of my own voice. Being alone in this world with no clear purpose or direction terrifies me to the core, and thoughts of ending my own life creep in. The future appears bleak and offers little to no hope for a brighter tomorrow. The little voice in my head calls me a hypocrite. Remembering my conversation with Isabel, I told her, *"I wanted to end my life. I wanted the pain I felt to be over. But trust me when I say someone needs you."*

Who needs me now?

No one.

More tears stream down my face.

I have no family left in my life.

A gentle knock on my door interrupts the chaos swirling inside me.

"Claudette, are you awake?" Eli calls out.

To be completely honest, I would rather not be awake right now. My pain is something I desperately long to be rid of.

When I don't respond, he walks right in. I quickly hide under the covers to hide my half-naked body. *What happened to not barging in?*

"You are awake. Why didn't you answer me?"

I let out an exaggerated sigh.

"Claudette, come out from under the covers," Eli pleads, sitting down on the edge of the bed.

I peek out from under the covers, my eyes red and swollen. I am not in the mood to face anyone.

"I just need some time alone right now," I murmur, avoiding his gaze. "I am completely broken, and I don't want to talk about it." Wiping the tears from my eyes, I turn away from him and curl up into a ball.

"I understand, Claudette," he says softly. "I'll be here when you're ready to talk, but just know that I *need* you. Please don't do anything that would cause you to leave me."

My breath catches in my throat, and I hold myself tighter. *How did he know what I was thinking?* He sees inside my soul.

When I don't respond, Eli gets up to leave, closing the door behind him. I stay curled up on the bed, closing my eyes to block out the world and drift off to dreamland.

A few hours later, I still don't feel any better. I do as Ms. Hudson suggested, grabbing my diary from my nightstand to write it all down.

Dear Diary,

Me again. To be honest, my current mental state is not very good. With each passing moment, I feel myself descending further into the dark, suffocating depths of the void. I thought I was past this. While I had convinced myself that I had successfully moved past this feeling of not wanting to be alive, the overwhelming grief and longing for my father have brought it back to the forefront of my mind. Why did he have to be murdered? I still don't understand God's plan for me. What is my purpose? I feel alone and broken. I loved Kevin. I still love him... How could I still love someone who used me? I hate myself for allowing him to deceive me. When I first met Eli, I knew we had an undeniable connection, but I was a fool. Instead of listening to Eli, I stayed with that demon. Eli is too good for me. Being happy is not something I deserve, and neither is being alive.

Closing my diary, I toss it to the side, closing my eyes once again.

Five days later...

Eli barges into my room and opens up the curtains, letting the sunlight flood in. I squint my eyes at the brightness, pulling the covers over my head to shield myself from the light.

"I can't stand to see you like this, Claudette! I am not letting you wallow in self-pity anymore," he says. "I called Ms. Hudson, and you have an emergency session with her today. Take a shower, get dressed, and eat. Now!"

I groan in protest. Who does Eli think he is, ordering me around like this? Still, deep down, I know he's right.

"Claudette!" he calls out, his voice stern.

Annoyance bubbles up inside me, and I roll my eyes, hauling myself out of bed.

Eli stands in the doorway, arms crossed, with a pointed look on his face. He knows me too well.

Dragging my feet and grumbling under my breath, I reluctantly head towards the bathroom to shower and get dressed.

I go through my morning routine, meeting Eli in the kitchen, where he has breakfast waiting for me.

A heavy silence hangs between us, a clear indication of his disappointment and anger. Sighing loudly, I lean on the kitchen counter. He prepared a simple breakfast of toast and eggs.

Eli snatches the butter off the counter and shoves it into the fridge, his jaw clenched tight.

I take a bite of toast, and his eyes bore into me.

He finally breaks the silence, his voice cold and clipped. "You are having a session with Gabriella and the twins today."

Spitting out a piece of toast. "I'm sorry. Repeat that back to me. I must have misheard you." I twist my index finger in my ear to clear out some wax because I want to make sure I heard him correctly.

Eli's eyes narrow. "You heard me right," he says deadpan.

Woah! What is with him today? He is usually so sweet to me, not this cold.

"What is your problem, Eli?"

His jaw clenches as he shouts, "*You* are my problem, Claudette!"

A knot tightens in my stomach, and I lower my gaze. I feel awful knowing that I'm the cause.

"Trust me, I get it. You experienced a lot of traumas. You lost both of your parents, and Kevin broke your heart. I know you're hurting, but life goes on, Claudette!" I flinch at his words, and he lifts my chin up gently, his eyes softening. "I love you, and I'm here for you. However, you have to let me in. Nicolette, Spencer, Mitch, Lin, Destiny, and Isabel all love you too. Don't shut us out. We all dealt with our own traumas, but we keep pushing forward. That's what you need to do. Push through the pain, Claudette. I know it doesn't seem like it now, but you are strong enough to overcome this." He holds my hand tight, his touch grounding me in reality. "My parents are evil people. They have never shown me any love." His voice trembles with pain as he continues, a rawness that cuts through the air. "My father has always been absent and never stepped up to protect my brother and me from our mother. My mother ran the show and called all the shots. She was emotionally abusive and manipulative, constantly tearing us down with her words. She belittled me, told me I was useless, and wished she never had me. Do you know what that does to a four-year-old? I wanted to be loved by my mom. And I wasn't.

I was four, wishing I had never been born. I remember feeling so small and helpless, and there were plenty of times I contemplated taking my life. The difference is my parents wouldn't have cared. Do you think your mother and father would agree with you taking your own life?"

I shake my head, tears well up in my eyes. *How does he know I want to die?*

"Claudette, you were put on this Earth for a reason, and it's time you start believing in yourself. God makes no mistakes!"

As I wipe away my tears, I lift my gaze towards him, speechless and unsure of what to say.

"I'm sorry, Eli." I choke out.

I need to get through this. *I will!*

He sighs. "Are you ready to go?"

Not really.

"Why am I having a session with Gabriella and the twins?"

"You were locked in your room for a week, not responding to calls or texts. Gabriella reached out to me. She seemed worried about you, so she suggested a session with her and the twins to make things right," Eli explains.

My eyes widen in surprise, and I nervously scratch the back of my neck. "I guess I'm ready."

This is my first therapy session in over a week. When I get out of Eli's car, I see Ms. Hudson with Mr. Handsome—the same man she was with on the day my father was murdered. Things seem to be getting serious between them. *Good for Ms. Hudson.*

"I'll see you later, Libby," he says to her, nodding in my direction as he walks past me.

A rosy hue spreads across Ms. Hudson's cheeks. *Libby?*

"I'll be here when your session is done," Eli calls out, and I give him a small smile.

"Hi, Claudette. How are you feeling today?" Ms. Hudson asks with a warm smile, inviting me inside.

"Okay, I suppose."

She leads me to her office, where I settle into the familiar chair. "We will give Gabriella, Marissa, and Crissy a few more minutes to arrive before we begin."

I shift uncomfortably in my seat. One therapy session won't undo the years of emotional and physical abuse they have caused.

Ms. Hudson notes my reaction in her notebook before looking up at me with a sympathetic expression. "Gabriella suggested we all meet as a family. This is a good place to start."

Scoffing internally, I resist the urge to roll my eyes. "Ms. Hudson, I don't mean to be disrespectful, but those people are not my family. My *real* family is dead."

She winces at the last part of my sentence, scribbling in her notepad. *I wonder what she writes in there.*

Gabriella, Marissa, and Crissy stroll into the room right when Ms. Hudson finishes jotting down her notes. *Oh great!*

"Excellent!" Ms. Hudson exclaims, clapping her hands together. "Now that everyone is here, we can begin. Please take a seat."

Gabriella sits down, and the demon twins reluctantly follow suit. Snickering to myself, I wonder how long this family session will last before the chaos begins.

"Why do we need to be here?" Marissa grits out, clearly not thrilled about being here either.

Gabriella tucks Marissa's hair behind her ear. "Because, sweetheart, we are a family."

Sucking my teeth. "We are not a family!" I sneer, crossing my arms defiantly.

"I agree," Crissy adds through gritted teeth. "Blacky is not our family!"

"Oh, wow!" My voice drips with sarcasm. "You can speak for yourself now, huh?"

Crissy shoots me a glare. "I hate you!"

"The feeling is mutual!" I retort, glaring back at her.

Crissy whispers something incoherent under her breath, which causes me to float into the air.

"Put me down!" I yell, "Right now, Crissy!"

Crissy smirks, and with a sudden jolt, I plummet to the floor, my knee colliding with it. The impact sends a sharp pain shooting up my leg.

"Now we're even," her smirk widens.

Oh, so we're using magic now?

I struggle to stand up, ignoring the pain in my knee. "Fine, let's play dirty." I summon my own spell to retaliate against Crissy, preparing to shatter every bone in her body when Gabriella suddenly intervenes.

"Enough!" she asserts, her voice cutting through the room. "We are a family."

My blood boils. She needs to stop saying that. We are *not* a family. When has she ever treated me like her own? How many times has she covered for her daughters when they bullied me? I clench my fists, my anger pulsing through me. *I've had enough!*

"We are *not* a family!" I growl, glaring at Gabriella. "You have never treated me as such, and now you want to act like you care? It's too late for that!" I limp out of the office as quickly as possible, leaving Gabriella stunned in my wake.

Chapter 25

Attack

Eli is waiting for me outside when I storm out of the office, and he knows not to say anything as I fume in silence. He starts the engine, and we head back to the apartment. Once we're home, I rush to the bathroom and slam the door shut, needing to be alone to cool off. Running the water as hot as I can stand, I try to declutter my thoughts under the soothing cascade of steam. Water brings me a sense of solace.

All these years, Gabriella has been an awful stepmother to me. She may have loved my dad, but she never showed me an ounce of kindness. She knew how her daughters treated me, yet she did nothing to stop it. There was always some lame excuse for their behavior. Now, she wants to play nice and pretend like everything is okay by saying *"We are a family."* Such nonsense. I am over her, and I am over the whole situation. My father is dead, and he was the last tie to those people. They will never be my family.

Stepping out of the shower, I wrap myself in a towel heading to my room to get dressed. I pass the living room, where Eli, Isabel, Lin, and Destiny are standing with worried expressions on their faces. *What's going on?* Hurrying to my room, I throw on a red T-shirt and gray sweatpants before returning to the living room to see what's happening.

Lin is pacing the room with his hands clasped behind his back when I walk in, and the others are waiting anxiously for him to speak.

"Lin, what's going on?" I ask.

He stops pacing and turns to face us, his expression grave. Sighing heavily, he says, "I have to tell you guys something important."

What is he about to say? Everyone's eyes are fixed on him, waiting for him to continue. If he says he had something to do with my father's death, I will lose it!

"I am an Earth witch." He pauses, letting the words sink in.

Destiny, Isabel, and I exchange confused glances while Eli remains neutral. *Does he already know?*

"What do you mean?" Destiny asks, breaking the silence.

Lin takes a deep breath before explaining the truth about his powers and how he has been hiding them from us all this time. "Kevin and his minions killed Jimmy. I received confirmation from Adam." Lin reveals.

The girls gasp while Eli clenches his jaw.

"You mean Adam, as in our teacher? Mr. Goatfair?" I furrow my brows.

Lin nods. "The battle has begun. Kevin needed to kill one more Earth witch to regain his powers. Jimmy was an Earth witch as well, hiding in plain sight. Kevin completed his final sacrifice, and now his powers are fully restored. He will be coming for all of us." Lin faces me with a rigid gaze. "Especially you, Claudette, and if he kills you, he will be invincible."

A cold shiver runs down my spine, and I have to sit down to steady myself. I bury my forehead in my hands, trying to process the gravity of Lin's words. *Kevin has his magic back.* Eli sits beside me, gently positioning my head to rest on his chest. I hear the rhythmic thumping of his heartbeat against my ear.

"Our History of Magic teacher, Mr. Goatfair, is actually an Earth witch–*warlock*?" Destiny asks, her eyes widened in realization. "How many Earth witches are there in town?"

"Yes," Lin confirms. "And there's only four of us left. Myself, Adam, Mr. Max, and Claudette." Destiny's and Isabel's eyes widen even further.

"I am sorry for deceiving you all for so long, but it was necessary for my protection," Lin apologizes. "Earth witches and warlocks are targets. My father was killed because he was one, and my mother died while trying to protect him. Mr. Goatfair took me in after their deaths. He knew of my lineage, and I don't know where I would be if he hadn't adopted me." Lin pauses, a somber expression crossing his face. "Adam sought help from Ms. Caron to create a potion to mask my true identity from the Witch Council under the assumption I took after my mother's coven."

"Ms. Caron knows you are an Earth witch?" Isabel asks in disbelief.

"Yes," Lin confirms matter-of-factly.

Eli clears his throat, and all eyes turn to him. "My parents told Jeremiah that Kevin's parents took his magic away before he turned seventeen in hopes that Antus would stop visiting him. His parents were removed from the council shortly after. Despite my parents being evil, they wanted no dealings with the likes of Antus. Jeremiah recently alerted me that Kevin's mother assisted in killing Earth witches against her will."

Lin's eyebrows snap together, creating a crease between them, and his eyes grow wide. "You mean to tell me Kevin's mother had something to do with the death of my parents?"

"And mine?" Isabel asks.

"My mother?" Destiny adds.

Eli nods. "She could have, but I'm not sure. We will get to the bottom of this."

"Don't you and Jeremiah hate each other?" Isabel asks, narrowing her eyes at Eli.

Eli shakes his head. "It's an act to throw off suspicion from our parents."

"What about the prophecy?" I say, and my friends turn to me. "Kevin said we are fated to be together."

Destiny scoffs, Isabel rolls her eyes, Lin raises an eyebrow, and Eli sighs.

"The prophecy states that there is one Earth witch fated to be with a Moon witch, born in the same month, and she would be the most powerful Earth witch the world has known. Together, the couple would be unmatched," Eli explains, fixing his gaze on me.

The room falls silent, and everyone looks between Eli and me. Butterflies flutter in my stomach, and I try to push them away by directing my attention to Lin. "How were you, Mr. Goatfair, and Mr. Max able to stop me that day at school?"

Lin's lips curve into a knowing smirk. "Ah, that was all thanks to the talisman, Ny-rob-son."

"A what?"

"There is no question that you are the most powerful witch to walk the Earth. We used the talisman to combine our magic to stop you from murdering Kevin and his clan. We were only able to use it because you haven't reached your full potential yet. We couldn't let you kill them, even if they deserved it. It would have taken you out as well," he elaborates.

Rolling my eyes, I scoff at his explanation. "Thank you for the mini history lesson." I get up and walk to my room, feeling the weight of his words sink in.

Pacing my room back and forth, annoyance settles in my chest. *Why does the fate of the world fall on me?* I am supposedly the most powerful being to walk this Earth, except I feel far from it. With Kevin now in possession of his magic, I feel powerless against him. I nearly lost myself when I tried to kill him and his minions, and he had no magic then. *"It would have taken you out."* Lin's words echo in my mind. What did he mean by that? *The magic was draining you.* My inner voice whispers.

There's a knock on my door. "Babe, can I come in?" Eli's voice breaks through my thoughts.

When I don't reply, he just waltzes right in. *It seems like neither of us has an issue with intruding on each other.*

"I can't do this right now, Eli," I tell him, my voice shaky. "I'm sorry I gave Lin an attitude. I am not upset with him. I am just overwhelmed by everything that's happening."

"I understand, Claudette. Still, we need to devise a plan. Kevin has his magic, and there is no telling when he will come after you." He tries to reason with me, but I can't focus on planning right now.

I let out a soft sigh, my eyes reflecting a mix of emotions. I know he's right—it is all just too much for one person.

"Eli, I still love him," I confess, my voice barely above a whisper and my eyes lowering to avoid his gaze. I am embarrassed to face his reaction. However, it's unrealistic to expect that I can simply erase my feelings within a matter of weeks. "I am heartbroken, depressed, and grieving all at once. How can I go up against him? I barely made it out the last time. My magic was draining me."

The mattress dips as he sits down beside me, running his fingers through his hair with a soft rustling sound. "Give me your hands."

Furrowing my brows, I meet his gaze.

"Do you trust me?"

Nodding slowly, I place my hands in his, unsure of where he's going with this.

He holds them tight, closing his eyes to recite a spell. "I call upon the Moon and Earth to combine our powers. Give us access and sight, and make us one with the Moon, Earth, and night."

The spell takes effect. Blue, brown, and gold lights swirl around us, filling the air with a mystical glow and merging our magic into an enchanting force. His magic courses through me, emanating from my chest and filling me with powerful energy. The sensation is a paradoxical combination of pleasure and discomfort, leaving a prickling sensation that's challenging to put into words. It taps into my inner strength, and a sudden surge electrifies my body, sending a vibrant jolt racing through my veins. I can almost see the crackling energy as it flows, like an intense lightning storm swaying beneath my skin. The tingling sensation intensifies, radiating from my core and spreading outward, reaching its peak at my fingertips. It's as if tiny sparks of power are eager to burst forth, illuminating the surrounding air.

The energy flows into Eli, and an exhilarating transformation unfolds before my eyes. His once ordinary eyes undergo a profound change, shifting into a captivating blend of dark brown and shimmering gold. With a sudden burst of power, he floats into the air, his hands slipping from mine. My magic is engulfing him as if it's devouring his very essence. As he descends to the floor, I feel an electric shock in my eyes, too.

My previous sense of power has transformed into an overwhelming feeling of invincibility. In a moment of complete certainty and without any hesitation, I find myself instinctively embracing Eli, desperate for the solace and reassurance that his familiar touch brings.

"What did you do to us?"

Eli smiles, a hint of allure and confidence radiating from his face. "I was only able to tap into merging our magic because you *love* me."

"W–what?" Chuckling nervously, my eyes dart from his face to the floor.

Eli tilts my chin up, locking eyes with me, and a sexy smile traces along his defined lips. "We are fated to be together, and you accepted that. Earth witches can access magic at any time of the day. And I am the strongest at night. Kevin is smart. He will most likely launch his attack against us during the day when I am at my weakest. But you finally admitted to yourself that you love me. *You. Love. Me.*" Eli's grin grows wider. "Our souls are intertwined, uniting our magic and granting us the strength we need to face him. Our powers wouldn't have merged if you didn't love me. And now, we are unstoppable together."

Before I can even respond, a commotion outside interrupts our conversation. The noise resonates through the air, resembling the deafening blasts of exploding bombs.

Eli and I sprint to the living room to see what is happening outside through the window. Kevin's minions wreak havoc in the streets, causing chaos and destruction wherever they go. My heart races with fear and adrenaline. My breath quickens. And a wave of panic washes over me as I start hyperventilating. The sound of my own rapid, shallow breaths fills the air, drowning out any other noise. My chest tightens. The weight of helplessness engulfs me as my knees tremble and my palms dampen with sweat. I struggle to maintain my composure. There is no way I will win, especially now that Kevin has his magic. With each rushing thought, a wave of dizziness consumes me, and the room slowly fades to black.

Resting against the wall to steady my breathing, Isabel sprints to my side. Lin, Destiny, and Eli rush outside to face the demon.

They don't stand a chance against him.

"This is ridiculous!" Isabel yells, rolling her eyes as she pulls me up. "Are you okay, mama?"

My eyes swell up with tears. "I don't think I can go up against him. My magic nearly drained me that day in school."

Isabel shakes her head. "That's because you were trying to take all of them out. You need to focus on one at a time. I need you to get yourself together. You can do this, mama!"

She is right. War is happening—the great fight between good and evil. I look out the window again, trying to build confidence. Kevin hovers mid-air, bathed in a swirling crimson mist. Sinister horns protrude from his head, and his eyes glow with a malevolent light, devoid of any trace of humanity. At the sight of him now, the little ounce of love I had left for him vanishes entirely. He is a demon.

"Where is she?!" Kevin bellows.

He is after me. This is payback for trying to kill him.

I start to pant heavily. "I can't do this. I don't think I can do it. I can't–"

Isabel smacks me on the arm, snapping me out of my panic. *"¡Tú puedes hacerlo!"*

Huh? My Spanish is a little rusty.

"You can do it, Claudette! *¡Tú puedes hacerlo!"* She repeats, "We must fight back!"

Isabel is right. We must fight back!

Moving towards the door, I exhale a sharp breath, preparing myself for the confrontation ahead.

Chaos surrounds me. People are running in all directions, screaming. Isabel joins Destiny to fight against the twins. Of course, the twins would side with Kevin. They have a deep-rooted hatred for me.

My eyes shift to Lin, who is taking on Tristan and Tanya by himself. Eli and Kevin are facing off, their faces contorted with rage as they clash. Eli hurls vibrant blue and pure white, shimmering gold fireballs at Kevin, crackling with energy as they explode on impact. Kevin retaliates with fiery red orbs, with searing heat waves emanating from each one. They soar through the air, leaving trails of smoke and scorch marks in their wake, attacking one another in a continuous loop.

Suddenly, Tanya breaks away from her fight with Lin, sprinting towards me with determination in her eyes. Using her extraordinary abilities, she effortlessly propels me into the air and back down, causing a resounding crash as I collide with the ground. My left wrist snaps upon contact with the hard pavement. I scream in agony, distracting Eli, and Kevin flings him into a tree. My eyes widen in horror as he crumples to the ground and his elbow bone protrudes from his skin.

"Nooo!" I screech, and Kevin grins sadistically when he sees me. He sends Tanya a knowing look, and she nods at his silent command.

Summoning all my strength to push through the pain, I stand up to get to Eli, who is currently incapacitated. Still, Tanya is blocking my path by conjuring flaming purple spheres and throwing them in my direction. The first strike sends a searing pain through my arm as the flames scorch my skin, leaving behind blistering burns. I grit my teeth and keep moving forward, determined to reach Eli. Tanya is on the brink of launching another fireball in my direction when a protective force field materializes around me, deflecting the attack and giving me a moment to assess the situation. My eyes dart around, trying to identify the individual–*individuals* behind the barrier, as I am determined to thank them. It's Ms. Billie, Ms. Caron, Mr. Goatfair, and Mr. Max.

They are shouting in unison and channeling their energy to help me. Mr. Goatfair and Ms. Caron combine their strengths to create a powerful counterattack, sending Tanya stumbling back.

"Get to Eli!" Mr. Goatfair shouts.

Sprinting towards Eli as fast as I can, I dodge the enemy along the way. He is unconscious but breathing. Struggling to lift his dead weight off the ground, I manage to hoist him up when a fireball comes hurtling towards us and explodes in a burst of flames, knocking us off balance. My good wrist breaks my fall as I shield Eli from the impact. Tristan hovers above us, bathed in a magnetic glow of red and orange lights. My pulse quickens, each beat resonating with the growing anger that boils inside me. All rationality is replaced by an unyielding and burning determination. *I've had enough!* While I may not be able to defeat Kevin at the moment, Tristan is no match for me.

Heal. Healing my wrists, I levitate, soaring above my enemy. Channeling all of my energy to Tristan and utilizing the incredible amplification provided by Eli, I trigger a rupture in the vein inside his brain, resulting in his swift and irreversible death. It is eerily quiet as his limp body crashes against the cement, fracturing his skull on impact. The sounds of bones crunching and blood spurting reverberate through the streets. Kevin soars to Tristan, scooping up his lifeless body in his arms, and all of them disappear in a gush of smoke before I can launch another attack.

Crouching down beside Eli, he is still unconscious; his breathing is shallow. His face is pale and twisted in agony from his broken arm. I gently place my hand on his chest, conjuring my magic to heal his injuries.

Heal.

Nothing happens.

Heal.

Still nothing.

Mr. Max, Mr. Goatfair, and Lin bolt toward us, transferring their magic into me, and I try again. I'm able to heal his arm, but he is still unconscious.

"Why isn't he waking up?" I look to everyone around me for answers, except no one has any.

Cradling Eli in my arms, tears stream down my face as I fear the worst. I hug him tight, hoping he will wake up and be okay. Still, the surrounding silence is deafening, broken only by the sound of my sobs.

This means war!

Chapter 26

Fated Lovers

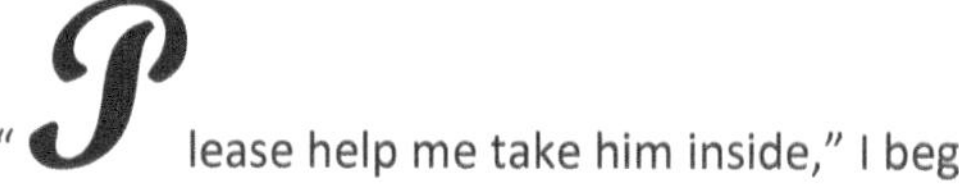

“Please help me take him inside,” I beg.

Lin and Mr. Max gently lift Eli’s limp body from my arms and carry him into the apartment. I follow closely behind, the sound of shuffling feet filling the air as everyone else mimics my movements. As we gently place him on the bed, his face remains pale and motionless.

“What do we do now?” I ask.

Everyone exchanges uneasy glances.

The silence stretches on, and my anger bubbles to the surface. “Someone, please answer me!”

“There is nothing more we can do but wait,” Lin says.

Wait for him to wake up or die?

Waves of shivers run through my body, and I instinctively clutch my elbows to steady myself. “I–I thought I healed him. Why isn’t he waking up?” My voice cracks, and a ripple of emotions threatens to overwhelm me.

Ms. Caron’s eyes fill with empathy. “You healed him physically. He was struck by magical fireballs, which will take time to recover from.”

“H–how long?”

Ms. Caron bends down to Eli’s still form, gently rubbing the back of her hand on his forehead. "It's hard to say. Hours, days, maybe even weeks." She says.

I watch over Eli's unconscious body. Ms. Caron's words repeat in my mind. *Hours, days, maybe even weeks.* There is no telling if or when he will wake up.

"We need to prepare for war in the meantime," Mr. Goatfair adds. "Kevin only gave us a taste of his powers. They'll be back stronger next time, especially since Claudette killed that little worm."

"Let's discuss strategies," Destiny suggests, and they gather in the living room, leaving me alone with Eli and Lin.

Sitting beside Eli, I hold his hand tight, hoping for a miracle.

"Anything you need, just let us know," Lin offers.

"There's one thing you can do," I say.

Lin looks at me expectantly, waiting for my request.

"What is Eli's favorite meal?"

Confusion spreads across his face as he processes my odd question. Still, he recovers and responds, "Uh, he loves pasta and seafood."

A plan forms in my mind. "Did Eli tell you where he took me when he told me Kevin had something to do with my father's death?"

Lin pauses, trying to recall the memory. "Ah, yes. He took you to his secret hideout."

Secret?

"How do I get there?" I ask, picking at Lin's brain.

When Eli wakes up, I want to plan a surprise that will leave him speechless.

"Caron can make a potion for a portal. If you remember what the place looks like, you can portal there."

"You wouldn't be able to take me there? Or can't I just portal there on my own?" I lift an eyebrow.

Lin shakes his head. "No, Claudette. I have no idea what Eli's hideout looks like, and I don't think it's in this realm, which is why you would need a potion." He looks down at his best friend's unconscious body. "Eli really loves you, you know. He never takes anyone there." With that, Lin gives me a nod and exits the room to join the others in the living room, leaving me to ponder his words.

After undressing Eli into something more comfortable, I settle down by his side.

The blame falls on me. I was the distraction that led Eli to this state. My heart is heavy with guilt as I watch him lie there. All he ever tried to do was warn me about Kevin, and now he's paying the price for my negligence. I was madly in lust with that demon—because that wasn't love—and I failed to see the danger Eli was trying to protect me from. *I wish I had listened to him sooner.* A deep sadness overcomes me, causing tears to well up in my eyes.

Kevin is now unrecognizable. His once charming features have crumbled, revealing the monster beneath. He glared at me with pitch-black eyes and a sinister grin. The red horns that protruded from his head made my blood turn to ice. How was I ever in love with such evil? *I was in lust, not love.*

A knock on the door distracts me from my inner thoughts.

"Come in," I call out, wiping away my tears.

The door creaks open, and Ms. Caron enters with two potion bottles in her hands. "This one is a protection spell for the apartment while Eli heals. It will time out in seventy-two hours, and I will give you another one if necessary," she explains, placing the first bottle on the nightstand. "This one is for a portal," she adds, positioning the second bottle next to the first with a reassuring smile. "Sweetie, listen to me. You are extremely powerful, and you have the strength to defeat Kevin. Still, you have to learn to channel the Earth's energy and the love that surrounds you when accessing your powers. Or it will destroy you."

"Thank you for the advice, Ms. Caron." I smile up at her. "And thank you so much for the potions. When did you have the time to make them?"

She cackles. "I have a bookshelf full of ready-made potions."

The cackling is peculiar, but I appreciate the potions that she has provided me with.

"I really appreciate you supplying me with both of these potions, Ms. Caron."

"Oh, honey, it's no trouble at all," she winks. "And you can call me Caron. We are not in school. No need to be so formal."

"Thank you, *Caron*," I correct.

Mr. Goatfair peeks his head into the room. "May I speak with you, Claudette?"

Caron turns her attention to Mr. Goatfair. "I was just leaving, Adam. She's all yours," she says, exiting the room.

He sits on the edge of the bed beside me.

"What do you need to speak to me about, Mr. Goatfair?" My brows furrow.

He raises his hand to stop me from speaking. "Adam is fine."

Clearing my throat, I start over. "Alright, *Adam*, what did you want to talk about?"

He looks at me with a serious expression. "We're one of the last Earth witches left in this town. You, me, Jessie, and Lin."

"My father left me a letter on a flash drive," I admit, and Adam nods knowingly. "He told me to reach out to you or Jimmy. Why would he tell me that?"

"Chance told me he would explain everything to you, but he was taken before he could." Adam's expression softens as he continues, "Your father knew there was danger coming, and he wanted to make sure you were prepared. He trusts me to help guide you in the right direction. Do you have your Earth book?"

"No. My father hid it in a safe place in the house, but I don't have the key. We need to find his necklace; it was stolen the night he was murdered."

Adam's mouth forms a small O. "We can do a locator spell to find it, but I need something of his for it to work."

"I don't want to go back to the house he was killed in, Adam. Please don't make me." I plead with him.

Adam nods in understanding. "I will figure something out with Caron, Billie, and Jessie. We will get you what you need. Even if it's a bit unorthodox." He says, rubbing his fingers together.

I give him a small smile. "Thank you, Adam."

Adam gives me a slight grin before turning to leave the room. "We are calling it a night. Rest up, kid, and let us know when Eli wakes up."

It is three in the morning when everyone leaves. The protection spell Caron casts will ward off any unwanted visitors, which also means Eli and I can't leave the premises unless through a portal.

I curl up on the soft, cozy bed next to Eli, hoping that the soothing rhythm of his breathing will lull me to sleep as I silently pray for a brighter tomorrow.

Upon waking up the following morning, Eli's condition remains the same. Throughout the night, I periodically woke up to check on him, hoping he would wake up. As the hours passed, my anxiety grew. *I don't know what to do.* My stomach growls with hunger. I haven't eaten since yesterday morning, so I head to the kitchen to make some breakfast. I quickly prepare some scrambled eggs and plop down on the sofa to eat. Despite my hunger, I struggle to swallow each bite. I feel helpless. My heart feels empty, and there is a void that can only be filled by my best friend.

Four hours of watching old sitcoms and movies on Netflix pass by in a blur. The apartment feels empty without Eli's usual banter and laughter filling the space. I drag my feet to the bathroom to shower and get dressed, but even a shower doesn't seem to wash away the emptiness I feel without my best friend around. I skim through Eli's Moon book, looking for something—anything that can help wake him up. As I mindlessly flip through the pages, I remember the flash drive my father had left me. There was a folder labeled *Fated Lovers*. I check on Eli once more to ensure he's still breathing, then grab the flash drive and plug it into my laptop. I open the folder and begin reading through the documents.

It states that fated lovers are two souls destined to find each other in every lifetime and bound to merge their magic to be the most powerful beings in the world. The merging spell that Eli cast on us is listed here. This spell is for all fated lovers—Sun, Moon, or Earth—to perform in order to unlock their full potential. *"Confess one's true self."* The bottom of the document reads. *What does that mean?* Confess one's true self. I repeat the phrase in my head, trying to decipher its meaning. Then it hits me—it was always Eli. *Not* Kevin. The sight of his true demon nature was the final push I needed to let him go and fully embrace my destiny with Eli. I had been suppressing my true feelings for him this entire time, never truly admitting how I felt about him.

Ejecting the flash drive, I hasten to Eli's room. Straddling his motionless body, I whisper, "Eli, I love you with all my heart and accept you as my mate." Electricity courses between us, and I press my lips to his, savoring the taste of destiny fulfilled. "Eli," I say softly, "I love you in every lifetime, in every universe. I confess my true feelings to you. I accept our fate. Do you accept me?" I wait with bated breaths for his response. Still, he remains motionless, his eyes closed.

"Please, Eli. Please wake up. I need you here with me. Please don't leave me alone in this world without you." I kiss his forehead, both sides of his face, and his lips, hoping to bring him back to me. Still, there is no response from him. My tears fall onto his cheeks as I plead for him to come back to me. "I need my best friend. Please wake up, Eli." I press my face against his well-defined chest, inhaling his familiar scent. I feel his faint heartbeat beneath my cheek. "I can't do this without you," I whisper, clinging to the belief that he will open his eyes, except he doesn't. *What will it take for him to wake up?* I confessed my feelings for him. How else can I show him how much he means to me?

Standing up, I quickly draw in a deep breath, allowing my lungs to fill with air. In an effort to convey my deep affection for him, I conjure a sphere that captures all my love. The orb shimmers with white illumination. Vivid memories of our time together flood my mind, causing the orb to shine and intensify. I have doubts about its effectiveness; however, I release it into the air. The luminous sphere hovers over Eli's body, emanating warmth and love. My hands tremble as I guide the orb above his heart. Eli's chest rises and falls, synchronized with the ethereal orb's rhythm. The transference of light from the vessel into his body ascends him toward the ceiling. Floating in mid-air, he emits a radiant glow before settling back onto the bed. The luminescence fades, and his eyes flutter open. He blinks a few times, taking in his surroundings.

"Eli! You're awake!" I shriek.

Clearing his throat, "Yeah, it seems like it. What happened?"

Leaping onto the bed, I straddle him.

"You have been unconscious for over fifteen hours," I tell him.

"Yet, I feel exhausted," he says, instinctively grasping my waist.

"Do you remember what happened?"

He shakes his head slowly, a puzzled expression on his face. "What happened?"

I recount the events that led to his unconsciousness, my eyes filled with tears. "You were knocked out by a magical fireball. How are you feeling?"

He listens intently, his expression shifting from confusion to amusement. "Fifteen hours?" he repeats. "I still feel exhausted."

Cracking a small smile. "You had us all worried sick," I admit, embracing him. "Don't do that again, okay?"

Eli chuckles. "Perhaps I should be knocked unconscious more often."

Pushing him back with my fist. "No! Don't do that to me again, okay?" Biting my bottom lip. "I–I love you so much, Eli. I don't know what I would do without you—I wouldn't survive without you."

His eyes soften, and his hand reaches up to wipe away a stray tear from my cheek. "I love you too, more than you'll ever know," he says with a sincerity that warms my heart. But you don't *need* me to survive."

I look at him, my brows furrowed in confusion. "What do you mean?"

Eli's lips curve into a sexy smile. "I mean that you are strong and capable on your own. I'll always be here for you, but we are not meant to live in this realm forever. If something were to happen to me, you would have the strength to survive, and I will be waiting for you in the Light World."

I don't want to think about life without him.

Sliding off of Eli, I lower myself onto the floor, my face reflecting a sense of seriousness.

He sits up on the bed, his eyes locked on me with a guarded expression. "Claudette?"

Savoring the intimate moment, I deliberately lower my shorts, feeling the material slide against my skin. Eli's eyes flicker with intrigue, and my gaze shifts to the pulsating bulge in his sweatpants.

Lost in the moment, I move closer to him without realizing that I didn't properly remove my shorts. As a result, I trip over the fabric and awkwardly land on the floor, the impact creating a soft thud. My cheeks flush with embarrassment, causing me to instinctively bury my face against the coolness of the tiles. In a matter of seconds, the atmosphere transitions from intimate to awkward. I wish the Earth would open up and swallow me whole, sparing me from this unbearable situation.

Eli peers down at me. "Claudette?"

"Yes?" I mumble, my voice muffled by the tiles.

"Are you okay?"

"I think I'll stay down here for a while."

He chuckles softly, crouching down beside me. "Let me help you up."

Exhaling a deep breath, I accept his offer and regain my footing. My gaze meets his, and we share a knowing look before bursting into laughter and falling back onto the bed. The awkwardness fades away, and when our laughter eases, he cocks his head to the side. "What are we?"

"We're fated lovers," I reply with a smile.

"No, Claudette."

My smile fades. *No?*

"You're sitting on my bed half-naked," he clarifies with a smirk, leaning in closer.

My breath catches in my throat. Just being near Elijah Powers is enough to make me lose all strength in my limbs.

His hand slowly slides up my thigh, and a rush of heat courses through my body. "What are we?" he asks again, his warm breath tickling my skin.

"We are one," I reply breathlessly.

His eyes lock onto mine, a dashing smile playing on his lips as a silent understanding passes between us.

"What do you want from me, Claudette?" His voice is low and husky.

My throat tightens, and I gulp nervously. "I–I want all of you."

He traces delicate kisses down my collarbone. "What do you need from me, Claudette?"

When he touches me, it feels like a surge of electricity, causing a tingling sensation all over my body.

"I need all of you," I reply; my pulse quickens as his touch sends shivers down my spine. "Eli, I want you to be with me in all ways possible. I am yours, and I love you."

With a seductive grin, he removes his shirt, showcasing his chiseled chest and toned muscles. My mouth is watering as I am unable to contain my admiration for his flawless physique.

He gently pulls my shirt over my head and unhooks my bra, momentarily leaving me disoriented. His gaze hungrily takes in every inch of my exposed skin.

"Do you want me to make love to you, Claudette?"

"Yes, please," I mutter, my body trembling with anticipation.

He quickly stands to his feet and kicks off his sweatpants and boxers, leaving nothing to the imagination, exposing his entire length to me.

Our eyes lock in a passionate gaze as he retrieves protection from the drawer and carefully slides it on. My jaw drops in awe, and he responds with a wide, toothy grin that brightens his entire face.

I love Eli with every fiber of my being, and I want to show him just how much. I reach out to him, grab his arm, and pull him back onto the bed. Adrenaline courses through my veins as I slide off my underwear and straddle him. “I love you, Elijah Powers.”

He grips my hips firmly. “I love you, Claudette Richardson.”

Lowering myself onto him, I bite my bottom lip to stifle a moan as our bodies become one. Eli groans softly, claiming my lips with his own in a passionate kiss. His hands explore every inch of my body as I rock my hips in rhythm with his. He whispers sweet nothings in my ear, caressing my skin with kisses and leaving a trail of fire in his wake. Our breathing is heavy, intermingling with the sound of the mattress creaking beneath us.

Eli grasps me by the waist and flips us over, taking control.

Every kiss feels like a drug.

Every touch intoxicates my senses, bringing me to the brink of ecstasy. With each thrust, our passion intensifies as I arch my back to meet his every movement. My body quivers with jolts of pleasure, and I grip the sheets. I have never experienced anything quite like this before. It’s pure bliss in every sense. The intensity of Eli’s thrusts escalates, sending waves of pleasure coursing through our bodies. In a fleeting moment, my body transcends into a fit of euphoria, and I am transported to a realm of pure bliss. As I come down from the height of passion, I can feel his body trembling with anticipation, leading up to his climax. Overwhelmed with exhaustion, we both collapse, panting and basking in the joyful aftermath of our passionate lovemaking.

I thought that when I lost my virginity to Kevin, we were making love, but I couldn’t have been more wrong. What Eli and I shared was more than just physical intimacy.

It was two souls merging as one.

Chapter 27

All is Revealed

My eyes flicker open, and I look to my left and admire Eli. Resting my head on his chiseled chest, listening to his steady heartbeat against my ear, his warm breath on my neck—it feels like home. This handsome man told me he loved me and showed me just how much he did last night. He was attentive to what my body needed and made sure I felt pleasure from every touch. My desire is to show him just how much I appreciate him.

I roll over to grab my phone on the nightstand and text Lin to come over to help distract Eli while I work on my surprise for him.

Leaning back, Eli meets my gaze, grinning from ear to ear.

"Good morning, Sunshine."

Returning his smile, I move closer to him and kiss him on the lips. "Good morning, baby. Would you like me to make you some breakfast?"

"So, this is the *girlfriend* Claudette treatment?" Eli teases, making me laugh.

Shoving him playfully. "I love the sound of being your girlfriend."

"Me too," he replies, pressing his lips against mine again.

"I'll make you some after my shower." I get up from the bed, but he pulls me back down, wrapping his muscular arms around me and holding me firmly in his grasp.

Melting into his embrace, I feel safe and loved in his arms. Feeling his frame against mine sends a comforting sensation throughout my entire body. Eli is different from Kevin. Thinking back, the whole time Kevin and I were intimate, he seemed distant and unengaged. While with Eli, he was present and attentive. Suddenly, guilt washes over me, weighing heavy on my conscience for comparing the two. I shouldn't be. Still, Eli is the second guy I've been with, and I can't help but notice the stark contrast between them.

Tracing my fingers along Eli's eight-pack. "Babe, I have to brush my teeth."

"Yeah, you do. Your breath stinks," he jokes, giving me a quick peck on the lips.

I playfully throw a pillow at his head. "Shut up. So does yours."

He chuckles, blowing out his stinky breath on my face. *Wow! I love him.*

Opening and closing the cabinets, I am trying to figure out what to make Eli for breakfast. Kevin usually cooked for me, and now that I think about it, he used his culinary skills to win me over and manipulate me. *That demon!* However, Eli is *not* Kevin. From the moment we met, there was a genuine connection between us—an unexplainable pull that defied logic. We are destined to be together. *Why didn't I just trust my instincts from the start?*

Opting for my father's famous buttermilk pancakes, I gather the ingredients and start whipping up a batch. Twenty minutes later, breakfast is ready. I place the pancakes onto the table and pour orange juice into two flutes.

Eli walks in shirtless, wearing gray sweatpants. "Breakfast smells good."

He is so sexy.

"It's my dad's infamous buttermilk pancakes," I reply gleefully.

His muscles ripple as he sits down at the table to dig in. I anxiously await his reaction, butterflies fluttering in my stomach.

"These are great, babe," he compliments between bites. "What did I do to deserve you?"

My smile falters slightly as guilt creeps in. "I am sorry it took me so long to reciprocate your feelings," I confess, looking down at my plate.

Eli reaches across the table, gently lifting my chin. "You were worth the wait," he says, making my heart skip a beat. "I am happy that we are here now."

We enjoy our breakfast, engaging in light conversation and sharing laughs.

Ring. Ring.

My phone interrupts our playful banter.

Caron is calling me. Back to reality: I answer the call with a sigh. She, Billie, and Adam are heading to my dad's house to steal something of his to perform the locater spell to find his Earth necklace and, hopefully, his ring, too.

Eli is loading the dishwasher when I end the call, and I quickly fill him in.

"My father left me a flash drive with important information about my family history, including the location of his Earth book. However, his Earth necklace and ring are missing. I need his necklace to unlock the box the book is in. Caron, Billie, and Adam are on their way to my dad's house to find something of his so that we can conduct a locator spell to find his Earth ring and necklace."

Eli nods in understanding and offers to help in any way he can.

When silence falls between us, he changes the subject to steer me away from gnawing over the situation. "What would you like to do today as an official couple?"

Smiling at the sound of the title *couple*. "I actually have something planned for us."

"Oh! You do?" He arches his brow.

As I nod my head, a bubbling excitement rises in my chest, like a sparkling drink ready to burst. "Yes, however, afterward, everyone is coming over to conduct the spell to locate my father's necklace." I say once again.

Eli squeezes my hand. "I'm here for you, whatever you need."

A knock sounds at the door, interrupting our moment.

Eli goes to answer it. Lin enters with a huge smile on his face, pulling Eli in for a bear hug. "I'm so happy you are awake. My brother!"

"I will give you two some time to catch up," I say, kissing Eli on the cheek.

Lin points between the two of us. "Oh! Are you two a thing now?" He asks, sporting a huge grin.

I wink at him before heading out of the room.

Rummaging through Eli's closet, I search for a blanket for our date later. I find a soft, cozy blanket and head to my room for supplies. I gather a crochet hook, some gold yarn, and scissors to crochet an E and C into the blanket.

Caron temporarily deactivated the protection spell to permit Eli to leave the apartment with Lin. I use the opportunity to cook a delicious meal for our date, opting for shrimp Alfredo, knowing that Eli's favorite dish is pasta and seafood. I pack the food into containers and into a basket with a blanket and a bottle of sparkling cider. With the potion Caron had given me securely in my grasp, I set my sights on embarking on a journey to Eli's secret haven. In this place, we can fully immerse ourselves in the breathtaking beauty of the sunset as we stand atop the highest point of the mountain.

Eli returns to the apartment just in time for our date, and I go to greet him. My smile falters when I notice the deep frown etched on his face.

"What's wrong, babe?"

"You killed Tristan, Claudette?" He asks, his eyes searching mine for answers.

Despite my reluctance, I lower my gaze to my feet and reply, "Yes, I did. I didn't know what else to do. There was rage brewing inside me, and I couldn't control my anger."

Eli's expression changes. His features relax, and his gaze softens as he reaches out to hold my hand. "The angrier you become, the faster your powers will deplete."

Sighing, I look down at our intertwined hands. "Caron told me to access my power from the Earth's energy and the love that surrounds me."

"Yes, that's correct. Access your power by channeling it from the Earth and the love you have for your parents, me, and your friends." Eli encourages me. "You have been filled with rage and anger every time you have used your power." He points out.

"How do I protect those I love if killing isn't the way to do it?"

Eli's eyes hold understanding. "Killing is the last resort, Claudette. You can protect your loved ones by using your power to defend, not destroy."

When I find out who killed my father, I plan to return the favor by executing them. I keep that thought to myself and smile. Retrieving my phone from my pocket, I send Spencer and Nicolette a text, informing them of everything.

Looking up at Eli. "I can't believe Kevin is evil and killed Jimmy."

"I expected nothing less; he is a demon, after all." He replies.

Putting my phone away, I place my hands on both sides of Eli's shoulders and look him straight in the eyes. He grasps my waist, his expression filled with concern. Taking a deep breath in and letting it out slowly, I focus on releasing the tension in my body.

"Let's not worry about our reality right now." I smile, trying to lighten the mood. "I have a surprise for you, babe."

His grip on my waist tightens. "I'm intrigued."

"You should be," I reply, pushing away from him before we get too distracted. I lead him by the hand to get the basket I had prepared and the potion bottle.

Eli raises an eyebrow in curiosity, his gaze shifting between the basket and the potion in my hands.

"You'll see soon enough," I assure him with a playful grin.

Closing my eyes, I envision the day Eli took me to the mountains. Shattering the potion bottle on the floor, I whisper, "Take me to Eli's secret spot."

The potion's effects take hold, and we transport to the mountain peak. Watching Eli's face light up as he recognizes the familiar view brings a warm feeling to my heart.

Breathing in the fresh mountain air, I unpack the basket and present the blanket crocheted with our initials. Eli's eyes widen in amazement as he carefully traces over my craftsmanship with his fingertips, a smile spreading across his face. "This is incredible, babe," he murmurs, pulling me into a tight hug.

We spread out the blanket and settle in, taking in the mesmerizing waterfall. *Just as I remember it.* Unpacking the pasta and sparkling cider, Eli pours us each a glass, and I feed him a bite of pasta. His eyes light up with delight, and he pulls me into his muscular arms. "I love you, Claudette." He kisses me as if it were our last.

I don't think I'll ever grow tired of hearing those three words from him.

"I love you too, Eli," I reply against his full lips.

He grins. "It's about time. It took you long enough."

"Oh, shush." I playfully slap his chest. "I have always had a thing for you since we first met," I confess. "I guess I was just in denial about it."

Eli embraces me tighter. "Well, I'm glad you finally came to your senses," he teases, making me laugh. "I like to believe that things happen when they're meant to. And this moment feels just right."

Eli leans in to kiss me again, his lips soft and warm against mine, but before things can go any further, we pull away to finish our dinner. We enjoy each other's company and conversation. Once we are done with our meal, we marvel at the sunset, painting the sky in an array of colors.

"Thank you, babe," he says, looking me in the eye. "For everything."

I smile, staring into his eyes. "You're welcome."

Enveloped in the beauty of the evening and consumed by the warmth of his love, Eli's sensual kiss ignites a passionate fire within me, and we find ourselves connecting beneath the breathtaking red and orange hues of the setting sun. Reflecting on the gradual buildup of our love, I can't help but wonder what it would have been like if I had met him first–the thought consumes me.

Ding.

I glance at my phone, and it is a text from Lin. He and the others are on their way to meet us at the apartment.

"It's time to go, baby. Back to reality." I tell Eli as we reluctantly untangle ourselves from each other. We gather our clothes from the ground and quickly get dressed. We pack the basket to head back to the apartment, where Lin, Caron, Adam, and Billie are waiting for us. Eli transports us back to the apartment in a flash.

Everyone is in the living room when we arrive, surrounding the table. Caron lights a candle and places the town map in the center. "Gabriella didn't give me a hard time when I went to your father's house. She agrees the twins have lost their minds and are not acting like themselves, and she doesn't know what to do. We chatted for a bit, and when she went to make us some tea, I snuck away to grab this ring from their bedroom," Caron explains, holding up a gold band.

"How were you able to go upstairs to their bedroom without her noticing?"

She cackles, "A lady never reveals her secrets." *Caron loves to cackle, I notice.* Tilting her head to the side, Caron adds, "The better question would be, is this your father's wedding band?"

Inspecting the gold band in her hand, I nod my head.

Adam joins us with a bowl, burdock root, and grass. Caron pours a bottled potion carefully into the bowl, making sure not to spill a single drop, and then delicately drops the gold ring into the mixture. A gray smoke billows from the bowl, and she skillfully wields a baster to extract the liquid that has formed. She then squirts the liquid onto the map.

"The locations of your father's possessions will be revealed," Adam explains.

We all watch in anticipation as the liquid slowly begins to spread across the map, dividing into two distinct locations.

Kevin's apartment. And Ms. Hudson's home.

My trust shatters like glass, and I swiftly retrieve my father's ring from the bowl.

Everyone's eyes widen as they exchange uneasy glances. *Is Ms. Hudson involved in my father's death?* My vision blurs with an overwhelming darkness, and an impenetrable sense of rage consumes me entirely.

"Wait! Claudette, don't leave!" Caron shouts.

"Claudette!" Eli yells, echoing Caron's plea.

Ignoring them both, I slam the door behind me.

The mere thought of Ms. Hudson's house triggers a magical teleportation. In an instant, I materialize in front of her doorstep.

Remaining calm, I ball up my fist and knock on the door, patiently waiting for her to answer.

The door swings open, and Ms. Hudson's eyebrows furrow in confusion. "Hello, Claudette. Did we have a session today?"

I direct my gaze straight into her eyes. *How could she help me cope with my father's death when she was the very person responsible for it?*

Forging a smile, I push down the rage bubbling inside me and politely respond, "No, Ms. Hudson. I just wanted to talk. May I come in?"

"Sure, sweetie, come on in." She gestures for me to enter her office.

I follow her inside, a flurry of fiery emotions swirling inside me.

"Please take a seat," Ms. Hudson says, motioning to the chair in front of her desk.

"No, I'd rather stand," I reply, unable to bring myself to sit down in front of the woman who shattered my world.

Clutching the ring in my hand, I pace back and forth. She opens the drawer of her desk to retrieve her notebook and pen to begin our unplanned session.

She opens her notebook, looking at me expectantly. "So, tell me. Claudette, what's been going on?"

There's a storm brewing inside me, and I know that once I start talking, there will be no turning back. "I know you like to stay out of witch business, but Kevin attacked my friends and me. He is evil."

Ms. Hudson fake gasps. "Oh no, that's terrible, Claudette! I had no idea. I'm sorry to hear that. Were you, or were your friends hurt? Is that why you are here today?" She pulls out her calendar and continues. "I know we weren't supposed to meet until next week."

She is lying through her teeth. It is remarkable how effortlessly she can pretend. What an incredible actress! She deserves an award! *Was it all an act to get me to trust her and open up?*

Walking closer to her. "Yes and no," I reply.

Ms. Hudson tilts her head slightly, waiting for me to continue.

My mind deliberates over the various spells at my disposal. "Turn the darkness into light, reveal the truth, and give me sight." My voice takes on a sinister edge as I chant this spell three times, the intensity building with each iteration.

The witch's eyes widen in despair, and she jumps to her feet. "W–what are you doing?" She stammers.

A visible light shines inside her drawer, and the color drains from her face. She quickly moves out of my way, and I find my father's Earth ring stashed inside, nestled under her notebooks from our sessions.

I collect the ring and play with it in my palm. Cocking my head to the side. "You see, this ring is why I am here today," I tell her calmly, holding up the ring for her to see. "Why do you have my father's ring, Ms. Hudson?" Fear flashes in her eyes, and a malicious grin spreads across my face. "Are you scared now, Ms. Hudson?"

"N–no. Why would I fear you?" She stammers, her shaky voice exposing her nervousness.

Because you should be. I catch a glimpse of my reflection in the small mirror on her desk. The darkness within me is reflected in the blackness of my eyes, a side of myself that I never believed existed.

With deliberate steps, I approach her. "Why did you do it?"

Her answer won't change her fate, but I derive a certain satisfaction from watching her squirm.

"Why did I do what, Claudette?" Ms. Hudson quivers under my gaze, feigning innocence.

"You know exactly what I'm talking about!" She flinches at my accusatory tone. "You killed my father!"

A painful recognition crosses her face. "I had no choice, Claudette. I am so sorry," she apologizes, her voice wavering with guilt.

A lousy sorry won't bring my father back. Extending my arm, I summon a fiery red fireball, feeling its warmth against my skin as it takes form in my hand.

Ms. Hudson's eyes widen, and a look of sheer horror flashes across her face. "Please, Claudette, I beg you, please don't do this," she pleads, her voice desperate.

Eli specifically emphasized the importance of not channeling my rage. Shaking off his warning, it's too late for mercy. All I feel is rage in its purest form, consuming me from the inside out. This lady—*my therapist*—convinced me to open up about my trauma, only to team up with Kevin and kill my father. That is the epitome of wickedness. Evil like that deserves to be met with an equal measure of inhumanity.

"Why did you kill my father?" I demand, playing with the fireball in my hand.

Her eyes dart at its fiery glow. "I...I..."

The flames flicker dangerously, and I shake my head at her incoherent stammering. "I...I...*What*?"

"I–I didn't have a choice. I–I swear it," she chokes out.

I scoff at her weak excuse. "Wrong answer." With a swift motion, I aim the fireball precisely at her heart, striking her with unforgiving force. She falls off balance, collapsing to the floor with a pained cry. As she writhes in agony, she conjures a fireball of her own, and with the last of her strength, she hurls it at me. It doesn't even sting. *She is pathetic.*

As I ascend above her, a malicious smirk forms on my face at her feeble pleas. I want this witch to suffer.

"Claudette, please don't do this," she begs, tears streaming down her face. "I didn't have a choice."

She will say just about anything to save herself, but she didn't spare any mercy for my father when she took his life.

"You had a choice, Ms. Hudson, or is it *Libby?*" I snort. "You chose to betray me. Now deal with the consequences of *your* actions!"

My lips curve into a malicious grin as I start breaking the twenty-six bones in her right foot, relishing in her screams of pain. Her anguish fills me with a twisted sense of delight as I break the bones in her other foot.

"Please..." she manages to say.

I proceed to break the bones in her legs, and she falls in and out of consciousness, her body battered and broken, as I carry out her fate. I heal her and break all her bones again. Repeating the process over and over again.

"Please... Claudette... Stop..." Her voice is barely a whisper now.

Even after she committed the heinous act of killing my father in cold blood, she had the nerve to still act as my therapist. I have no sympathy for her! She brought this upon herself.

I continue to fracture every bone in her body—the cracks echoing in my ears like sickening symphonies—inflicting bruising, bleeding, and irreversible deformation. I heal her just enough to keep her alive, prolonging her suffering for as long as possible. A quick death would be too merciful for her.

Her whimpers are hoarse and barely audible now, begging for mercy that will never come. When I grow tired of her torment and incessant pleas, I regard her with a cold, unsympathetic gaze and say, "Any last words? Witch?" I ask, raising her above me toward the ceiling.

She opens her mouth to speak, but strangled cries escape her lips as I seal her fate with a snap of my fingers, fatally breaking her neck. The life drains from the witch's eyes, and her limp body falls to the hard floor, lifeless and broken.

I glide toward her and lower my ear near her body. "I'm sorry, I didn't hear you."

Stepping over her motionless body, I open and close my hands, torching her residence and leaving nothing but charred remains behind.

Chapter 28

Consumed by Rage

The moment I appear at the apartment, the room starts to spin, and I feel drained of all energy, causing me to collapse to the ground.

Several hours later...

What happened? As I slowly regain consciousness, a wave of dizziness hits me, making it difficult to focus. In the background, I can hear faint voices murmuring, but I'm unsure of whose voice belongs to whom.

A hazy figure looms over me. My vision is blurred, making it hard to see their features; however, I immediately recognize their scent. *Eli!*

"Claudette," Eli calls out, shaking me gently. "Are you okay? Can you hear me?"

I try to focus on his words, yet everything sounds distant. *Why can't I see clearly?* My head is pounding, and there is a throbbing sensation behind my eyes.

"Claudette, can you hear us?" Another voice joins in. I attempt to reply, but my mouth feels dry as a desert, yearning for raindrops from the sky. *Why can't I move or speak?*

The tightness in my chest intensifies, making each breath a struggle. Despite my best efforts, I strain to open my heavy and unresponsive eyes. *What's happening to me?* The voices in the background call my name and echo in my ears until everything goes silent. The world around me fades to black, accompanied by swirling white spots in my vision as I succumb to unconsciousness once again.

Eli's point of view:

Kneeling beside Claudette's sleeping form on the sofa, my fingers tremble as I reach out to touch her clammy skin. Even in her vulnerable state, her beauty is enhanced by the gentle rise and fall of her chest as she breathes. I shake her gently, calling out her name. Still, she remains unresponsive. Panic takes hold of my heart, squeezing it tight. Kevin and his minions are expected to retaliate soon, and Claudette is not waking up. *What do I do?* A sense of urgency sets in as I frantically shake her, but she shows no signs of waking. Her breathing is steady and her pulse is strong, but she is lost in a deep slumber.

"What are we going to do now?" I shout to no one in particular. "Claudette killed Ms. Hudson. It is only a matter of time before Kevin shows up."

Claudette has already killed two of their own. Kevin will not take that lightly, and we need to prevent him from finding out Claudette is unconscious.

Caron steadies me by squeezing my shoulders. "Eli, she is drained. There is nothing more we can do. She has to wake up on her own."

Nothing? I shift my gaze towards Claudette, and my shoulders sink in defeat. Carefully, I cradle Claudette in my arms and gently transfer her to the comfort of my bed, ensuring she is tucked in with a soft, warm blanket. Brushing her locs away from her face, anguish settles in my chest. If only I had taken the necessary precautions, maybe this could have been avoided. We should have been better prepared. I suspected Claudette would react emotionally when she found her father's killer. She was shocked and devastated. The revelation hit her like a ton of bricks—her therapist was the murderer all along, and none of us saw it coming. This blindsided me, and I can only imagine how much more it affected Claudette. *What did Kevin have on Ms. Hudson?* There must have been some sort of leverage he had over Ms. Hudson to manipulate her into doing his bidding. I always knew Kevin was evil, but *Ms. Hudson?* She and Jimmy were the only two members of the Witch Council that I didn't hate. Now, Jimmy, Ms. Hudson, and Tristan are dead. Claudette's father is dead. And all the Earth witches sacrificed for Kevin's ritual. *How many more lives need to be lost in this fight?*

Allowing Claudette to rest, I return to the living room, pacing back and forth. Everyone exchanges worried glances. *Think, Eli. Think.* Claudette is a good witch, yet she keeps channeling rage to harness her magic. She won't listen to reason, especially now that she's lost so much. However, there must be a way to reach her. *I got it!*

I barge into Claudette's room, my eyes scanning the space for something specific among her belongings. What am I looking for? I don't know yet. *How can I help her channel love and not rage?*

There it is—I spot her laptop on her desk; I quickly grab it and open it. It's password-protected, and I need four numeric digits to unlock it. I try a few common passwords, like her birthday and her dad's birthday. Luckily, she has the obituary sitting on her shelf. However, none of them work. I only have one more attempt left before the laptop locks me out. Tapping my fingers on the desk, I rack my brain for any other numbers that could be significant to her. I try my birthday, typing in 0-3-1-7, and to my surprise, the laptop unlocks. I smile, shaking my head. *I love this girl.* Claudette informed me that her father left her a flash drive; perhaps there is something on there that could help wake her up or at least speed up the process. Where would Claudette hide a flash drive? Closing my eyes, I gesture my hands around the room, focusing my mind on the object. "I call upon the moon of the night; give me a clear vision and sight. Reveal to me what my heart desires; reveal to me what I might require." I chant.

Claudette's mattress is bathed in a dazzling light, emanating an incredible and exquisite glow. Lifting it up, I find what I need. Her jewelry box. The flash drive is safely tucked away inside of it. Plugging in the drive, a series of files and folders appear on the screen. I groan internally. It will take hours, maybe days, to go through all of this.

I begin the long process of sifting through the folders on her laptop. Still, after forty minutes of searching, I stop to rub the bridge of my nose, feeling a headache coming on. Scrolling through more files, I exhale when I stumble across a spell that permits people from the Light World to crossover. I write down the spell on a piece of paper and close the laptop, returning the flash drive to its original spot.

Heading to my room, I check on Claudette, who is still knocked out on the bed. Closing the door behind me, I make my way to the living room to find Caron talking with Adam, who is listening intently.

"Hi, have you ever done this spell before?" I politely interrupt them, showing them my scribbles on the paper.

She takes the paper from my hand and studies it carefully before shaking her head. "No," she says, glancing at Adam.

"I have done this spell before with Chance." He clears his throat. "He wanted to speak to his, um, Claudette's mother."

"Do you think it could wake Claudette up?" I ask.

Caron and Adam exchange a knowing look before Caron replies, "I don't think so, sweetie."

"Her father left this spell for her as a way to see him again," Adam adds. "The spell is for speaking with the dead." He continues.

A heavy sense of hopelessness engulfs me, making it hard to breathe. *What now?* Kevin is plotting. It is only a matter of time before he makes his move.

"There has to be something we can do!" I shout.

Caron, Lin, Adam, and Billie watch me warily as I pace back and forth.

Now that the roles are reversed, I can empathize with how Claudette felt when I was unconscious. *This sucks!*

"How did Claudette wake you up?" Lin inquires.

I stop pacing and turn to face him. *I have no idea how she woke me up.* I remember feeling an overpowering sensation of warmth and light, but beyond that, it's all a blur. It felt like she was channeling all her love into me, forcing me to wake up. *Maybe I can manifest the same power?*

"That is a great question, Lin! I'll be back in a few minutes. I need to try something." I head back to Claudette's bedside, hoping that my love can have the same impact on her.

Here goes nothing. In my quest to connect with my emotions, I find myself fixated on one particular feeling: my overwhelming love for Claudette. Her smile, infectious and radiant, lights up the room whenever she enters. *There are so many reasons why I love her.* Letting the feelings engulf me, a luminescent white orb materializes in my hand, emanating a soft buzzing sound. I direct it toward her still form; a lingering vibration tingles through my fingertips as I release the orb, merging it into her body as gently as possible. Her entire body glows with a warm light, her chest rising and falling with each breath, but she doesn't open her eyes. My shoulders slump in defeat. "What am I doing wrong?" As my voice echoes through the air, a burst of magic surges from my body, filling the surroundings with a spectacle of white and gold lights.

Everyone rushes into my room, wearing worried expressions.

Lin places a hand on my shoulder. "Eli, she needs time to heal. She did this to herself."

"In the meantime, we need to devise a plan of attack to defeat Kevin and his tribe of maggots," Adam warns.

"We *need* Claudette to be at full strength when that happens," I argue.

"I agree. However, Claudette cannot help us now," Adam replies.

"How do you propose we defeat Kevin and his followers without her?" I ask.

"I think we should strategize an attack on his territory at night," Lin suggests.

"I second that," Billie says, tapping her fingers together with a callous grin. "Get those little bastards when it's nighttime when they least expect it. I'm talking two or three in the morning."

"I think that's a solid plan," Adam chimes in.

Caron nods in agreement and adds, "Catching them off guard should work."

The group collectively nods.

"It is settled then. We will launch a surprise attack in the dead of night." I glance at each of their unwavering faces. "We all have our own Ce-Ja daggers ready, right?" I ask, receiving nods of confirmation from everyone. "We will use the daggers to eliminate their powers. Who else is fighting with us?"

The group looks around at each other.

"You know how this town is. Besides Isabel, Destiny, and Jessie, I don't see anyone else joining us," Lin says.

My brows snap together, creating a deep furrow on my forehead. "What about Principal Deanwall? This town is brimming with witches and warlocks, and no one wants to rid our home of all this evil?"

"Billie, Jessie, Adam, and I are the only ones willing to get our hands dirty," Caron replies, rubbing her hands together.

"I'm going to head home and grab my spell books," Billie announces.

"We need all the help we can get," Adam adds.

Billie and Adam share a knowing nod as she exits the room.

The fate of this town falls on Claudette's and our shoulders. That is a heavy burden for us; however, we must protect our home.

"We need Chance's Earth ring to locate the book. We may need it for the battle." Adam says.

I collect the ring from Claudette's nightstand and hand it to Adam before he leaves.

"I am going to grab more potions from my shelf. I also need to place another protection spell on the apartment until Claudette wakes up." Caron meets my gaze. "We will defeat them. Don't you worry," she reassures me before following Adam out the door.

Despite her encouraging words, I am worried. *What if Claudette doesn't wake up?* What are we going to do? How will we defeat Kevin without her? Claudette is the most powerful being in this world. She is our only hope against him, and without her, our chances are slim—she just needs to learn to channel her love and not her rage.

Lin sits on the sofa beside me, flipping through Netflix. I try to focus on the TV, but my mind keeps wandering back to Claudette. Pulling myself up from the sofa, I check on her again, and there is still no change in her condition. If only I had the power to wake her up like she did for me.

Pressing my lips against her forehead, I whisper, "Please come back to us, Claudette. I love you." She doesn't move. I can't help but think that, somehow, she is aware of my presence, even in her unconscious state.

Sitting by her side, I'm deep in thought. The location spell Caron cast revealed two locations: Kevin's and Ms. Hudson's. Ms. Hudson had Mr. Richardson's Earth ring; perhaps Kevin has his Earth necklace. As for the Earth spell book, where could it be? Shouldn't the spell have shown us its location since it belonged to her dad? A sudden thought crosses my mind.

I walk back to the living room, where Lin is sitting. "Lin, I have a question."

Pausing the show he is watching, he looks up at me, tapping the remote. "What is it?"

"Why didn't the spell work on locating the Earth spell book? It belongs to Claudette's father."

"He is dead, so the book is passed down to his next of kin, which would be Claudette. The Earth ring will show us where the book is located, though.

Adam is working on a spell as we speak," Lin replies matter-of-factly.

My phone rings, and Adam's name flashes on the screen. *Right on time!* I answer the call, and he informs me that the Earth spell book is at Gabriella's house.

Hanging up, I propose a crazy plan.

"So Lin, what do you think about breaking into Gabriella's house and stealing back the book?"

There has to be something in that book that can help wake Claudette.

Lin looks at me like I've lost my mind. "Bro, Claudette is in a coma. Her magic is drained by rage. She will wake up when her body is ready. No spell can change that."

Feeling defeated, I let out an exasperated sigh and place my forehead into my palm. Perhaps all we can do now is wait and hope for the best.

I head back to my room, feeling helpless. Holding Claudette's hand in mine, I whisper. "Please, Claudette, wake up. I love you."

Chapter 29

Dream Realm

What happened? Where am I? How did I get here? Where is *here*?

I was lying on the floor in Eli's living room for one moment, and then I was here the next. Standing to my feet, I look around the room, taking in its all-white walls with no doors or windows.

Panic grips me as my knees tremble, making it impossible for me to stand upright, eventually causing me to collapse to the floor. I pull my knees close to my chest and hug them tight. Swaying back and forth, my heart races beneath my chest like a stampede of animals fleeing a predator.

Is this heaven? Am I dead?

Closing my eyes, I count backward from ten. Maybe this is a nightmare, and I will wake up soon from this terrifying place. I pinch my arm. *Ouch!* The pain confirms that this is real, and I am not dreaming. I rise to my feet once more, feeling the hard ground beneath me as I take a step forward. The space around me starts to elongate; the walls of the room—or wherever I am—seem to stretch out into infinity.

"Hello?" With unease, I call out, my voice filling the vast emptiness and creating an eerie echo.

No response comes, only the sound of my own heartbeat pounding in my ears. I take another step, the ground beneath me feeling unstable and uncertain.

I am trapped in a never-ending void. There are no doors or windows; there is no one else here with me. And there is white *everywhere*. Tears stream down my cheeks like a waterfall. As I sink to the floor, the realization hits me that I am completely alone in this endless expanse with no way out. White noise rings in my ears, clouding my mind with the root of my deepest fears. I cover my earlobes, trying to block out the overwhelming noise, but it only seems to grow louder. The realization hit me like a ton of bricks: *Ms. Hudson!* The person I trusted—my therapist—manipulated me all along. She murdered my father, taking away the only family I had left. And I tortured and killed her in cold blood. A choked sob escapes my throat as the weight of my actions crushes me. The horrid look in her eyes as she took her last breath haunts me, and the twisted satisfaction I felt at that moment sickens me to my core. Her death brought me a sense of peace, but it also gave me a new level of guilt. While she deserved it, I can't bring myself to justify it. I am not God!

Grappling with the overwhelming emotions swirling inside me, I bury my tear-streaked face in my hands, feeling the warmth of my palms against my cheeks.

A thunderous roar jolts me awake, my heart racing in my chest as I realize the nightmare is not over. I don't know how long I have been asleep, but the room is no different than when I closed my eyes. *White everywhere.* I rise to my feet, my body stiff and sore from sleeping on the hard floor, when my eyes catch sight of a miniature black dot. *What is that?* Squinting my eyes, I realize it's a hole, barely visible against the stark whiteness of this place. My curiosity is piqued, and I inch closer to inspect it further. However, this time, the room or whatever I am in does not expand; the hole does. As I approach it, I lean in closer, pressing my face against the surface to peer inside. Suddenly, the hole widens, and a figure appears. I jump back in surprise and clutch my racing heart as a girl walks through the opening, joining me in the nothingness. She looks just as bewildered as I am, her eyes scanning the void around us.

"What? Not again!" she shouts into the emptiness.

Without uttering a single word, I hasten towards the hole she recently came out of, except it vanishes when I reach it.

Sighing in defeat, I turn back to the girl, who is now crying with her shoulders slumped.

I stare at her, unsure of what to do or say.

She notices me staring and rubs her eyes with the back of her hand.

"Do you speak English?" She says with a heavy accent.

I open my mouth to speak, but nothing comes out.

"Ou pale kreyol?" She asks, quirking an eyebrow.

I shake my head.

"English?" she repeats, sniffling.

I nod, "Y–Yes."

She offers a small smile, then walks towards me, extending her hand. "I'm Josephine. What is your name?"

I take a hesitant step backward.

Josephine narrows her eyes at my reaction and lowers her hand. "What's wrong? I promise I am not going to hurt you."

Watching her cautiously, I continue to back away from her.

She holds up both hands in surrender, trying to show that she means no harm.

"Okay, okay. I am going to sit here, and you can stay over there." She sits yoga-style on the ground and begins to hum a beautiful tune with her eyes closed.

Relaxing slightly, I lower my guard and take a seat on the ground with a safe distance between us. She peeks at me with one eye, followed by a slight smile.

"Where–where are we?" I stammer.

She opens her eyes fully and replies, "We are in the dream realm."

My eyes bug out. "What?!"

"Magical beings are transported into a dream realm when they are in a coma." She says matter-of-factly, as if everyone, or rather I, should know. "The better question is, why are you here? The sooner you figure that out, the quicker you can wake up."

"I have no idea why I'm here!" I stand up, throwing my arms in the air.

She smiles knowingly.

Why is she so calm about this?

"Why are you so calm?" I blurt out, echoing my thoughts.

Josephine stands to her feet and walks towards me. "Because I've been here before. Trust me, panicking won't help you wake up any faster."

"You are in a coma too?"

She chuckles, shaking her head. "No. I have visions, and sometimes, I am transported here when the vision is particularly overwhelming. It's so frustrating, and I never know when I will be able to return to my own reality."

My mouth forms a small O.

"You didn't tell me your name," she says.

"Because I don't know you."

Josephine sits back on the ground, cross-legged, and sighs heavily. "I don't know you either, but I told you mine. And it seems we'll be here for a while, so we might as well get to know each other."

With a graceful flick of her wrist, a gentle swish fills the air, and delicate snowflakes form in her palm.

Is she a witch?

"Are you a witch?" I ask with wide eyes.

"Maybe I am, maybe I'm not." She challenges me with a smirk. "Are *you* a witch?"

I concede, moving to sit in front of her. "My name is Claudette."

Her gaze softens, and a smile spreads across her face. "It's nice to meet you, Claudette."

"It's nice to meet you too."

Josephine opens and closes her hand. "I have the power to manipulate water and transform it into ice or snow." As she opens her hand, the snowflakes start dissolving one by one into thin air, disappearing completely when she closes it.

Ice? She must be from Jajuville, but how is she here? *How did I end up here?*

"How did I get here?"

"Hmm... that's a great question. What were you doing right before you woke up in this realm?"

"I was on my way to meet someone," I admit, a sense of unease creeping into my chest. Thinking back to that moment, a knot forms in my throat, and I swallow hard. I don't want Josephine to know that I murdered someone. That wouldn't be a great first impression. "And I can't recall anything after that, and the next thing I knew, I was here."

Josephine raises an eyebrow, her expression unreadable. "Interesting," she says, her voice calm. "Perhaps your meeting didn't go as planned. Or it went exactly as planned."

I shift uncomfortably.

She smiles and grabs my hand. Immediately, white smoke billows around us, creating a mystical embrace. The air around us crackles with otherworldly energy while her piercing eyes emit a frosty glow. A chill seeps into my bones, and icy formations dance around us, creating a mini snowstorm that envelops the space. I attempt to take my hand away from her, but she has a tight grip on me, and I am paralyzed in place.

"What are you doing?" I shout, confusion and alarm coloring my voice.

She doesn't respond and remains deep in thought, her magic consuming me.

"Let go of me!" I demand, but she only tightens her grip, her expression blank.

"You are an Earth witch from Mashalville." She finally speaks.

I don't reply, but she gives me a knowing look. "It's okay, Claudette," she says, her grip finally loosening. "You did what you thought you had to do."

What?

"I have visions of the past and the future," she continues, her eyes searching mine.

When I open my mouth to speak, the black hole appears again, but my legs give out beneath me before I can run to it.

"Claudette, you need to focus on the love and purity of this world to defeat the enemy. We will see each other again." Josephine says, disappearing through the black hole.

I lift myself from the ground and sprint towards it, feeling the adrenaline pumping through my veins; however, it closes when I reach it. Collapsing to my knees, tears stream down my face as I sob into my hands.

How do I wake up from this nightmare?

Chapter 30

Awake

Three days later...

A thick fog clouds my vision, creating a blurry atmosphere that makes it hard to distinguish anything. Blinking repeatedly, I finally regain focus, and my surroundings come into view. I am in Eli's arms, his soft snores filling the room. I shake him gently, and his eyes flutter open, adjusting to the sudden brightness.

He rubs his eyes to shake off the remnants of sleep until the realization dawns on him. "Claudette! You are awake!" He kisses my forehead, my nose, and my lips, relief flooding his handsome features. "Thank God! I thought I had lost you," he says, holding me tight.

How long was I out? Opening my mouth to speak, my throat is dry and scratchy, and my voice comes out as a whisper. "H–How." Eli snaps his fingers, and a glass of water materializes. He hands it to me. As I take a sip, I notice the worry lines on his face, and my heart aches at the thought of causing him distress.

"I'm okay, Eli," I manage to say, my voice still raspy. I reach up to touch his cheek, reassuring him that I'm here and safe with him now.

He exhales a long sigh of relief, his shoulders relaxing as he leans in to kiss my forehead once again. "I was so worried," he murmurs into my hair.

Destiny rushes into the room. "Eli, Kevin—Oh! Claudette, you're awake! Thank goodness!" Destiny shouts, her expression shifting from serious to relieved when she sees me sitting up in bed. "You had us all scared," she adds.

My lips form a weak smile as I nod my head.

"You were saying something about Kevin," Eli reminds Destiny.

Destiny nods and continues. "Oh, right! Kevin and his minions just left. We plan to attack them in two days."

I blink, taking in this new information. "How long have I been out?"

Destiny and Eli exchange a look before Destiny answers, "Almost four days." She continues. "Kevin, his parents, Tanya, and Eli's parents have been attacking us every morning, trying to breach Caron's protection spell. We plan to attack Kevin's home at night to end this once and for all. You have two days to regain your strength." She says.

Nodding my head. "I'll be ready."

"Destiny, I need to speak to Claudette privately," Eli requests and Destiny nods, leaving the room with a knowing look.

What's that about?

Once we are alone, his expression turns serious.

"What is it, Eli?" I touch his arm.

"You need to channel your power from love, Claudette," he begins, his tone grave. "Your love for your mother, your father, your friends, and me. You cannot do what you did before."

I open my mouth to speak, but he places a finger on my lips, silencing me. "Let me finish."

His eyes bore into mine. "I get why you killed Ms. Hudson. However, look what it did to you—it knocked you out. I understand the betrayal you felt, but you have to control it. You have to use your love as a source of strength, not your rage."

Shaking my head. "How do you expect me to channel my love when all I feel is anger? I am *still* angry. My *therapist* killed my father. I trusted her, and she took him away from me. The only family I had left, that witch stole that from me!" My breathing quickens, and rage threatens to consume me.

Eli tilts my chin up; his eyes are full of empathy. "When you woke me up from my coma, you showed me that love is stronger than anything. *Love* is what brought us back together. It is a choice, not just a feeling. It's okay to feel angry, but you have the power to choose how you respond to that anger. You can't go around killing everyone who hurts you."

Exhaling slowly. "I know you're right, Eli. I will try to remember this when I face Kevin."

Eli's face drops to a frown, and he sighs. "Claudette, I am serious! It will take a lot of magic to defeat Kevin, and you won't be able to do it if you let your anger control you. You don't win by losing yourself."

"Okay, okay, I hear you." I surrender with my hands up in defeat. "I will do my best to keep a level head and not let my emotions get the best of me."

He's not entirely convinced. Still, he doesn't say anything more.

It's been days since I last felt like myself, and a haunting feeling lingers inside me after taking Ms. Hudson's life. Kevin is the ultimate enemy. He is the source of all my pain. *I want to kill him for everything he has done.*

Eli helps me to my feet, and we head to the living room to regroup with the others. Jessie, Billie, Lin, Destiny, and Isabel are sitting in a circle on the floor brainstorming strategies. Adam and Caron are in the kitchen mixing potions and pouring their contents into numerous bottles.

"Claudette! You're awake! It's great to have you back," Lin says as I join them, and everyone looks at me with a warm smile.

"It feels good to be back," I reply, a small smile forming on my lips. "You guys plan to catch me up on what I've missed?"

Lin begins explaining. "In two days, we will launch an attack on Kevin's home at night. They have been attacking us every morning, so we will repay the favor."

"And we will not fail like they have," Isabel snorts.

"You have to practice conjuring the fireball you used to wake Eli from his coma," Adam instructs. "We need you to incapacitate Kevin long enough for us to stab him with the Ce-Ja dagger to take his magic away and imprison him."

I was on board with the plan until the last part.

"Stabbing him with the dagger won't kill him!" I roll my eyes. *Why does he get to live while my father had to die?*

Caron's eyes widen at my outburst. "Sweetheart, our goal is to remove Kevin's magic, not kill him. We will be the new Witch Council, and our plan is to handle things differently than before by creating a magical prison. We want to end this without any more bloodshed, if possible."

"Claudette, we talked about this," Eli reminds me. "Killing is our *last* resort."

My blood boils at the thought of sparing Kevin's life. "Kevin pretended to love me. He took my virginity. He had my therapist murder my father—the only family I had left—and you expect me to let him live?"

"What gives you the right to take someone's life?" Caron asks, her voice firm.

"What gives him the right to do it?" I retort, my anger rising.

She doesn't reply, and everyone in the room exchanges uncomfortable glances. *How do they expect me to let that demon live after all he's done to me?* I storm to my room, their distinct chatters fading into the background as I slam the door shut behind me.

Pacing back and forth, I struggle to calm the rage burning inside me. I'm not God, and I don't have the authority to decide who lives and who dies. Still, of all people, Kevin is the last person who deserves mercy—he deserves a ruthless death.

Eli barges into my room, arms folded. "Are you ready to practice?"

Is he serious? I am not in the mood to practice magic and use *love* as my inspiration. *Perhaps I can distract him in a different way.*

"How about we practice something else instead?" I suggest, giving him my best sexy eyes.

"What are you doing with your eyes?" He asks, chuckling, breaking his serious exterior.

"I'm trying to distract you." I tempt him by batting my eyelashes. "I think we both could use a different kind of release right now."

Eli clears his throat. "No, Claudette. As much as I want to, and trust me, I do," he says, tugging at the bulge in his pants, and my eyes follow. "We can't. We need to focus. I need you to conjure the same white fireball you used to wake me up."

Sighing dramatically. "Fine. I guess this isn't the right time."

One thing I know about Eli is that if he doesn't want to do something, there's no changing his mind. He has self-control. *Maybe I should learn a thing or two from him.*

He looks at me expectantly to start practicing, and I comply.

Closing my eyes, I try to replicate the white fireball, using *love* as an inspiration and focusing on the energy within me, but it's not working. I attempted it a few more times. Still, nothing happened. Eli watched me patiently as I continued to struggle. This is a lot harder than I thought it would be.

After three hours of unsuccessful attempts, I slumped onto the bed, feeling overwhelmed and overstimulated.

"Maybe we can try again tomorrow," I suggest in defeat.

"No, keep trying. I'll be right back," Eli says, leaving me alone in the room and returning with Caron and Adam.

"Hit me with your best shot," he challenges them, causing my eyes to widen in disbelief.

"Wait, what? W–what are you doing, Eli?" I stammer.

"Motivation," he replies eagerly.

Before I can protest, Adam and Caron join in, holding hands and chanting a spell, conjuring a captivating sphere of swirling purple and gold energy. They aim the sphere at Eli, firing it with precision and knocking him unconscious.

"What did you do to him?!" I gasp, rushing over to Eli's side.

Caron and Adam shrug, exchanging a knowing look.

"We knocked him out. Now wake him up," Caron demands, and she and Adam exit the room.

Eli is annoying. I love him, but seriously, dude, what was he thinking? I have been practicing for hours to replicate the fireball, and I just can't seem to get it right.

Closing my eyes again, I channel all my energy and push myself to manifest the luminous fireball once more. Peeking through my eyelids, nothing seems to be happening. *What am I doing wrong?*

"Channel your love." The faint sound of a woman's voice whispers to me.

Who was that?

Concentrating even harder, I focus on love. Memories of Eli flood my mind. His unwavering support, his belief in me, and the way he always makes me feel like I can do anything. Newfound sensations of warmth course through my body as I focus on the feeling of love. His gentle touch when we made love, the way he looked at me with adoration, and the safety I felt in his embrace. With these thoughts in mind, my emotions evoke a renewed sense of purpose. I think about the love I have for my parents—they are the pillars of my strength. And my love for my friends—my chosen family. Suddenly, a celestial sphere materializes, emanating a radiant white light.

I did it! With force, I push forward, striking Eli and jolting him awake in an instant.

He blinks rapidly, regaining his bearings as recognition dawns on him, and a grin spreads on his lips. Rushing to him, I plant kisses all over his face. "I did it, babe, I did it!" I squeal between kisses.

Eli wraps his arms around me, pulling me close. "I knew you could do it. I never doubted you for a second," he hums on my lips.

Straddling him, I scold him. "Don't do that again, and that's an order, Elijah Powers."

He chuckles, his hands gripping my waist and his intense gaze meeting mine. “Understood, Claudette Richardson.”

Chapter 31

Attack

Flipping through the pages of my Earth spell book, I search for ways to force Kevin into a slumber. There are so many spells in this book that it is hard to determine which spell I should use.

Eli is beside me, thumbing through his book, when suddenly, Lin barges into the room. “We have to go now!”

We dress in comfortable clothing armed with a Ce-Ja dagger in hand and are ready for war.

Destiny and Isabel join Eli and me in one car, and Lin is with Billie, Caron, Jessie, and Adam.

Planning our next move, we park three blocks away from Kevin’s residence. Splitting into teams of two, we each take different blocks toward Kevin’s apartment. We arrive in front of his home simultaneously, and a bright red light emanates around its barriers. Like us, they placed a protection spell to keep us from breaking in.

Caron gets into position, holding her hands together. “We need to break the protection spell.” With each lightning bolt she conjures, her eyes emit a radiant hue of light purple toward the barrier.

“If they weren’t able to break through our barriers, how can we break through theirs?” I ask.

“Good always wins,” Adam reassures us as if that explains everything.

Good always wins. I repeat silently to myself.

Billie cracks her knuckles and her neck. "Let's get these little bastards!"

Lin exhales slowly, his hands tracing a circular pattern in the air, materializing a captivating purple sphere of energy.

Isabel and Destiny share a knowing glance and follow suit.

"Let's do this!" Destiny shouts.

In an impressive display of teamwork, the three of them charge forward with incredible speed, simultaneously hurling mystical purple fireballs at the force field. Adam and Jessie materialize burning daggers, aiming with precision to weaken the impenetrable barrier. With each strike, the barrier crackles with an electric surge, sending sparks of vibrant explosions that reverberate through the air. Fragments from the magical shield begin to shatter, forcing them to cover their eyes from the blinding light.

With the barrier weakening, Eli and I clasp hands, our magic merging into a powerful force that effortlessly lifts us above the apartment.

"Babe, channel our love," Eli urges as we soar higher and higher.

Nodding, I think about our love. We concentrate hard on our bond, allowing our emotions to intertwine with our magic. Our brows furrow with determination and sweat beads on our foreheads as we pour all our energy into breaking through the remaining fragments of the force field. The last remnants of the barrier shatter with a resounding crack, sending shards of light scattering in all directions.

"I guess their spell wasn't as good as Caron's." Isabel snickers, kicking down the door with force.

"Oh, please. No one can make a potion like me," Caron gloats, emitting her infamous cackle as she charges into the apartment with Isabel, Destiny, and Billie following closely behind.

Mr. and Mrs. Powers and another stranger who looks oddly familiar are waiting for us inside with bleak expressions. *Is that Ms. Hudson's man?*

"You're so predictable," Elizabeth remarks. "We figured you would strike your attack in the middle of the night."

"We have been expecting you," Joseph states, his gaze cold and unwavering.

With a firm grip, Eli clenches his fists as he listens intently to what his parents are saying.

The stranger steps in front of Elizabeth and Joseph, and a grim line forms on his lips as he addresses me directly. "It is a pleasure to meet you! Witch! I'm Malcolm, and this is for Libby!"

Elizabeth, Joseph, and Malcolm join forces against Eli and me, their magic swirling and crackling in the surrounding air, causing my thoughts to scatter. In a state of confusion and vulnerability, I struggle to regain my footing, pondering the mysteries of my own identity and the purpose of my presence in this place.

What is happening? What am I doing here? Who are they?

There's a strange fog clouding my mind, making it difficult to think clearly. The confusion is overwhelming as I try to piece together the puzzle of my existence. Holding my head in my hands, I try to shake off the disorientation, but the answers remain elusive, leaving me feeling lost and alone in this unfamiliar world.

Someone interferes, clasping my hand in theirs. *Who is this?* His touch sends a jolt of recognition through me, snapping me out of the mind-clouding spell they cast over me.

"Their magic doesn't work on me," Eli says, alerting me back to reality. "I protected my mind from their tricks."

That's my man.

Elizabeth throws a tantrum over Eli's interference and retaliates by launching a gust of gold energy directly at him. I swiftly step in front of Eli, shielding him. Conjuring a purple ball of energy in my hands, I deflect Elizabeth's attack and strike her with a powerful blast. The impact knocks Elizabeth off balance, causing her to sprawl to the ground and rendering her unconscious.

Joseph's reaction to what I did to his wife is far from forgiving. A look of fury crosses his face as he forms an orb of energy, its colors shimmering in a mix of purple and gold. The blast hits Eli and me with such force that we are both thrown backward, landing hard on the ground. Excruciating pain shoots through my body as I struggle to get back on my feet. Joseph and Malcolm share a knowing look, their expressions dark and menacing as they prepare to launch another attack. Jeremiah intrudes from the sidelines, and Joseph turns to his oldest son, communicating a silent plea for him to aid in our ultimate downfall. When Joseph is about to fire another blast of energy, Jeremiah steps in front of us, his arms outstretched in a protective stance. The looks on Joseph's and Malcolm's faces are priceless when they realize Jeremiah is on our side and not theirs.

They recover quickly, their expressions turning from shock to fury. Joseph and Malcolm join forces to launch a coordinated attack towards us, hurling orbs of energy in our direction. We brace ourselves for impact, deflecting the orbs with our powers. The air crackles with energy, with orbs and blasts flying in all directions. Our magic clashes with theirs with enough force to knock them out cold, and its impact slams Eli and me to the ground once again.

Jeremiah helps us to our feet.

The fight is far from over.

"Thank you, Jere." Eli thanks Jeremiah, and they share a brotherly nod before Jeremiah ushers us inside Kevin's apartment.

"Hurry! You don't have much time before they find out what I've done and come after me next." Jeremiah shouts, joining Adam and Jessie in the fight against Kevin's parents.

We enter the apartment with caution. The moment we step inside, we are greeted with a lightning bolt striking the floor in front of us. Losing our balance, we stumble backward, barely avoiding the impact.

The twins and Tanya hold hands, reciting a spell. "We call upon the leader of the Shadow World. Give us the strength and the power we need to end the lives of our enemies."

Caron, Isabel, and Destiny are unconscious on the floor. Eli, Lin, and I are on our knees, holding our heads in agony. The vessels in our brains pulsate with intense pressure as if they are about to rupture. *They are giving us aneurysms.* How original. That's my move.

As the pressure builds, the blood vessels in my head throb with pain, weakening my body and blurring my vision. The pain is unbearable. I feel my existence slipping away as I struggle to maintain consciousness until the faint sound of a male's voice breaks through the haze. *"You can do this."*

Forcing my eyes open, I see my friends in need of help. Caron, Isabel, Billie, and Destiny are incapacitated on the floor. Lin and Eli are both clutching their heads in agony. It's up to me to save us all. *I have to stop this.*

Summoning every ounce of strength left in me, I push through the pain and focus on saving my friends. With each slow and steady breath, my determination grows stronger. Mustering all my willpower, I break through the haze and rise to my feet to take charge of the situation. With a clear mind and a steady hand, I manifest a ball of energy, striking Tanya with a powerful blast that sends her flying into the wall and crashing to the floor, unconscious. When Crissy sees Tanya not moving, she focuses her energy on me. She launches a counterattack, firing magical red and gold spheres toward me. However, I deflect Crissy's feeble attack and send the orbs back towards her with even greater force. The impact knocks Crissy off balance and gives me the opportunity to seize control. I channel my powers with *love*.

Concentrating on protecting myself and my friends, a bubble of energy forms around me, its colors shifting between shades of blue, gold, and brown. It acts as a barrier that repels any further attacks while I ascend above Crissy. From my elevated position, I propel my Ce-Ja dagger with precision, piercing into her chest. She passes out from the impact. Marissa retaliates by using her magic to fling Lin across the room, knocking him unconscious. Descending to the floor, I rush to his side, checking his pulse and making sure he is stable. His pulse is weak but steady.

Marissa targets Eli next, levitating him above us. Her magic brutally stretches his limbs from their sockets, causing him to groan in agony.

"Enough!" I shout, propelling energy forward into Marissa's chest and breaking the spell she has on Eli. He descends, his limbs snapping back into place.

"What are you waiting for? Do it!" Marissa yells. "Go ahead, kill me! You know you want to."

She's taunting me, trying to provoke a reaction. I *want* to kill her!

"Dark Thunder!" she mocks.

Marissa is trying her best to get me to do it. However, when I meet Eli's gaze, I know he will disapprove. It would make me no better than her. Neglecting my anger, I focus on channeling something far more significant—*mercy*. The Ce-Ja dagger from Eli's pocket teleports to my hand, and with a swift movement, I plunge it into Marissa's stomach, knocking her out cold.

Eli's parents, Malcolm, the twins, and Tanya, have been neutralized. It's time for me to face Kevin. *Alone*.

No one else is getting hurt under my watch.

No more innocent lives are at stake.

This fight is between me and Kevin.

The sun is beginning to rise, and I know this is when Kevin will be the most powerful. But I am ready. I will defeat Kevin Evans for my parents, my friends, my boyfriend, and ultimately for myself. This is the final showdown.

"Get everyone out of here!" I shout to Eli. "I'll handle this alone."

Eli helps Caron, Billie, Destiny, and Isabel to their feet. Jeremiah and Adam carry Lin out of the apartment.

With my friends safely out of harm's way, it's finally time for me to confront this menacing demon.

Before exiting the apartment, Eli locks eyes with me, and time stands still for a moment. He mouths, *I love you*, tugging at my heartstrings before evacuating the apartment.

I can do this.

Pacing the apartment, I search for any sign of Kevin. He is hiding in plain sight, waiting for the perfect moment to strike. Still, I am prepared, mentally and physically. "Kevin, come out, come out wherever you are," I tease. "I know you can hear me. It's time you stop lurking in the shadows and face me."

Suddenly, I hear a faint sound that comes from behind me, causing me to spin around quickly, only to find that there is nothing there. A sinister sneer hangs in the air, unsettling my senses. Again, I call out into the empty room, feeling his lingering presence taunt me. There's more movement, this time louder, and I see a flicker of a shadow out of the corner of my eye. With caution, I pivot on my heels, my heart beating rapidly in my chest, only to find myself engulfed in an eerie darkness yet again. Kevin is playing mind games with me. I turn back around and nearly jump out of my skin when I see him walking through the wall behind me. In his complete demon form, his beady black eyes glint with malice as he approaches, a chilling smirk on his face. My breath catches in my throat, and I stumble backward. The sight of his intimidating presence causes goosebumps to rise on my skin. Black claws extend from his fingertips, two prominent horns protrude from his head, and a distorted face leers at me. There is no trace left of the handsome man I was once deeply in *love* with. The demon before me is frightening and unrecognizable, a stark contrast to the person I thought I knew. With a wave of his hand, a force pushes me through the wall and into a room I don't recognize. A shooting pain sears through my body as I hit the floor, adding to the confusion that grips me. Kevin grasps me by the throat and flings me across the room, again and again, until I am barely conscious, giving me no chance to heal myself.

Why did I think I could beat a demon?

He launches at me again, but this time, I manage to summon a burst of energy and hurl it back at him. It has no impact on him whatsoever.

Um, what? With each breath, I gather my strength and unleash a series of energy blasts in his direction, which does nothing to him.

"You'll never win!" With every word he utters, his voice rumbles like a deep growl. The sound of his voice is bone-chilling, almost as if it's not his voice at all. *He sounds like a monster.*

"I won," he snarls, grabbing hold of my hair. "And now I will kill you."

The force of his punch connects with my nose, causing bones to crunch and blood to splatter, creating a horrifying scene. I hit the floor hard, struggling to stay conscious. Kevin conjures a flaming red and orange fireball, penetrating the searing force into my chest, causing me to gasp for air as darkness impairs my vision. The pain is like a thousand knives stabbing into my body all at once. Holding on by a thread, I can feel my strength waning. The room is spinning around me, making it difficult for me to see clearly. Leaning my head back against the cold floor, a sinking feeling tells me that this might be my final moment.

I don't have the strength to defeat him.

I am not the most powerful being to walk this Earth.

This is how I will meet my end.

My eyelids grow heavy, and I think I am starting to see the light at the end of the tunnel. This is it! The light is beautiful, peaceful, and inviting. I slowly reach out my hand, and the radiant white light seems to be beckoning me towards it, flooding every corner of my sight. My body floats toward the bright light, and the soft hum of energy resonates in the fresh air around me; I can almost taste the purity of the ethereal glow. I continue to reach towards it, a comforting warmth enveloping me like a gentle embrace from the great divine. *Is this the Light World?*

Two silhouettes, a woman and a man, appear in the distance. They seem familiar, but their faces are masked. They gently touch my shoulders, chanting in unison, "We call upon the Earth's greatest power to defeat the demon in this hour. Give her the strength that she needs to annihilate our enemy."

A force instantly snaps me out of my thoughts and brings me back to the present moment; my soul returns to my body, fully aware of my surroundings. Kevin is now hovering over me, wielding a dagger above my heart. Time freezes still for a brief moment just as he is about to dive the dagger into my skin. I swiftly grab his wrist with both my hands, pushing the blade away with all my might. His demonic eyes stare into mine with pure hatred, and mine mirror back with defiance. He pushes back with equal force, both of us trying to gain the upper hand. I squirm and twist, using every ounce of strength to keep the dagger at bay. It is just inches away from my neck now; the sunlight rising is glinting off its sharp edge. The blade grazes my flesh, drawing a thin line of blood. *My hands are confined, but my legs are free.* Bending my knees, I kick my legs upward with force. He lets go of my wrist, and I am able to wrap my legs around his neck and use all my power to pull him down to the floor and spin, pinning him beneath me. The dagger clatters to the floor near our entangled bodies. He stretches his hand out, reaching for the blade. I channel the Earth's energy to maintain my advantage and keep him subdued under me, grabbing the dagger before he can reach it. His own weapon is now pressed against his throat, nipping at his skin. *The tables have turned.*

It takes everything in me to resist the urge to end him right here and now, as opposed to neutralizing his magic. He deserves it after all the pain he has caused me, and the bitter look in his beady eyes tells me he knows it, too.

"I will kill you," he spits out, a distorted smirk twisting his lips.

Taking his life would only make me just like him, and I refuse to let him have that satisfaction. Instead, I think about my love for my parents, my friends, and my boyfriend, who are all counting on me to make the right choice and end this without losing myself in the process.

"Not today," I reply, a small smile forming on my lips. Exhaling a sharp breath, I muster all of my strength and resolve, choosing to channel love and not rage. Throwing his weapon to the other side of the room, I then open and close my free hand, summoning the Ce-Ja dagger to my side, and with one swift strike, I stab the blade into his neck, watching as his eyes widen in shock. Red smoke expels from his body, and he twists and turns, reverting back to the familiar form of the man I once knew.

Standing to my feet, panting heavily, I exhale and wipe the sweat from my forehead.

It's over, I won!

Chapter 32
Peace

Eight weeks later...

Dear Diary,

Life is great! Eli and I are doing fantastic. I love him more every day, and he loves me just as much. Eli makes me so happy, and he is not using me for an evil plan. Yeah, I know I'm still working on letting it go! The summer is almost over, and I look forward to my senior year of high school in a few weeks.

I have learned so much at Mashal High and can't wait to continue studying in college next year. My plan is to attend SME University once I graduate from Mashal High. There are three schools: one for warlocks, one for witches, and one for both. Eli and I have decided to attend the same school; we are not enrolling in the same classes, though. That would be too much. I love him, but I don't need to see him at home and in all my classes. Now, let's get to the good part—my enemies.

Kevin and all his trusted minions are now locked away in an impenetrable magical prison, thanks to Caron—Mashalville's Potions Master. And Adam conjured cuffs that dampened magic. Even though all of their magic was removed with the Ce-Ja dagger, it's better to be safe than sorry.

The new Witch Council consists of Eli, Lin, Adam, Jessie, Caron, and me. Destiny stepped down as a Witch Council member to spend more time with Isabel. We have meetings on Fridays to discuss all things magical. There is a greater evil brewing out in the atmosphere, and we are keeping our eyes peeled should we need to get involved. Our goal is to protect Mashalville from all threats.

We found out that Elizabeth Powers was behind the deaths of Destiny's mother and Isabel's parents. Destiny's mother, as well as Isabel's parents, got caught investigating Earth witch killings, and Elizabeth admitted her involvement in silencing them. The police in this town are no longer under Elizabeth's influence, and I hope she and her husband rot in prison for the rest of their lives. Jeremiah and Eli are closer than ever now that their parents got the punishment they deserved. Jeremiah even joined the police force as a rookie.

Oh, and Lin's parents… Kevin's mother confessed to killing them on behalf of Antus. Eli's suspicions were correct. That poor woman is so disoriented—she has not been in control of her own thoughts or actions. I had a notion that something was off about her the very first time I met her. The Witch Council deliberated and decided on a lighter sentence for her due to her mental state and the influence of Antus. She received a five-year prison sentence, and her husband agreed to serve his time until his very last breath. His words, not mine.

With the twins in prison, Gabriella and I have been on civil terms. She apologized for being an awful stepmother and wished she had done things differently. There was remorse in her eyes. Sometimes, I wonder what life would have been like if things had turned out differently between us. It's not like she forced me to do chores or be the housemaid… she was just unkind to me, and, of course, she did try to kill me with peanuts that one time. I know, I know. Water under the bridge.

It's been so long since I've actually been happy. I still miss my parents every day, but the pain no longer weighs me down like it used to. I accept they are gone, and I know I will see them again one day. Ms. Cameau, my guidance counselor from my previous high school, schedules phone call sessions with me once a week to check-in, and the Witch Council is okay with my two best friends knowing about magic. I am still working on convincing them to let Mitch know as well. This may take some time.

As far as school goes, the mags and the norms now interact more freely. I didn't enjoy being a part of a school implementing modern-day segregation among its students. It wasn't a great idea years ago, and it's not a great idea now!

Eli barges into my room with a goofy grin on his face. "Babe, I have done it!"

Closing my diary and hiding it underneath my pillow, I tilt my head to the side. "What have you done?"

"Follow me," he says, grabbing my hand and pulling me out of the room.

I follow him to the living room, curious about what he could be so excited about.

Our friends are sitting on the floor and gathered in a circle, each holding a flickering candle. Adam and Caron sit in the center, holding hands. They have broad grins on all of their faces.

My brows snap together. "What is this, Eli? What's going on?"

He turns to me with a grin, kissing me on the cheek. "This is your victory against the greater evil's surprise!"

Bursting into laughter. "My what?"

"You defeated Kevin! That's huge!" Eli lifts me up and spins me around in circles, and my friends cheer us on. "This is your present from all of us," he says, placing me back down on the floor. "You deserve it."

Joining my friends on the floor, I sit cross-legged and smile from ear to ear. Anticipation fills my heart as I wait to see what surprise they have planned for me.

Eli pulls out a crumpled piece of paper from his pocket. He unfolds it and reads aloud, "In this sacred hour, we call upon the leader of the Light World to allow us time with the ones Claudette loves and honors."

Everyone else joins in, chanting in unison two more times, their words echoing through the dimly lit room.

Adam and Caron pass out when the spell is complete, and the lights flicker, casting a mystical glow around us. A haunting and pungent scent fills the room, and white smoke billows out from the center of the circle, forming two figures that look eerily familiar. The air becomes frigid, and a brisk wind cuts through me, biting at my skin and sending shivers down my spine. The smoke begins to dissipate, and the two distinct figures—a man and a woman—emerge from the haze. I blink repeatedly, rubbing my eyes to make sure I'm not hallucinating. *I'm not!* A wave of shock washes over me, hitting me like a ton of bricks—*it's my mom and dad!*

I slowly rise to my feet; however, they feel like they're glued to the floor. Overwhelmed with emotions, I stand there paralyzed, struggling to process the surreal sight of my parents magically morphing into living flesh-and-blood beings right before my eyes. The tears well up in my eyes, and the realization hits me like a thunderbolt—they're back from the dead!

Tears stream down my cheeks. "What is happening?! This can't be real."

Eli steadies me with a reassuring hand on my shoulder, his voice calm as he says, "I know it's hard to believe, but they're really here. Caron and Adam are temporarily taking your mother and father's place in the Light World. The crossover process is almost complete."

His words sink in, and my mouth goes dry. This is really happening!

"We will give you some privacy," he says when the crossover is complete.

My mother and father step forward, their faces filled with love and familiarity.

"Mom! Dad!" I rush forward, tears streaming down my face as I embrace them.

"How is this possible? How are you here?" I ask through choked sobs. "I am so sorry for everything. I–"

My father kisses my forehead, cutting me off. "It's okay, Cheetah. We saw everything. We understand."

"Daddy," I wail, sobbing into his chest, and he squeezes me tighter.

My mother cups my face in her hands, wiping away my tears. "We are so proud of you, my darling daughter. We have been watching over you all this time. You have grown into such a strong and beautiful person." She says, smiling.

I missed her smile; she is so beautiful.

I grasp her hands, bringing them to my nose and inhaling her familiar scent. I have missed her so much. "Mommy," I choke out, my voice cracking with emotion.

"I miss you, too, sweetheart," she says, kissing our clasped hands. "I know how much pain you have felt without me by your side, but know that I am always with you, guiding you every step of the way."

A thought occurs to me, and I swallow hard. "Was that you on the day of the train incident?"

She nods, her eyes glistening with tears. "Yes, my love. The veil was open that day and I was able to change the train tracks to keep you safe. I will always protect you, no matter what."

"And it was you two who helped me defeat Kevin?" I ask, already knowing the answer.

They nod in response, and more tears fall from my eyes. I can't stop crying. My parents hug me tight, soothing me with their love.

"Cheetah, don't cry. You are never alone," my father says while my mother strokes my hair.

"We don't have much time left." Her voice fills with sadness. "I love you so much, my darling daughter." She kisses my forehead, and my father squeezes us into a bear hug.

"We will always be with you, although we're not physically here," he says.

I wipe my tears and smile at them. "I love you both so much. I will miss you every single day." The weight of their impending departure settles in my chest, and I try to hold back the flood of emotions threatening to overwhelm me.

"We will miss you too, sweetheart," my mother says, her eyes brimming with unshed tears.

"But we will always be watching over you," my father adds.

Despite the lump in my throat, I try to maintain my composure.

"One more thing, sweetheart," my mother says, smiling through her tears. "We love Eli. He is definitely a keeper."

My heart swells. Their blessing means everything to me.

With one last hug, they release me, and I step back as they disappear into the haze of smoke.

I drop to my knees, tears streaming down my face—tears of happiness, not sorrow.

Caron and Adam wake up from their slumber, and Eli and my friends return to the living room.

"Thank you! Thank you so much for this wonderful gift! I don't know how to express how much this means to me." I squeal, overwhelmed with gratitude. "I love you all so much."

"We love you too, and we are so glad to see you happy," Destiny says with a smile, wrapping her arms around me, and everyone joins in for a group hug.

I love these people! They are my chosen family, and I am beyond blessed to have them in my life.

Two days later...

We are at the prison gates.

"Are you sure you want to do this today?" Eli brushes his lips against mine.

"Yes, I need to do this," I reply, gripping his hand. "I'm ready."

He squeezes my hand in silent support. "Okay, Claudette. I'll be right here waiting for you when you come out."

"Thank you, babe." I plant my lips on his one last time before heading down the long corridor towards the staircase.

Descending ten levels below the prison, a wave of anxiety washes over me as I approach the heavy metal door leading to Kevin's cell.

When his gaze meets mine, his brows rise in surprise. There are noticeable dark circles under his eyes, and his face looks older than before.

"What brings you here, Claudette?" He asks, spitting into a mason jar he keeps by his cot.

I take a deep breath, trying to steady my nerves. Inching closer to the cell bars, I muster the courage to speak. "Why did you do it?"

"Do *what*?" He smirks, a bitter edge to his voice. "I need you to be more specific."

Confronting him head-on, I look him straight in the eye and ask, "Why did you go through the trouble of dating me?"

Kevin chuckles, the sound echoing off the cold stone walls. Rising from his cot, he pushes his face against the metal bars, his gaze cold and calculating. "That's why you came to visit me?"

I can see the hatred and resentment in his eyes. Taking a step back, I steady myself and reply, "Yes, that's why I'm here."

"Very well, Claudette. It won't be pretty," he warns, rubbing his dirty fingernails against his shirt. "I never loved you. I never cared about you. I only wanted my magic back. You were just a pawn in my game." He pauses for my reaction, but I have none. "You were nothing to me," he continues. "And every time we had sex, I was thinking about Tanya." He pauses again, waiting for my response. I won't give him the satisfaction. "I was thrilled when your father was murdered. It meant I was one step closer to getting what I wanted. You were just a means to an end." He laughs coldly, finishing his cruel confession.

I simply stare at him, blinking. His words have no effect on me now. I needed to hear him say it with his own mouth.

With a calm voice, I say, "Thank you for finally being honest with me," and I turn on my heel to walk away, leaving him alone in his own bitterness.

"That's it?!" He calls out after me, gripping the metal bars. "You're just going to walk away?"

I don't look back.

"These bars won't hold me forever! I will get my magic back again. You have not won, Claudette!"

My feet come to a sudden halt, and for a split second, I consider turning back. However, I don't.

"Good always wins!" I shout over my shoulder, and with a wave of my hand, I close the door behind me with a resounding clang.

The End

Thank you for reading Claudette's story!

If you have enjoyed reading this story, please consider leaving a review on Goodreads, Amazon, Bookbub, Storygraph, or anywhere you can to spread the word. Reviews are extremely important for Indie Authors.

Keep reading for the Bonus Chapter.

Bonus Chapter

Escape

Six weeks later...

K*evin's point of view:*

It has been weeks since Claudette visited me. Good riddance, but the confinement of this cell is pushing me to the brink of insanity with each passing day. I must escape this prison at all costs! If only I still had my magic. Antus hasn't visited my dreams since I lost my gift. I failed him, and now, without his guidance, my chances of getting out of here are slim. *What am I going to do?*

I pace back and forth, pinching the bridge of my nose in frustration. The walls press in on me, suffocating me with their oppressive weight.

"Ahh!" I shout, throwing my cot against the stone-cold wall with a resounding thud.

"Kevin?" Tanya calls out from the neighboring cell. "Are you awake?"

Rolling my eyes, I mutter, "Yeah, I'm awake," my voice strained with frustration at the relentless confinement. "Not that I can sleep in here anyway."

Every day follows the same monotonous routine. A guard brings me the bare minimum of food and water. I shower in the freezing cold liquid. Then, I spend the rest of my time confined in this cramped cell, counting the cracks in the walls as the hours drag on endlessly. And thanks to Claudette, I am only allowed sunlight once a week for an hour, despite her supposed kindness. It's a cruel and inhumane existence! The other cellmates get to go outside and eat in the cafeteria, but I am stuck here alone. Good old Eli thought it was best for me to be isolated from the others and have Tanya's cell nearby. I guess he felt having her so close but not being able to see her would bother me. He was wrong. My only priority now is to find a way to escape this place and get revenge on Claudette and everyone who failed me. Even Antus!

"Are you okay?" Tanya calls out from her cell again.

"Yes, I'm fine."

"I heard a crash from your cell. What happened?"

Sighing heavily, I respond, "I just dropped something. No big deal."

She falls silent for a moment before speaking again. "I wish we weren't trapped in here. I miss you."

Rolling my eyes, I mutter, "I agree, Tanya, but from the looks of it, we're stuck here for a while. Claudette and her friends took their time creating this *elaborate* prison for people like us. With no magic, it's nearly impossible to escape."

My voice trails off as the weight of reality sinks in—I am trapped here indefinitely.

Suddenly, the walls begin to shake, and a rumbling noise fills my ears.

"Uh, Tanya?" I shout over my shoulder.

"Yes?"

The bricks begin to crumble. "Are you hearing this too?"

"Hearing what?"

I shield myself as debris falls around me. "The walls are collapsing!"

"No, it's not, Kevin. Do you need to go to the infirmary?"

The rest of the bricks fall to the ground, and I stare in disbelief at the open space where the walls once stood. A figure emerges from the dust, but I can't make out who it is.

"Uh, no, Tanya. I think I might be hallucinating."

She mumbles, something that I ignore as the figure becomes visible. It is a man with caramel skin, fierce hazel-green eyes, and a scar right above his left eye. I don't recognize him.

My brows snap together. "Who are you?"

"What did you say, Kevin? I missed that," Tanya replies.

I shake my head. "Nothing, Tanya," I reply to her with my eyes still fixed on the man in front of me. "I won't ask again," I say to him, my voice firm and preparing for any possible threat in case he is a foe.

He stares back at me, his expression unreadable. "I am here to help you escape and bring you back to my realm."

"Are you talking to someone?" Tanya asks.

His gaze shifts past me, his attention fixed on something behind my back. "She needs to be eliminated."

"Why?"

"Because she is a liability." He replies, shrugging his shoulders. "You have to kill her, and I will take you back to my realm."

I bite my knuckles, weighing my options. "Can't we take her with us?"

The man shakes his head. "No, my mission is to bring you back alone."

"Who assigned you this mission?"

"Antus."

My blood runs cold as the man's eyes narrow. "Kill her now! We don't have much time."

He clenches his fists tight and then opens them, letting out a blazing fire. The intense heat radiates through the air, bending and melting the metal cell bars, which pool onto the floor with a sizzling sound. My eyes widen to their limits, almost popping out of their sockets, as I witness this incredible display of power.

He extends his hand, placing a cold steel knife in my palm. "Finish the job," he commands.

Tanya stands frozen in her cell. While I don't want to harm her, she is the only person who can expose my escape to the council. She is a loose end that needs to be tied up. I approach her slowly, and her beautiful eyes widen in fear as she sees the knife in my hand. Tears drip down her rosy cheeks, and I hold her in my arms before carrying out my orders. I watch as her life slips away, then gently lay her down on the cold, hard ground. Kissing her forehead one last time, I whisper, "I'm sorry, Tanya," before leaving her cell.

"Let's go!" The man barks at me, shattering a bottle of liquid on the ground.

As the liquid shimmers, a transparent bubble forms, revealing a stunning array of black and brown stars. He nods his head to follow him. We walk through the portal, and I look back to see Tanya and the prison disappear behind us, and nothing but black and brown stars surround us. The man shoots fire from his fingertips, drawing a path in front of us, and we continue to stride with purpose. The next thing I know, we are transported to a living room bathed in deep charcoal shades. The distinct smell of burning wood engulfs my senses as I walk further into the cozy room, and the crackling sound of a blazing fireplace fills the air, casting a warm glow on the two tall bookshelves beside it. The room is decorated with monochromatic portraits and paintings depicting Fire and Ice, surrounded by Sun, Moon, and Earth symbols. The abstract throw rug in the center ties everything together with its white, gray, and black tones, complementing the sleek black sofa that invites me to sink into its plush cushions.

"Have a seat," the man instructs, gesturing toward the green chairs in front of us.

He waits for me to comply, and I walk to the chair before settling in and meeting his gaze. "I didn't catch your name earlier."

"That's because I didn't give it," he responds, leaning back on the sofa and crossing his legs.

His gaze is fixed on me, and I don't know if I should be thrilled or skeptical—maybe both.

"My name is Pierre," he finally says, breaking the silence. "I rescued you because I have a proposition for you."

I raise an eyebrow. "What kind of proposition?" I ask, leaning forward in my seat.

His lips twist into a wicked grin. "I want you to join me in wreaking havoc on Jajuville and Mashalville," he proposes, and he stands to his feet to collect two books from the shelf. "Here, I suggest you start reading to learn our history. I'm sure the simpletons have learned of your escape by now and will be searching for you soon, but don't worry. My home is protected, and they won't be able to find you here. They won't even know that we are in a different realm."

Grinning from ear to ear, I take the books from him. "Count me in. I look forward to causing chaos in Jajuville and Mashalville with you."

He nods in approval. "Excellent."

We shake hands, solidifying our alliance.

*****

All good things must come to an end. However, the end marks the start of an exciting new journey.

Keep reading for a sneak peek into the enchanted realm of Jajuville!

Welcome to the enchanting realm of Jajuville.

Separated at birth, fraternal twins Josephine and Marie will reunite on their eighteenth birthday. One twin has the power of fire; the other has the power of ice. However, what should have been a joyous reunion takes an unexpected turn when they least expect it. An evil threat known as the Shadow King plans to sacrifice the twins on their birthday. The twins must join forces, harness their unique abilities, and cooperate for the greater good.

Can they rise above their contrasting perspectives and find common ground?

Join the Toussaint Sisters on an adrenaline-pumping adventure as they face off against the most formidable villain in the enchanted realm of Jajuville.

Kindly be aware that this Young Adult Dark Fantasy does not adhere to the traditional Happily Ever After narrative and is associated with the Magic is Real series.

Introduction to

FIRE & ICE
The Toussaint Sisters

One thousand years ago, two brothers fell ill, their bodies succumbing to the ravages of disease. Their mother, desperate to save them, performed an ancient ritual that miraculously healed her sons and bestowed upon them extraordinary abilities. They soon became powerful brothers, each with their own distinct personalities and strengths. As they continued to age, one of them started embracing evil, while the other chose the path of goodness.

Antus had grand ambitions, aspiring to be worshipped as a god and dominate the entire world. On the other hand, Jaju had a simple desire–he wanted his people to have a life filled with serenity. The two were at odds, unable to find common ground on their purpose.

Jaju desired to create a realm where witches could reside, while Antus aspired to rule over the real world along with the witches.

After years of resentment, fights, and exposure to the humans, Jaju went on to create Jajuville, the Magical Realm, where his people were gifted with the powers of Fire and Ice. At the same time, Antus and his followers were trapped in Mashalville.

Antus became a formidable threat, prompting witches to unite in a mission to eliminate him and condemn him to the Shadow World. He placed his curse on the Sun, Moon, and Earth witches for banishing him there. Every child born from the same coven was engulfed with darkness and forced to serve Antus, granting him the ability to seek revenge on Jaju and his people by creating the very first Shadow King from beyond the grave. In doing so, the magical veil was broken, and the people of Mashalville were able to leave if they wanted to. The people of Mashalville needed order, and the Powers family was the first family to form the Witch Council and set their rules in place.

Pierre was tired of living in the shadow of his twin brother and made a dark deal with the Shadow King that Antus created. Pierre didn't know that he would be the very first twin to merge, causing him to remain young and alive for decades.

It is time for another merger. Will he succeed in killing and absorbing Josephine and Marie's powers on their eighteenth birthday?

Brace yourself for the upcoming release of Fire & Ice: The Toussaint Sisters.

(TBA)

AUTHOR'S NOTE

Thank you for purchasing the Special Edition! I hope you enjoyed my story as much as I loved writing it. If you enjoyed the Magic is Real series, stay tuned for more details regarding Fire & Ice; like Josephine said, she will see Claudette again.

Let's be friends!

I enjoy connecting with my readers and would love to hear from you.

Please find me on any of the social media platforms below and join my newsletter.

My website: https://kcmcmillian.mailchimpsites.com/

Newsletter: https://eepurl.com/iJtSzA

Instagram: www.instagram.com/kcminspired_author

My Broadcasting Channel on Instagram:

https://ig.me/j/AbbtqGM3rQEE4wwD/

Facebook: www.facebook.com/kcmcmillianauthor

Facebook Group: https://www.facebook.com/groups/931639820833941/

TikTok: www.tiktok.com/@kcminspired_author

GR: www.goodreads.com/author/show/22481124.K_C_McMillian

Books by K.C. McMillian

- Bright A Forbidden Love Story, available now.
- Seventeen Magic is Real Part I, available now.
- Earth Magic is Real Part II, available now.
- Magic is Real Seventeen & Earth Hardcover Special Edition, available now.
- Loving Reign: A Fake Dating Romance Novel (Book One) 18+ and older coming 2025!
- The Forbidden Fruit: Tales of the Remi Clan (The Nosis Series) 18+ and older (TBA)
- Fire & Ice: The Toussaint Sisters (TBA)

ACKNOWLEDGMENTS

Thank you for taking a chance on me. I really hope you enjoyed reading Claudette's story and the sneak peek at Fire & Ice. It means so much to me that you took the time to read my story and purchase this special edition copy.

Huge thanks to Shalinie Rohit for once again joining me on this journey.

Thank you to my wonderful husband, Troy, for all of your support and for being my true love. I love you with my all.

Thank you, Amy Sobel, for all of our chats, your encouraging words, and your support. Thank you for always being on my side.

Thank you so much, Alicia Marcia, for joining me on this journey and for your support and encouragement.

Thank you to my parents (Shirley and Charlie Carter) and my Aunt Lucille Brown for all of your continued support! Also, thank you to my friends Fabiola Cameau and Michelle Azizi for the words of encouragement and continued support!

I love all of you!

ABOUT THE AUTHOR

When Kiana "K.C." McMillian was a child, she would make up stories in her head and write them down. While attending high school, her favorite play was Romeo and Juliette, and she enjoyed reading it, but she sometimes fumbled over her words while reading in front of her classmates. And, of course, children can be cruel. Kiana didn't like being made fun of and lacked confidence in herself, and she felt that if she couldn't read in front of a crowd, then perhaps she wasn't good enough to write. She didn't think her stories would be well received and feared failing at something she loved. Kiana knew back then that she would one day want to share her imagination with others, but she wasn't sure about putting herself out there.

Fast forward twenty years later, after the death of her husband's grandmother on January 13th, 2022, she decided she wouldn't let the fear of failure hinder her from following her dreams. Before "Gran," as she and her husband called her, left this earth, she said, "I have lived my life, and I've done everything I wanted to do; I'm ready." K.C. knew that if her life suddenly came to a tragic end, she wouldn't be satisfied. That statement inspired her, and she decided to follow her dream of becoming an author.

www.ingramcontent.com/pod-product-compliance
Lightning Source LLC
Chambersburg PA
CBHW020326030826
48979CB00020B/303
* 9 7 9 8 9 8 7 8 7 2 3 4 5 *